"Our ranch isn't for sale!"

"I'm sorry you feel that way, but we have a binding verbal agreement with your father. We'll do whatever it takes to hold him to that agreement," John stated with an air of finality that made Marah cringe.

"Well, give it your best shot. But I can promise you my sisters and I will do whatever it takes to fight you on this," Marah said.

John Stallion came to his feet, moving to stand directly in front of her. He was so close that Marah imagined she could feel the heat from his body teasing hers. Perspiration suddenly pooled between her breasts, her temperature rising rapidly. She took a step back, dismayed at the way her body was suddenly betraying her.

He stared her in the eye, and Marah fought to hold his gaze, his piercing look seeming to undress her where she stood. When he spoke, his voice was low and even. "I look forward to the challenge, Ms. Briscoe."

DEBORAH FLETCHER MELLO

is the author of seven romance novels. Her first novel, *Take Me to Heart,* earned her a 2004 Romance Slam Jam nomination for Best New Author. In 2005 she received Book of the Year and Favorite Heroine nominations for her novel *The Right Side of Love.*

For Deborah, writing is akin to breathing, and she firmly believes that if she could not write she would cease to exist. She loves to weave a story that leaves her audience feeling full and complete, as if they've just enjoyed an incredible meal. That is the ultimate thrill for her. Born and raised in Connecticut, she now calls Hillsborough, North Carolina, home. She resides there with her husband and son.

TO *Love* A STALLION

DEBORAH FLETCHER MELLO

KIMANI™
ROMANCE

KIMANI PRESS™

ISBN-13: 978-0-373-86054-8
ISBN-10:   0-373-86054-4

TO LOVE A STALLION

www.kimanipress.com

Printed in U.S.A.

Dear Reader,

Where do I begin to thank you for the love and support you have shown me since I embarked on this wondrous journey? I have been so blessed, and I understand that it has been a generous and loving God who has led me to this point.

I also know that if it had not been for your heartfelt expressions of love and the generous accolades for my many characters, none of this would have been possible. I am grateful for the kindness you've shown me, the criticism when you didn't think I'd gotten it right and all the words of encouragement and support that have kept me writing. Thank you again and again.

I'm hopeful you will fall head over heels in love with each of the Stallion men. They embody the strength of their convictions and their integrity, and the sheer beauty of men of outstanding character. As always, please don't hesitate to let me know what you think.

Until the next time, take care and God bless.

With much love,
Deborah Fletcher Mello
www.deborahmello.blogspot.com

Chapter 1

Marah Briscoe sat in a line of early morning traffic that seemed to be going absolutely nowhere. Vehicles were bumper to bumper on I-35, everything slowed from Zang Boulevard to Illinois Avenue. After a seriously long night with almost no rest, Marah was not in the mood. Sleep had been alluding her for days, ever since the last family meeting when her father had shocked her and her sisters with what he had called "good news." Since that moment, her mind had been a random mush of reflection, her concentration challenged. Some sleep would have helped because the lack of it was truly messing with her thoughts and this morning was surely not the one for her to be unfocused.

From the moment she'd risen from her bed, her day

had not gone well. The alarm on her clock radio had not gone off, setting her thirty minutes behind schedule, and a previous problem with the plumbing in her apartment had resurfaced with a vengeance. There had only been a short burst of hot water for her shower and premenstrual cramps were wrecking havoc on her body. With the traffic now holding her hostage, making her drive downtown a tedious chore at best, Marah was wishing she could crawl back into bed, pull the covers up and over her head and forget any of this was happening.

She was grateful when she finally pulled into the lower parking deck of the highrise offices and quickly found an empty parking spot in the front row. It felt as if she'd been given a minor reprieve from her misery. Exiting the vehicle, she took a series of deep breaths before entering the lobby of Stallion Enterprises' executive office complex. Anxiety swept through her as she maneuvered her way past a uniformed officer sitting at the front security station and eased over to the building's office directory. The oversize display case was recessed into a marbled wall, the black surface and bright white lettering illuminated by a hint of light that seemed to seep from somewhere in the back of the unit. She scanned it slowly, confirming the location of the corporate boardroom. When she located the appropriate floor and wing she depressed the up button for the elevator, waiting with the small crowd that had quickly gathered around her.   · ·

Taking a glance over her shoulder Marah noted the security guard eyeing her curiously, his gaze sweeping the length of her size-four frame with much appreciation. She tossed him a wry smile, then turned her attention back to the opening doors of the conveyor. Stepping inside she pushed the button for the fifty-fourth floor and eased her body in among the others who were riding up with her. The doors closed quickly and Marah blew a sigh of relief, cementing her decision to follow through with her mission.

Marah had been having second thoughts about what she planned to do. But what she was doing had become necessary. Six weeks ago she'd gotten word that Stallion Enterprises had made a bid to purchase her father's ranch, one of the last black-owned granges in the county of Dallas. Some egotistical, corporate demagogue had preyed on her father's soft nature and had conned the old man into actually believing this was in his best interest.

Since his wife's death five years ago, Edward Briscoe had been beside himself with grief, his bereavement consuming every aspect of his life. He'd lost his one and only love and, besides his children, all he had left was that ranch. Marah was willing to go to any lengths to ensure her father didn't lose it and definitely not to the likes of a silver-tongued, snake-oil salesman by the name of John Stallion.

Taking a glance down to the gold-toned watch on her wrist, Marah was suddenly concerned that she'd missed her window of opportunity. The executive committee of Stallion Enterprises would already be gathered together, preparing for the annual board meeting that would be commencing later that morning. Marah knew that slipping into the boardroom and interrupting their planning session before someone called security and tossed her out on the heels of her Abilene cowboy boots would be no easy feat.

A few stops later the elevator was exceptionally full when the doors opened and another crowd of bodies pushed their way inside. Marah took a step back to make room, pressing herself against the people already standing behind her. She tossed a quick look behind her, suddenly aware that she had stepped into someone's space. A woman standing just over her right shoulder met her gaze, a slight smile of polite acknowledgment pulling at her thin lips. Marah couldn't see the man at her back without turning all the way around, but she was acutely aware of his seductive cologne and imposing stature, and had caught a glimpse of his expensively tailored dark gray suit and classic Bostonian cap-toe shoes.

Marah found the small accommodations disconcerting. The man behind her was standing so near that she could feel the heat from his body mixing with her own. She was also aware that it had been some time since any man had been that close to her. His body heat teasing hers suddenly felt like lighter fluid being tossed on a raging flame. Marah felt a mist of perspiration rise between her cleavage.

The tall stranger stood with his back pressed against the elevator wall, his arms crossed evenly over his chest. He was unconsciously tapping the toe of his leather shoes, everything about his body language announcing his eagerness to reach his destination. The elevator jerked harshly, causing the woman in front of him to fall awkwardly against his body. A soft voice muttered a quick apology as she fought to regain her footing.

"No problem," he responded, his gaze moving to focus on her female frame.

The woman's attire was conservative but casual. Too
casual for her to be an employee of Stallion Enterprises. Form-fitting Levi's jeans hugged narrow hips
and a small waist. She was leggy, the appendages seemingly a mile high for such a petite woman. A bright
white blouse dressed her torso and from where he stood
he imagined it was buttoned well up to her chin. He was
suddenly aware of the faint scent of lavender wafting
up from her space into his, the delicate aroma inciting
a current of electrical energy through his bloodstream.

She tilted her head ever so slightly, just a hint of
movement as though she were listening for something
in particular to sound above the static breathing and the
occasional cough of the other occupants. The elonga-
tion of her neck as it dipped, as if in invitation, suddenly
made him want to lower his mouth to her flesh. He was
suddenly lost in the thought of himself laying a path of
damp kisses against the soft skin that peeked below the
loose bun atop her head, a wealth of cinnamon-colored
curls shimmering beneath the fluorescent lights. The
moment was disturbing and he found himself fighting
to resist the urge that had instantly consumed him.

The elevator stopped short, shuffling them one
against the other. Marah's heart dropped into the pit of
her stomach as the sharp movement caused her to fall
back on the man.

The stranger leaned forward slightly, moving to
whisper into her ear. "I'm very sorry," he said, his voice
a low gust of breath against the back of her neck. His
voice was a throaty, deep rumble, the seductive vibra-
tion of it and the warmth of his breath only serving to
aggravate Marah's discomfort. She nodded ever so

slightly, not bothering to respond, not quite sure what she should say, if anything at all.

The elevator climbed three more floors. As the conveyance approached the twentieth floor and came to a halt, it emptied enough for Marah to make a quick exit. Maneuvering her way to the front of the conveyor she stepped out into the corridor. Unable to resist, she turned to look over her shoulder, her gaze meeting the man's fully for the first time. She was suddenly taken aback by his rugged good looks, rock-solid body and imposing stature. He had stepped to the forefront of the elevator behind her and was staring as well. Their gazes locked for just a brief moment, then the elevator doors closed shut between them and the stranger disappeared out of sight.

Marah inhaled, a deep influx of air filling her lungs. She eyed her watch one more time, then glanced around to see where it was she stood. A neon sign directed her to a restroom and Marah rushed inside to regain her composure.

Minutes later, she resumed her trip up the elevator to the fifty-fourth floor intent on doing the one thing she'd come to do. As the elevator doors opened, pointing her toward her destination, Marah knew there would be no turning back.

Determined to get an audience before chairman and chief executive officer John Stallion, Marah eased her way down the short length of corridor. The man had steadily refused to take her calls over the past few weeks, not even bothering to acknowledge her efforts to reach him, and Marah fully intended to give him a very large piece of her mind.

The robust black woman seated at the oak desk in the foyer was ill-prepared for Hurricane Marah as she stormed toward the closed doors, pushing her way past without seeking permission first.

"Excuse me, but where do you think you're going?" the woman demanded as she jumped to her feet, rushing behind Marah.

Marah paused momentarily, turning in the direction of the booming voice. "I need to speak with John Stallion. And I need to speak with him now," she responded, her hand wrapped around the doorknob of the executive conference room.

"I don't think so. Mr. Stallion is in a very important meeting."

"Well, this is important, too," Marah intoned, the knob turning in the palm of her hand.

"You can't go in there," the woman reiterated, her voice rising sharply.

Marah snapped back, her own tone loud and crisp, "Watch me!"

Before either woman could utter another word, the door to the room swung open, pulling Marah over the threshold so abruptly that it took every ounce of effort not to fall flat on her face. As she stumbled through the entrance someone caught her by the elbow, stalling her fall to the carpeted floor.

A familiar baritone voice rumbled at her side. "May we help you?"

The matronly figure on Marah's heels answered before Marah could collect her thoughts. "I tried to stop her, John. Do you want me to call security?"

Marah shook off the large hand still clutching her

elbow. Pressing a palm to her abdomen, her gaze swept around the room, acknowledging the four pairs of eyes that were suddenly fixed on her, her own stare finally resting on the exceptionally tall black man at her side. The man from the elevator.

Heat flushed her face, a wave of embarrassment coursing through her. She took a deep inhale of air, stalling the quiver of nervous energy that rippled through her center. "I need to speak with John Stallion," she finally muttered, her attempts at a commanding tone failing her. Marah struggled to fight past the rise of anxiety, trying to maintain a firm hold on an icy demeanor.

The older woman motioned as if to speak, her words stalled by the nod of her employer's head. "Thank you, Miss Hilton," he said, dismissing her. "We'll take it from here."

"Yes, sir."

Marah glanced over her shoulder to see the woman close the door behind her, suddenly leaving her, and them, alone.

John Stallion moved to the conference table, taking a seat in an oversize leather chair. He crossed an ankle over a knee and his arms over his chest as he eyed her curiously. A faint smile pulled at his mouth as he and the three men sitting around him appraised her, their gazes sweeping from the top of her head down to the floor beneath her feet and back again.

Marah was not amused as her own gaze shifted from one cocky face to the other. It was obvious that all four men were related, each possessing the same distinctive features: black-coffee complexions, chiseled jawlines, seductive bedroom eyes, plush pillows for lips and the same sexy, smug smile.

The man seated at the head of the mile-long conference table gestured in her direction. "So, Miss...?"

"It's Ms. Ms. Briscoe," Marah answered curtly, taking two steps in his direction.

"Well, Ms. Briscoe, what do you need to speak with me about?"

"Are you John Stallion?"

"I am and these are my brothers." The man pointed with his index finger. "That's Matthew, Mark and Luke."

Marah looked from one to the other, her expression voicing her amusement. Back in the day Ma and Pa Stallion obviously didn't realize their biblical brood was going to grow into evil incarnates set on stealing other folks' life savings. Marah could only shake her head at the absurdity.

Reaching into the leather satchel slung over her shoulder, she pulled a stack of legal documents from the inner lining, tossing them onto the table in front of the man. "I think these belong to you," she said, her ire ringing in her tone. "My father won't be signing them anytime soon."

John lifted the package of paperwork into his hands, scanning the documents briefly. He nodded slowly, then lifted his gaze toward brother number two. "Mark, it would seem that Ms. Briscoe is refusing our offer to purchase the Briscoe Ranch."

The brother named Mark extended his hand in the direction of the paperwork. He shook his head as he scanned them as quickly as his brother had done.

John turned back to Marah. "I think we might have a problem, then. Mr. Briscoe has already verbally voiced his intent to accept our initial offer. And that is prime real estate that Stallion Enterprises isn't willing to let pass."

Marah's hand moved to her lean hips, her head gyrating against her neck like a bobble-head doll. The index finger of her right hand waved from side to side in midair as she spoke. "Excuse me? Listen, I really don't care what Stallion Enterprises is willing or not willing to do. All I know is that you have taken advantage of an old man, preying on him at a vulnerable time in his life and I'm putting a stop to it right now. The ranch isn't for sale," she pronounced, snapping her fingers in the air.

The four of them were still smiling at her, annoying Marah even more. Mark nodded, his eyes meeting John's briefly before John spoke again.

"We're sorry you feel that way, Ms. Briscoe. But again, we have a binding verbal agreement from Mr. Briscoe. We're more than willing to consider renegotiating the deal if your father requires more time, but we will do whatever it takes to hold him to an agreement." It was stated with an air of finality that made Marah cringe.

She bristled, hostility raging from her eyes. Both hands fell against the line of her hips as her head waved from side to side. "Well, give it your best shot. But I can promise you my sisters and I will do whatever it takes to fight you on this."

John Stallion came to his feet, moving to stand directly in front of her. He stood close, his tall frame hovering easily over hers, the woodsy aroma of his cologne teasing her nostrils. Thoughts of their time in the elevator together flashed like cinematic photographs through her mind. A rise of perspiration suddenly puddled between her breasts, her temperature rising rapidly. She took a step back, dismayed at the way her body was betraying her.

The man stared her in the eye and Marah fought to hold his gaze, his piercing look seeming to undress her where she stood. When he spoke, his voice was low and even, so controlled that Marah imagined him to be the kind of man who was never unnerved by anything.

"I look forward to the challenge, Ms. Briscoe," he said, that smug smile resurfacing to his face.

Inhaling swiftly, Marah spun around on her heels and rushed out the door as quickly as she'd rushed in. Behind her she could hear a rise of laughter; the Stallion men were no longer able to contain their amusement.

Chapter 2

John stood facing the slammed door, the walls still seeming to vibrate from the violation. His hands were pushed deep into the pockets of his slacks; his thoughts had followed after the woman when she'd stormed out of the room. The roar of laughter from the table behind him pulled at his attention.

"Yo, John, what just happened? Looks like you might have met your match. I thought you were more persuasive than that?" Mark Stallion said with a deep chuckle.

"You surely don't see that every day," Luke mused. "Edward was right about his daughter."

John shook his head from side to side. "It would seem that we have a problem with that project of yours, Mark," he said, changing the subject.

Mark nodded. "It would seem so. How do you think we should handle it?"

John paused, reflecting on the brief moments he'd just shared with the stunning Ms. Briscoe. The three men at his side sat watching him intently, curious as to what was on his mind.

The woman had spirit and John was rarely afforded an opportunity to be in the presence of a woman who wasn't fawning for his attention like a lovesick puppy dog. Clearly, this woman was a force to be reckoned with. Not only had Ms. Briscoe not overreacted to their time in the elevator, but she'd barely given him a raised eyebrow as she'd thrown down her challenge. He was intrigued as he found himself imagining what it might be like to get to know her better.

His mouth lifted into a full grin. "I think I'll handle this one personally," he said finally. "Leave Ms. Briscoe to me."

In the parking garage below, Marah was still shaking with anger as she pushed the speed dial on her cell phone. Three rings later her twin sister Marla picked up the line.

"Hello?"

"Hey, it's me."

"Marah, where are you? Daddy is having a fit."

"Downtown. I'm just leaving Stallion Enterprises."

"What did you do?"

"I told them Daddy's not selling the ranch."

"Marah, honey, you can't…"

"Don't start, Marla. You know as well as I do that Daddy shouldn't sell that land. He and Mommy spent their entire lives building that business. I'm not going to sit back and do nothing while John Stallion tries to steal it."

As she mentioned his name, Marah found herself breaking into a cold sweat. Admittedly, whether it had shown on her face or not, the good-looking man had unnerved her. But she was on a mission and not even a man as fine as that one was going to get in her way. And admittedly, John Stallion was one fine specimen of maleness.

Marla called into the receiver. "Marah? You still there?"

"Sorry. What did you say?"

"I said you better come on home so we can all talk about it. Eden is already here."

Marah nodded into the receiver. "I just have one more stop to make then I'm on my way."

"See you soon," Marla responded, disconnecting the call.

Pulling out of the garage, Marah stared up at the Stallion Enterprises logo that marked the front of the building. She heaved a deep sigh. John Stallion might be laughing now, she thought, but she promised herself he wouldn't be laughing for long.

An hour later, Marah pulled into the circular driveway of the Briscoe Ranch. As she stepped out of her Lexus sedan she allowed her eyes to roam the landscape, taking in the familiar sites that always reminded her that this was her true home. Even the sleek, three-story, penthouse apartment she owned on McKinney Avenue with its spectacular downtown views didn't give her the sense of homecoming she felt when she stepped back on the wealth of property that had been her parents' dreams come true.

Briscoe Ranch was well over eight hundred acres of working cattle ranch and an equestrian center. Back in the day, her father, Edward Briscoe, had been one of the original black cowboys. Not long after the birth of their three daughters, Edward and his wife, Hazel Briscoe, had expanded his Texas longhorn operation, adding an entertainment complex that specialized in corporate and private client services. The ranch now housed two twenty-thousand square feet event barns and a country bed and breakfast. With the property being central to Austin, Houston, Dallas and Fort Worth, Briscoe Ranch had soon made quite a name for itself. Marah couldn't begin to imagine her father ever giving it up.

Familiar chatter greeted her at the front entrance, her father's booming voice calling her name from the kitchen. Marah could tell by the tone of his voice that he wasn't so happy with her. Before she could make her way into the family room, her older sister Eden appeared at her side, her head waving from side to side.

"I swear, Marah! Why do you have to keep Daddy riled up?" she said with a hushed breath.

Marah shrugged. "Don't start, Eden," she answered, her eyes rolling as she followed on her sister's heels.

Her twin was seated in the kitchen at the center island, shaking her head knowingly at Marah. The two women were spitting images of each other from the wealth of their curls to their warm café-au-lait complexions and thin lips. The only physical attribute that separated one from the other was the last of the excess baby weight Marla still carried around her hips and mid-section.

Where the twins were the spitting image of their father, older sister Eden had taken after their mother with her deep chocolate-brown complexion, large, round, blue-black eyes and jet-black hair. Every time the family looked at Eden they were reminded of the woman, a thought which sometimes brought joy and sometimes dropped a cloud of melancholy over their spirits, knowing that Hazel Briscoe wouldn't be there for times like now when one or the other needed to be kept in line.

"What?" Marah said, tossing the other women an icy glare.

"You know what, young lady," Edward said, turning from the pot of chili he was cooking on the stovetop to face her. "What did you think you were doing?"

"Stopping you from making a big mistake."

"Munchkin," he said, calling her by the pet name he'd christened her with when she'd been just weeks old. "My selling this ranch is not a mistake."

Marah rolled her eyes, moving to take the empty seat beside Eden. She leaned into her sister's shoulder. "Which one of you told on me?"

Eden shrugged, tossing a look toward Marla.

"Well, I didn't," Marla said. "Daddy was the one who called to tell me."

Marah looked toward her father, an air of defiance painting her expression.

"Don't you worry about how I found out, girl. Just know that I did. Now what did you do with dem papers I needed to sign?"

Marah said nothing, her gaze dropping to the floor.

Edward waved a spoon in her direction. "Don't make me ask you again, Marah Jean."

"I gave them back to the Stallions."

Edward rolled his eyes, shaking his head from side to side. "I swear!" Dropping the spoon onto the counter he wiped his hands on a cotton dishcloth, them moved out of the room toward his office. When he was well out of earshot, both Eden and Marla started to laugh.

"Did you really just barge into their board meeting?" Marla asked.

"Kind of."

"So what was he like?" Eden asked, curiosity pulling at them all.

"Who?"

"This John Stallion guy. I've heard he's a real business shark."

Marah suddenly blushed, a rush of color heating her cheeks. She stammered, searching for words. "He… well…he was…"

Before either of the Briscoe women could say another word, Edward moved back into the room. A wide smile filled his face as he cuddled Marla's two-month-old son in his arms.

"Look who was wide awake," the man gushed, nuzzling his face into the infant's neck. "He was just laying there waiting patiently for his mama. This here's one good baby. Boy wasn't even crying."

Marla extended her arms as her father passed her the child. Marah grinned, moving from her seat to her sister's side. "He gets bigger and bigger each time I see him, Marla," she said, pressing her lips to the baby's forehead.

"And heavier and heavier," Marla chuckled.

Edward fanned a hand in her direction. "You need to feed that boy some real food, that'll fatten my boy up."

Marla rolled her eyes skyward. "He'll get real food soon enough, Daddy. Breast milk is just fine for now."

Her father scowled. "You kids don't know nothing. Need to give him a real bottle with a little cereal in it. That's what your mama and I use to give you three."

"And I'm still trying to get the weight off my hips!" Eden exclaimed.

They all laughed as Edward moved back to his pots. He peered in quickly, giving the concoction another quick stir.

They all fell silent for a quick minute as they watched Marla and the baby, marveling at the new life that had blessed their family. Edward broke the quiet.

"You need to get dem papers back, Marah."

"But, Daddy…"

"But nothing. I've made my decision, honey. It's time. I'm tired and running this ranch takes more out of me than I have to give." The man let out a deep sigh.

"But, Daddy, if Marla and Michael keep running the day-to-day operations and I know Eden and I would be more than willing to take over some of the other responsibilities."

"Munchkin, for all you know Marla and Michael might have other plans. Marla needs to be thinking about little Mike there, not this place. She's got a family now and Eden needs to be thinking about having one with that new husband of hers. And you don't need any more distractions keeping you from finding your own man. This ranch has just become an excuse for all of us to not go on with our lives. Besides, if you and Eden want to see that new business of yours do well, then you two will need to invest all the time and energy that you have there and not be worried about this ranch."

Marah persisted. "I don't think that's fair, Daddy. This ranch is our lives, too. You haven't even asked us what we wanted to do. I really think we should all talk about it."

"I don't need to talk about it. I've made up my mind," the man said, his expression showing that he had no intentions of discussing it further.

"But, Daddy—"

Edward held up his hand and stalled her words. "Just get dem papers, Marah. That's all you need to do."

The family had all gathered for lunch, not another word spoken about the Stallions or the sale of the family home. After excusing himself to go take a quick nap, Edward had retired to his room and his children had discussed their options. Marah was only slightly dismayed by her sibling's attitudes: Eden and Marla not wanting to rock Edward's boat, but all agreeing that none of them wanted to see what their parent's had built sold away—and definitely not to a corporation that didn't have a clue.

Down in the stables, Marah groomed Brutus, the chestnut gelding that had been gifted to her on her twenty-fourth birthday. Her mother had been the one to select the horse as well as the palomino that Marla had named Chester. The stables and the animals that dwelled there had been her sanctuary for so long that

Marah couldn't begin to image her life without them. Somehow they had to make their father understand how important the ranch was to them all.

Hearing her name being called, Marah stroked the horse one last time, then headed out of the barn. Looking toward the homestead, she couldn't miss the black sedan that was parked in the yard or the man standing in conversation with her father. She could feel her body tense as she stood staring in their direction.

Directly ahead of her, Eden and Marah were making their way to her side.

"If I wasn't already in love and married," Eden chimed, a wide grin filling her face.

"That brother is one good-looking man," Marla exclaimed, giggling with her older sister.

"What's he doing here?" Marah asked, her palms gripping the sides of her waist.

"He came to speak with you."

Marah tossed Eden a quick look. "Me?"

The other woman nodded. "We assume you're the *Ms. Briscoe* he wants to speak with."

"And Daddy says to not keep Mr. Stallion waiting. Something about him being a busy man," Marla said with another giggle.

Marah sneered as they all three headed in the direction of the house, but as they approached the two men, she was suddenly conscious of the fact that she reeked of horse and barn, and her face and hands were smeared with dirt and grime. Marah couldn't believe this was happening to her. She brushed her palms against the front of her jeans, willing the dirt away.

John Stallion turned as she approached, his eyes

· widening with amusement as she drew near. He nodded in greeting.

"It's very nice to see you again, *Ms.* Briscoe," he said with more emphasis on the Ms. than necessary.

"Mr. Stallion."

"John came to talk to me about your meeting this morning," Edward said, eyeing his daughter with raised eyebrows.

Marah found herself wishing for a hole to crawl into as her father continued, turning his attention back to the man at his side.

"Marah is just like her mother—headstrong and stubborn as a mule. Did you meet my other girls, John?"

"No, sir. I haven't yet had the pleasure," the dark prince said, his tone full and deep. He extended a hand toward Eden and then Marla as Edward made the introductions.

"This is my oldest girl, Eden Waller and this is Marah's twin, Marla Baron. Marla and her husband Michael just gave me my first grandbaby. As you know, they run the daily operations here. Girls, this is Mr. John Stallion."

"It's a pleasure to meet you both," John said.

"It's nice to meet you as well," Eden chimed.

Marah rolled her eyes at her sister, crossing her arms over her chest. Her gaze fell back on John, who was watching her intently, his stare more than obvious.

"Ms. Briscoe, I was telling your father that since you're not happy with the details of our preliminary offer that it might be in his best interest if you were to participate in the final negotiations."

"Excuse me?" Marah cut her eyes from one man to the other.

John smiled, the beauty of it sending a torrent of heat straight into Marah's southern quadrant. "That's right. Your father has agreed that you should handle his end of the negotiations."

Marah tossed her father a shocked look. The old man was grinning in her direction. He nodded his head.

"That's right, munchkin. I still plan to sell, but I'm going to trust you to get me a deal that will make everyone happy."

"But, Daddy—"

He interrupted, changing the subject as he turned to face his other daughters. "Marla, we have five weddings here this month and my grandson needs a diaper change so you've got work to do. Eden, don't you have a business of your own to run?"

"Yes, sir, Daddy," both chimed simultaneously, following behind the man as he headed back into the house.

Both women tossed a quick look and grinned at the duo standing toe-to-toe.

When her family was out of earshot, Marah blasted him. "You really are an arrogant ass, Mr. Stallion. I told you he's not selling."

"And I told you that we have a deal on the table that will go through, with or without your approval, Ms. Briscoe. But your father has decided he would like your approval and I support that."

"I just bet you do."

John stepped in, his thumb brushing against her cheek. "You really are quite beautiful when you're angry," he said, his voice dropping two octaves.

Marah stammered, rage flashing across her face. "I don't believe you just said that," she hissed, her tone incredulous.

"Well, I did." The man moved back in the direction of his car, that smug grin filling his dark face. "The executive board is having dinner tonight to discuss the Briscoe acquisition. I'll send a car to get you. Be ready at seven. And, Ms. Briscoe?"

"What?"

"Please wash. We'll be in black tie tonight," he said with a quick wink before sliding into the driver's seat of the vehicle.

Marah watched as he pulled out of the gate and onto the main thoroughway. When he was finally out of sight she allowed herself to relax, stalling the shakes that had taken control of her muscles. For some reason things weren't going at all the way she'd planned.

Chapter 3

Her sisters were waiting for her when she entered their childhood bedroom. The decor was as it had been when they'd been children. Bubblegum-pink walls, princess-white furniture with gold trim, gray-and-white shag carpet and white lace curtains adorned the space.

Marah groaned loudly as she threw her lean body across the twin bed that had been Eden's bed back in the day. Marla and Eden sat on the bed across from her, both grinning from ear to ear. Baby Michael slept soundly between them.

"I think she could use some professional advice," Marla giggled, jostling Eden's shoulder.

"I agree," Eden joked, crossing her legs as she reached for a pen and tablet that sat on the nightstand.

Marah drew her arms up and over her head, her eyes

closed tightly as Eden continued. Her twin sister giggled as if something were actually humorous.

"First," Eden said, switching to her serious business tone as she pretended to scribble a note across the notepad. "When you meet a man you're interested in, try not to smell like manure."

Marla burst out laughing.

"Neither one of you is funny," Marah responded, not bothering to look in their direction.

"Definitely not as funny as you and that man," Eden quipped.

"Leave it alone, Eden."

"Leave what alone? Your obvious interest in a man you've deemed your enemy hardly went unnoticed. Even Daddy noticed."

Marah sat upright on the bed. "Did he say something?

"Who?"

"Daddy."

Both women grinned broadly, cutting a glance in each other's direction before turning their gazes back to Marah.

"No," Marla said, her expression saying otherwise. "Did you hear Daddy say something, Eden?"

Eden shrugged. "Not me. I didn't hear anything."

Marah reached for one of the plush pillows that decorated the room and sent it sailing toward Eden's head. Her sister ducked and giggled, the pillow bouncing against the pink wall behind them.

"Don't you hit my baby," Marla admonished, a protective hand reaching across her son's back.

"What did Daddy say?" Marah implored, her voice dropping to a loud whisper.

Eden smiled. "Daddy said that it's going to be interesting to see what's going to happen with you and Mr. Stallion."

"Actually, he said it's going to be *very* interesting," Marla interjected, her head bobbing against her shoulders.

"Can you believe the audacity of that man?" Marah questioned, her eyes flicking from one sister to the other. "And did you get a good look at his rear end? That man has a body to die for!"

In a flash, the memory of John Stallion and their elevator ride resurfaced. Marah could feel her body temperature rising rapidly, her breathing becoming static as she recalled the moment.

"What's wrong with you?" Eden asked, eyeing her curiously. "You're all flushed all of a sudden. You're not getting sick on us are you? You can't get sick, Marah. You have a dinner date tonight, remember?"

Marah did remember, a wave of anxiety sweeping through her. "I can't go," she said, her head waving emphatically from side to side.

"What's going on?" Marla asked, leaning forward in her seat.

Marah swallowed hard before responding. "Stallion and I had a close encounter in the elevator of his offices this morning," she said. "A very close encounter."

Marla looked confused. "Why doesn't that sound like it was good thing?"

"Oh, it was a very good thing. That's part of the problem. I find him irresistible and that's so wrong. He made me remember what I'm missing."

Eden rose to her feet; Marla reached for her baby

before doing the same. "You better go shower and get ready. I imagine that at least one of those Stallion brothers might be just what you're looking for."

The spray of hot water felt good on Marah's bare skin. She was in dire need of relaxation and allowed herself to revel in the aromatic scent of the floral body wash in the steamy mist that billowed warmly around her. Leaning back against the shower wall, Marah relished the sensation of the tiles against her skin. Her senses had been off-kilter since her encounter with that man, her awareness of her own longings and desires more acute. The sensitivity was like nothing she could explain, the weight of it heavy in her feminine spirit.

Although she didn't want to admit it, she still burned hot from his body heat, her skin feeling as if it were on fire. Her blood boiled as she thought about him, and Marah imagined that if it were at all possible her insides might easily combust. She could never admit to him that she wanted to feel him near her again, his body moving with hers. She shook her head vehemently, shaking the thoughts from her mind.

She stood still beneath the flow of warm liquid that rinsed the suds from her flesh. She had to have a game plan. She had to be ready to counter whatever John Stallion and his so-called executive board threw at her. She had to do whatever it took to regain some control and do what was in her father's best interest.

Control. I have lost control, she thought. And if someone were to ask her how and why, she couldn't begin to give them an answer. Something about that man, damn him, had made her lose control.

Marah heaved a deep sigh. Obviously, appealing to his sense of honor wasn't going to do her any good. The man was clearly a snake in sheep's clothing who had no honor. Or at least that's what Marah was working hard to convince herself. As she stood thinking about the man and their very brief history together, the obvious suddenly shifted her mood and she found herself smiling.

This was going to be easier than she'd realized. John Stallion was, in fact, just a man. The look he gave her after she exited the elevator served to prove that he was a man who could easily be moved by a woman. And not just any woman, but a female like Marah Briscoe.

Marah grinned broadly, tilting her face into the flow of water. John Stallion might be the shark of all sharks, but Marah was a barracuda in her own right. A barracuda with the body of a goddess. John Stallion didn't have a clue what was about to hit him.

Marah stood in the foyer of her family's home, appraising the black stretch limousine that sat in wait in the driveway. Behind her, Eden shook her head, her gaze evaluating her baby sister's wardrobe choice. Reaching into the foyer closet she dug through the coats and jackets until she found a lightweight silk shawl that she passed to Marah.

"Here, put this on," Eden commanded. "Daddy is already in a mood about what you did. We don't need him starting in about you and that tattoo."

Marah rolled her eyes skyward, but took the garment from her sister's hands and wrapped it around her shoulders to cover her back. She met Eden's gaze, her mother's eyes scolding her from her sister's face. Her tattoos had always been a bone of contention between her and her family, her parents vehemently disapproving of her body art. She took a deep breath and then a second, blowing warm breath out slowly.

"Wish me luck," she intoned, reaching out to hug the two women who had been her best friends since the day she'd been born. Their father's booming voice sounded from the top of the stairwell.

"What's luck got to do with anything?" he asked as he made his way down the stairs. "You're playing in the big leagues now, Marah Jean. Them Stallion boys wheel and deal every day. They're making multimillion dollar decisions for breakfast and spitting out the small players for lunch. They're at the top of their game because they're supersmart. You're going to need your brain, munchkin. Not luck."

His daughters stared at him, all three standing with their mouths wide open. Before either of them could say anything, his eyes narrowed into thin slits.

"Where's the rest of your dress, young lady?" he asked, his stare racing the length of Marah's body.

The young woman stammered, her mouth opening and closing as she sucked in air. She looked toward her sisters for help, heaving a sigh of relief when Marla came to her rescue.

"That's the style now, Daddy. That dress is too cute on her!" she exclaimed, Eden nodding her agreement.

"Humph," Edward grunted, not at all convinced.

Marah quickly changed the subject. "Where are you going?" she asked, admiring the black tuxedo he sported.

Eden reached to adjust the patriarch's bow tie and collar. "You look quite dashing, Daddy," she said.

Edward grinned. "Why thank you very much! And, I'm joining you for dinner," he said to Marah as he extended his elbow in her direction, his palm pressed flat against his abdomen. "Shall we?"

Marah smiled back, her eyes wide with surprise as she pressed her arm through her father's. "I'd be delighted, Mr. Briscoe," she answered as she allowed him to guide her out the front door to the waiting vehicle. "Simply delighted!"

Chapter 4

The drive to the magnificent Preston Hollow estate on Audubon Avenue would have taken Marah's breath away had she been breathing. But Marah felt as if she'd been holding her breath since she and her father stepped into the vehicle, the patriarch chatting away as if this was something that they did every day. Edward didn't seem to notice that Marah was twisting her fingers together nervously, anxiety flushing her face with color. She was nervous and excited about seeing John Stallion again and she couldn't ever remember being nervous or excited about any man.

The driver stopped at the entrance to the grand home. Constructed of Austin stone with copper accents and a tile roof, the European-style residence easily encompassed some fifteen thousand square feet of living space. It sat on some sizeable acreage as well, and Marah took in the expanse of landscaping that boasted a putting green, an Olympic-size swimming pool and tennis courts. It didn't, however, begin to compare to the ranch.

Edward barely blinked as they made their way to the iron-and-glass entrance, moving as if this was all an everyday occurrence. At the door he depressed the button for the doorbell, tossing Marah a quick wink as they waited for someone to answer.

Their wait was brief as the receptionist Marah had encountered that morning at the entrance to the Stallion conference room opened the front door. The woman smiled warmly as she greeted them both by name and then leaned to kiss Edward's lips.

The gesture took Marah by complete surprise, and the expression across her face showed her displeasure. In all her life she had only seen her mother kiss her father like that and so the moment did not sit well with Marah at all. She could feel herself bristle, tension adding to the stress she had already been feeling.

The other woman's voice intruded on Marah's thoughts.

"It's very nice to finally meet you, dear. I've heard a lot about you and your sisters."

Imagine that, Marah thought to herself. *We've never heard anything about you.* Marah forced a smile onto her face. "Thank you," she said. "How do you know my father?"

His eyes avoiding hers, Edward answered the question, clearing his throat before he spoke. "Juanita and I are old friends."

It was on the tip of Marah's tongue to ask how old "old" was, but the moment passed as Juanita Hilton escorted them into the formal living space of the home, her arm now looped through Marah's father's arm.

Conversation stopped as Marah and her father stepped from the foyer into a handsome study that was complemented by Brazilian cherrywood floors, wall-to-wall built-in bookcases and a beamed ceiling. The four Stallion men had stood in deep discussion, debating the merits of a mutual fund portfolio when their attention was diverted in her direction. Those four pairs of eyes were appraising her for the second time that day. And Marah stared back, meeting each gaze one by one, noting the expensive tuxedos each wore to perfection. Black suits adorning picture-perfect, rock-hard physiques. She suddenly felt like a kid with a sweet tooth in a candy shop.

Matthew Stallion greeted them first, extending his hand toward her father before formally introducing himself to Marah.

"We're glad you and your father could join us this evening, Marah."

"Thank you," she responded politely.

Edward shook hands with each of them in turn, an easy camaraderie obvious between them all. Marah suddenly had a long list of questions she intended to ask the old man before the evening was over.

John Stallion was the last brother to step forward to greet them.

"Let me take your wrap for you," he said as he stepped behind her, his fingers grazing hers as she allowed the garment to slip from her shoulders.

The man was awestruck. He couldn't take his eyes off of Marah. He was held hostage by bare skin, her attire screaming for attention. Her entire back was exposed. She wore just the hint of a forest-green silk dress, a triangle of fabric that draped into a valley of deep cleavage and stopped mere inches past her southern quadrant to wrap around the shelf of her buttocks. The halter-style dress was tied with a wisp of silk ribbon at the neck and waist.

John found himself dazzled by the expanse of tattoo that painted the woman's back. Starting just below her hairline, an intricate depiction of scrolls and flowers was detailed in magnificent color against her warm complexion, seeming to stop somewhere past the curve of her buttocks. He marveled at the tattoo's intricacy, having never seen such a display of artwork on a woman before. Not one other blemish marred her skin, the tone so smooth and even that one could only imagine how soft and sweet she might be in a man's arms. He resisted an urge to draw his finger against her bare flesh.

He wasn't used to the sensations sweeping through him, his blood surging as it simmered through his veins. Since their brief encounter in the elevator and their abrupt introduction in his boardroom, John felt as if his whole world had changed and John wasn't one to like a whole lot of change. But everything felt different. He felt different, as if some piece of that woman was crawling just beneath the surface of his skin, pleasant but irritating. With her suddenly in his presence, standing so close that the fragrant scent of her perfume was teasing his nostrils, it was almost too much for him to take. He suddenly pondered whether or not a shot or two of straight scotch might calm his frazzled nerves. John shook his head, trying to clear the rush of confusion that threatened to consume him as he still stood staring like he'd lost his mind.

Marah could feel his eyes burning over her flesh and she smiled slyly. Working her assets came naturally and she paused just long enough for him to get a good look before she spun slowly in his direction to face him. She shifted her weight from one hip to the other, accentuating the curve of her buttocks and the narrow line of her thin waist. "Cat got your tongue, Mr. Stallion?"

John blinked, forcing his focus back to her exquisite caramel-colored eyes, the forest-thick lashes batting in his direction. "I'm sorry. You were saying…?"

"I was admiring your home," Marah said, a soft smile brightening her face. "Have you lived here long?"

"We built the house back in 2002, right after the company started doing well.

Marah's smile widened. "And you all live here?" she asked, her gaze skating from one to the other.

Mark shook his head, the appendage waving from side to side. "Not anymore. Luke and I are the only two still here at home. John and Matthew both have their own places."

"Interesting," Marah said, nodding slowly.

John shrugged. "Not really. We entertain clients here and occasionally a business associate or two might stay here if they need to be in town for an extended period of time."

"We like to make our guests feel at home," Juanita chimed, her gaze resting on Edward's.

Marah couldn't help but note the look that passed between them. Her discomfort did not go unnoticed as John looked from her to the older couple and back again.

"Miss Hilton has been our surrogate mother. She lives here as well and keeps us in line," he said.

"Now that's right," the woman chimed, a warm chuckle passing over her lips.

"Do you have any other family here?" Marah asked curiously. "Your parents?"

The man shook his head. "No. It's just us four," he said, an air of tension rising from his center. Marah sensed that she had struck a sensitive nerve and immediately regretted having asked the question.

Luke changed the subject. "Why don't we move this conversation to the dinner table. I'm starved."

"I second that," Mark echoed.

Juanita Hilton moved ahead of them. "I'll let the kitchen know you're ready to be served," she said, shifting into assistant mode.

John took the seat at the head of the table, guiding her to the seat at his side. Her father was seated at the other end, Juanita taking the seat on his right side as the Stallion brothers occupied the remaining chairs. The table was set immaculately, the Stallions displaying their finest china and crystal. Eden, with her pretentious airs, would have been duly impressed, Marah thought to herself.

The conversation was casual as they all chatted easily over a meal of prime rib, glazed carrots and garlic mashed potatoes. Marah knew that her father was truly comfortable when he starting telling a few of the many cowboy jokes he'd become famous for.

"Okay," Edward was saying, everyone's eyes on him. "This old cowhand comes riding into town on one of them hot, dry, dusty days. Now the local sheriff is standing at the front of the saloon watching as the cowboy climbs on down off his horse and ties the mustang to a rail a few feet from the entrance.

"The sheriff, he says, 'Howdy, stranger.' and the old cowboy gives him a 'Howdy, sheriff' right back. The cowboy then goes to the back of his horse, lifts its tail and places a big kiss on that horse's ass end. He drops the tail, steps up on the sidewalk and heads through the swinging doors into the saloon.

"Now, the sheriff can't believe what he's just seen and he says, 'Hold on, mister. Did I just see what I think I saw?' And the man says, 'Reckon you did, sheriff. I got me some powerful chapped lips.' The sheriff is still floored by what the man did so he asks him, 'Does kissing that horse's ass cure them lips of yours?' And the man says, 'Nope, but it does keep me from lickin' 'em.'"

The men bust out laughing. Marah could only shake her head having heard that joke and most of her father's others more times than she cared to count. As the evening wore on, Marah was beginning to think the night was about everything except the acquisition of her family's homestead. Throughout the evening she could feel John stealing glances in her direction, his timid behavior reminiscent of an adolescent in the cusp of a first crush. Marah figured she would be well served to take full advantage of the situation.

She leaned closer in his direction, her eyes widening with intrigue as she gave him a wry smile.

"Mr. Stallion?'

"Please, call me John. Too many Mr. Stallions for us to know which one you're looking for," he said, tossing a quick wink toward his brothers.

"John, about the ranch…" she started.

Her father interrupted, clearing his throat to draw their attention in his direction and away from whatever it was Marah was about to say. "John, my boy. I didn't get a chance to tell Marah about your hobby. She's quite the art collector. I was thinking that she might like to see your studio one day."

Marah turned back to face the man, her annoyance dispelled by her curiosity. "You're an artist?"

John shrugged his shoulders, a shy smile filling his face. "I dabble on occasion."

"He does more than dabble," Juanita interjected. "He's quite talented."

"Quite," Mark teased, elbowing Luke. The two men chuckled and John rolled his eyes. Marah smiled.

"I have two sisters," she said with a warm laugh. "I understand perfectly.

"Where do you fall in the lineup?" John asked, leaning his chin into his hands, his elbows propped against the tabletop.

Marah met his intense gaze. "I'm the youngest. My sister Eden is six years older than Marla and me, and Marla is ten minutes older than I am."

The man nodded. "I'm the oldest. Matthew's next and there's a two-year age difference between us. Then comes Mark who is one year younger than Matthew, and Luke here was the family accident."

Luke snarled. "I was too planned!"

"Like a heart attack," Mark joked. "I was six when Mom got pregnant with him. He wasn't planned."

The table chuckled as Luke flicked a carrot at his brother's head.

As if reading her mind, John answered the question that had been on her mind. His tone was edged in emotion that seemed to pierce straight through Marah's heart.

"Our parents died in an automobile accident when Luke was eight."

For a brief moment, all the men grew quiet, a hushed silence dropping down over the table.

Matthew continued the conversation, breaking the awkward moment. "John stepped in and took responsibility for us. Big brother here became our parent."

John clasped his hands together, looking from one brother to the other.

"He did a fine job with all you boys," Juanita interjected, her head bobbing up and down. "A fine job."

"Your folks would be very proud," Edward said.

Marah nodded, sensing the man's discomfort talking about losing his parents and hearing the accolades for all he'd accomplished. She smiled sweetly as she focused all her attention on him. "I imagine it wasn't easy for you," she said softly. "When my mother died I don't know if my sisters and I could have gotten through it without our father."

Marah turned to meet her dad's stare, the man watching her intently. "I know how you must feel because our mother was everything to all of us," she said, her eyes shifting to meet Juanita's. "Everything."

As dinner came to a close, the group savoring the last

bites of a New York cheesecake with a strawberry rum sauce, John tapped Marah against the back of her hand, his thick fingers sending a current of heat up the length of her arm.

"Care to walk with me, Ms. Briscoe?"

"Only if you drop the Ms. and call me Marah, John."

He nodded his head, and they excused themselves from the table. "So, now that we're on a first name basis, what was it you wanted to ask me earlier?" he asked, guiding her out the room, his large hand pressed lightly against her elbow.

"This evening wasn't what I expected. You said the executive board would be discussing the purchase of our ranch. This doesn't seem like your typical board meeting to me."

John chuckled as they maneuvered their way toward the rear of the large home and then down the length of a short corridor. As he turned the knob on the door at the end of the hallway and gestured for her to enter first. "Nothing that my brothers and I do is typical, Marah. And, we are all the executive board that we need."

Marah stopped short, turning abruptly. "Why are you taking advantage of my father?"

John smiled, the motion brightening his face. "I wasn't aware that I was. Your father has been very eager to negotiate the sale of that property."

"That ranch has been his whole life. Since my mother died that ranch is all he has."

"He has you and your sisters. That's more important to him than that land is."

"You wouldn't understand," Marah said, exasperation tingeing her voice.

"I think I understand your father better than you do. He's ready to shake things up a little," John said matter-of-factly. "He wants to make some changes in his life while he still can."

Marah crossed her arms over her chest, her eyes narrowing sharply. "What do you know about what my father wants?"

"He and I have become good friends over the last year or so. We've spent a lot of time together talking."

A look of confusion washed over Marah's expression. "How did you two meet?"

"Aunt Juanita introduced us."

At the mention of that woman's name Marah bristled, even more baffled by the relationship Juanita and her father appeared to share. The moment passed as she was suddenly distracted. She took in the space surrounding them, John stepping in behind her. The room was a Victorian conservatory, a light-drenched glass chamber that looked out over the landscape outside. The afternoon sun had disappeared, replaced by the brilliance of a full moon and a flood of flickering stars that lit up the dark sky. It was an intimate retreat surrounded by a wealth of vegetation and blooming flora. The glow of nightfall was enchanting and Marah found herself mesmerized by the sheer beauty of the moment. It also helped that they had polished off a bottle or two of bubbly at dinner and she'd been feeling warm and mellow in his company since they'd finished dessert.

"It's beautiful," she whispered as she tilted her head skyward. She turned to stare at him, a coy expression painting her face. She leaned against the back of a wing chair, her arms resting on the edge, her gaze sweeping around the room. She was lean and elegant, temptation standing on two legs and every ounce of her body was beckoning him to her.

"Yes, you are," he answered, pushing his hands deep into the pockets of his slacks, his gaze still locked on her as he fought the urge to move to her side. "You clean up nicely," he said, a hint of teasing in his tone.

Marah cut her eyes in his direction. She suddenly couldn't remember the last time a man had looked at her as intently as John Stallion was watching her now. She shook her head, disturbed that she was being swayed so wantonly when it was she who was supposed to be doing the swaying.

"Thank you," she muttered, turning an about face to stare out through the wealth of glass that separated them from the gardens outside.

She could feel John step in closer to her, his gaze boring a hole straight into her soul. Marah felt warm, too connected to the moment, and she shook the sensation from her mind. She jumped as he drew a hand down her back, the pad of his index finger outlining the ink coloring her skin.

"Did it hurt?" he asked, stepping in even closer to exam the design.

"A little. Not much," she said, trying to contain her breathing. She closed her eyes, sensations sweeping like fire through her body. All of his fingers were gently caressing the expanse of her back.

"It's absolutely exquisite," John said, his own breathing coming in short, quick gasps. "What possessed you to do it?"

Marah paused, relishing the warmth of his touch, the sensation distracting her from any coherent thoughts. "I…I…liked…" She was unable to form the words to explain the edge to her personality that allowed her to take risks and do things other people wouldn't. She stepped away from his touch, wrapping her arms tightly around her torso.

"Look," she said, taking a deep breath and holding it for a quick minute. "I don't know what kind of game you're trying to play, John, but I'm not interested," she said, her tone everything but convincing.

"Aren't you?" he answered, that smug smile pulling at the line of his mouth.

Marah was suddenly overcome with emotion she didn't like. No, she didn't like how she was feeling at all. "No, I'm not," she said firmly, a bald-faced lie slipping past her lips. "All I want is to know what it will take for you to let go of this deal and leave my family alone?"

"Is that all?' John asked, taking a step toward her, the look he gave her overwhelming.

Marah was consumed with emotion, her mind and body suddenly doing battle for control. The expression across the man's face was edged with something that Marah could only describe as wicked. The man was playing her, she thought suddenly. John Stallion was trying to beat her at her own game. She nodded her head slowly. A slight smile blessed her face. If he wanted to play, then she would pull him into a game that would surely leave him wishing he'd found someone else to play with.

"Maybe not," Marah said, lifting her coquettish gaze to stare into his.

There was a moment of quiet hesitation as both stood contemplating each other.

"I suddenly have an overwhelming desire to kiss you," Marah said softly, taking a step toward him.

John stepped in to meet her, a torrent of heat flooding his senses when she pressed a perfectly manicured hand against his chest. A large hand fell to the curve of her waist as he snaked his arm around her body to pull her close. When her pelvis met his, John felt like he might explode right there. Marah gasped, her own body awed by the intensity of his touch.

"What's stopping you?" he asked, his voice dropping to a husky whisper as he moved to lower his mouth to hers.

Marah paused, smiling sweetly, then took two steps back, her hand falling down to her side as she slipped out of his grasp. "The urge passed," she answered, her eyes flickering with amusement.

John laughed, a wide grin filling his face. "You're a tease, aren't you?"

"Not at all, Mr. Stallion. I'm just tired of brothers like you who think they can get over on their good looks and smooth lines. This deal is nowhere close to being done. Believe that. Now, either you want to take this to the table or you don't, but I guarantee you that my father will not be signing any time soon, if—" she paused, allowing her gaze to meet his evenly "—he signs at all."

John nodded, still smiling smugly. "Tomorrow afternoon. Two-thirty. I think you know where the conference room is, Ms. Briscoe."

"I do, but then you know where the ranch is. Meet me in the stables, Mr. Stallion. Shall we say three o'clock?"

"Three o'clock," he responded, nodding his agreement. "I look forward to it."

As she disappeared in search of her father, John turned to stare out to the starry sky. The image of Marah lingered in his memory as he replayed the evening over in his head. Picturing the woman's sweet smile made him hard with wanting. Picturing the length of her lithe legs made his stomach hum with appreciation. Picturing her sparkling eyes made him hungry with desire. As he imagined what could have happened between them, he couldn't help but picture what kissing her could have been like.

Chapter 5

The four men sat lost in their own thoughts when Juanita came into the room to wish them all a good night. "Sweet dreams, boys," she chimed, her tone as comforting as it had been when she'd come to help eighteen-year-old John assume responsibility for his siblings.

Juanita had been their mother's best friend since the two women had been children. The deaths of Irene and James Stallion had devastated her world almost as much as it had destroyed the four Stallion children. With no family of her own, she'd made it possible for them to remain together as a family, stepping in to enable John to have guardianship over his brothers. Juanita had been a rock and all four of them adored her.

John smiled, swirling a tulip-shaped glass slowly in his hand. "Thank you, Aunt Juanita. I'll be heading out in a few minutes," he said, coddling the last sips of a vintage cognac.

"Why don't you stay the night?" the woman asked, concern warming her voice. "I can have your room ready in a few minutes."

He shook his head no. "I want to go home tonight."

"Well, I'm staying, Matthew interjected. "If I have to sleep alone tonight, I can do it here just as well as I can do it at my apartment."

His brothers laughed.

"John," Mark said, his amusement seeping into his voice. "Are you sleeping alone tonight or might you be entertaining company?"

"Yeah, bro. Who will you be discussing contracts with later this evening?" Luke asked.

Juanita waved her hand. "You all need to stop now. Take that nonsense someplace else. Leave your brother be."

"That's okay, Aunt Juanita. They're just jealous," John responded.

Matthew laughed. "I know I am. You and Ms. Briscoe seemed very comfy with each other. Something you want to tell us?"

John could feel them all staring in his direction. "No," he said, waving his head from side to side. "There isn't anything to tell."

"I'm not so sure about that," Mark said. "I saw how you were looking at the woman."

John glared in his brother's direction, not bothering to respond.

Juanita shook her head. "Marah's a sweet girl. You should get to know her better."

Matthew came to his feet, moving toward the door. "I'm sure that's exactly what John wants, Auntie. To get to know her better." He winked an eye at the other men. "Isn't that right, big brother?"

John sipped the last of his drink, rising from his own seat. He ignored the grins plastered on his sibling's faces, not bothering to respond to what Matthew had just said. "Good night, Aunt Juanita," he said, leaning to kiss the older woman's cheek. "Love you."

"Love you, too, baby," she said, patting his back lightly.

As John moved through the door and out of the room, Matthew continued to grin at him. Unable to resist the temptation, John swung a fist in the man's direction, landing a punch against his brother's shoulder.

"Ouch!" Matthew exclaimed, caught off guard by his brother's behavior. He rubbed the bruised spot, a look of surprise gracing his face.

John laughed. "Keep being a wise ass. You forget I can still whip your butt, little brother. Mind yourself before I hurt you," he said, waving good night to the others.

Behind him, Luke and Mark rolled with laughter.

Not even the flicker of candlelight, the lull of soft music or the soft scent of lavender bubbles could dispel the frustration Marah was feeling. She dipped a perfectly painted toe in and out of the bath of warm water.

On the ride home, her father's answers to her many questions had been less than enlightening. He would only acknowledge that he and that woman were good friends, giving her no other information about their relationship. As well, it would seem that his friendship with the Stallion men had bloomed months prior with neither her nor her sisters having any knowledge that they even knew each other.

Marah shook her head, shifting her body against the porcelain pool. What her father had been eager to discuss, though, was John Stallion and his more favorable attributes. It had become quickly obvious that Daddy was keenly interested in Marah being interested in that man. Marah had admonished him for trying to play matchmaker and Edward had simply laughed, reminding Marah that daddies always knew best. In this case though, Marah was determined to prove her daddy wrong.

Admittedly, John Stallion intrigued her. On one hand, there was something about his casual aloofness and commanding demeanor that made her want to know more. She was excited by the prospect of getting to know him better. On the other hand, John Stallion stood poised to wreck havoc on her life. He wasn't interested in understanding what Briscoe Ranch meant to her and that made him her adversary. A very worthy adversary, Marah surmised, and one who didn't appear interested in backing down from his position.

Marah took a deep breath, then two, holding both briefly before blowing the warm air past her lips. She couldn't begin to imagine what was going to happen between them, she thought, but she wished she could stall the rise of wanting that seemed to originate from her center and span through her body each time she thought about him. The man unnerved her, making her quiver at the possibility of his touch. She wished she could get all thoughts of John Stallion out of her head.

Settling into the warmth of the water, Marah was

suddenly aware of the song playing on her CD player.
The Dixie Chicks were singing about not being ready
to make nice. Natalie Maines was crooning about not
being ready to back down. And truth be told, Marah
wasn't ready, either.

The short ride to his Edgemere Road home took
John longer than it should have. He couldn't resist
driving past the gates of Briscoe Ranch first, stopping
his car just at the edge of the extensive property. He sat
watching as the limousine pulled out of the driveway,
away from the house. He sat with the engine running,
lingering long enough to see the flash of lights come
on and go off inside the home. He sat allowing himself
to imagine for just a moment what Marah might have
been doing inside before continuing on home.

The woman was intoxicating, but he was astute
enough to know that her obsession with the ranch would
prove to be even more problematic than it already was.
He never mixed business with pleasure and the business
of Briscoe Ranch would surely come between them
and any pleasure he might want to imagine the two of
them having. Unfortunately, the deal was signed and
sealed whether Marah was willing to accept it or not.

John heaved a deep sigh as he pulled into his garage.
Under any other circumstances, he would never have
entertained the thought of appeasing any woman with
a meeting after a deal had been signed and delivered.
But for Marah, he realized he was willing to go to extensive lengths to make her feel good about what his
company planned to do with the acquisition. For the life
of him, though, he couldn't figure out why.

They barely knew each other. The woman had stormed into his life and may well storm back out when all was said and done, but she had struck a nerve that no other woman had even remotely been able to touch. Making his way inside, John reflected on all he knew about her.

Edward Briscoe had told him story upon story about his three daughters. The man adored his children and it was evident in everything he did and said. He was also a concerned father, worried about what would happen with each of them when he was no longer around to help them toe the line. He had high hopes for his youngest child, the daughter most like the wife he'd loved and adored. And he worried more for her than he did the others.

Edward had told him the tragedy of losing their mother had touched Marah more than the other girls. John could understand what she had gone through, remembering his own devastation when learning that both his parents were gone. Edward feared that Marah's obsession with the ranch was more about her being afraid to let go and move on with her life than anything else. He was concerned because he himself was ready to think about moving on.

John had watched as Edward and Juanita had grown closer over the last few months. They had slowly moved past the bounds of friendship toward something more and John, for one, was happy for them. He couldn't help but notice, however, that his Aunt Juanita's presence had been a source of consternation for Marah. It probably hadn't helped that her father hadn't shared the news of the woman in his life with his youngest child. John had admonished him for that while Edward had tried to make John understand why the news was not

going to sit well with his daughters and how Marah
would be the child least accepting of his choices. They
had politely agreed to disagree.

He took a moment to reflect back on his conver-
sations with the woman while she'd been in his
family home. At one point he'd been able to pull her
aside, to apologize for the experience in the elevator.
Marah had shrugged it off. He wasn't quite so eager
to do the same.

After changing out of his tuxedo, he moved from his
bedroom into his studio. John settled himself in front
of an easel and began to paint. He was ready to lose
himself in something that didn't have to do with
business—or that woman. Because that woman was
beginning to crawl knee-deep beneath his skin and John
wasn't quite sure he liked how that felt at all.

As she'd been doing every evening before retiring
for the night, Juanita Hilton dialed the private number
she'd been dialing for months. As it rang, she couldn't
help but think back on everything that had happened
over the course of the evening. When Edward answered
his line she was anything but happy with him.

"You shouldn't have done that, Edward."

"I'm sorry, sweetheart."

"I told you that you need to tell the girls about us.
Poor Marah. That child looked like she was ready to
cry." She paused as the man drew a deep sigh on the
other end. "What were you thinking?"

"I don't know, Juanita. When John extended the invitation I just thought it would be as good a time as any
for Marah to see us together."

"This was not the proper way for you to introduce me to your child."

"You're right. I should have warned her first."

"Yes, you should have."

"Do you still love me?" Edward asked, his voice dropping low on the other end of the telephone.

Juanita giggled, the length of her gray hair waving from side to side. "Don't be silly, Edward Briscoe. Of course I still love you."

The man smiled through the receiver, the brilliance of it seeming to flow over the line. "Good, because I love you, too."

"Do you have any plans for dinner on Thursday?" he asked, shifting his body against the pile of pillows atop his bed.

"I would love to have dinner with you," Juanita responded. "Are you asking me?"

"I am. In fact, I would be honored if you would come have dinner here at the house with me and my family. I would like to introduce you to my children."

"Are you sure about that, Edward?"

The man nodded as though she could see him. "It's past time, Juanita. I've asked you to be my wife. I don't want to keep our relationship a secret any longer."

The woman nodded slowly. "I would love to meet your children, Edward."

"Thursday, then."

"Thursday it is. Sweet dreams, Edward."

Chapter 6

"Seventy-five percent of all new businesses fail in the first five years," Eden Briscoe was saying just as the telephone began to ring.

Marah rolled her light eyes toward the ceiling as she reached for the telephone receiver. "And where did you get those statistics?" she asked as the phone rang for the second time, vibrating against the palm of her hand.

Eden pointed to one of the many business start-up books lying atop the new oak desk. Before she could say anything else, Marah picked up the call.

"Thank you for calling The Post Club!" she chimed sweetly, her professional tone just shy of seductive. "This is Marah."

"Hello, this is Marah. This is your big sister!" The voice on the other end laughed warmly. "I was just calling to check up on you. Wanted to make sure you're not storming any business meetings this morning."

"You're so funny, Marla. What did you really call for?"

"I just wanted to make sure you and Eden remember that we're all having dinner at the house with daddy this week. I think something's up. He's reminded me three times this morning and he said a friend of his will be joining us."

"It's probably that Juanita woman. Did you know about her?"

Marla went quiet on the other end.

Marah's expression was incredulous. "You knew and didn't tell us?" she exclaimed loudly, catching Eden's eye.

"Well, I wasn't sure, but I know the two of them have been spending a lot of time talking back and forth on the telephone. I just thought maybe it might have been about the ranch," Marla said.

Marah shook her head. "I can't believe this is happening."

"Don't make a big deal out of it, Marah. You can be so dramatic sometimes."

Marah bristled. "Here," she said, tossing the phone to Eden. "Talk to your sister. I'm not speaking to her anymore."

Eden pulled the receiver to her ear and said hello. The duo chatted briefly as Marah pretended to pout from her desk on the other side of the room. Eden laughed, her gaze skating from Marah down to her desk and back again. When all was said and done, she nodded as if Marla could see her through the telephone.

She then heaved a deep sigh. "All right. Well, I'll see what I can do with her before then."

"It's always a pleasure, big sister. Tell my twin I said behave and we will see you two soon," Marla concluded before disconnecting the line.

Eden dropped the receiver back onto the hook.

"What was that all about?" Marah asked, leaning forward in her seat.

Eden shook her head. "Nothing yet. Your sister was just trying to help, is all."

Marah nodded and laughed. "She's your sister, too."

"That has yet to be proven."

"Where does that leave me then?"

Eden shrugged. "In the same boat with your look-alike."

Marah shook her head as Eden changed the subject.

"Marla's concerned about how you're going to act when we meet Daddy's friend."

"Did you know about that woman, too?"

"Marla told me that he was becoming friendly with someone. I didn't know anything else."

"And neither one of you told me?"

"Marah, you always blow things out of proportion. We didn't know if anything was happening between them or not and we were waiting for Daddy to say something. Now that he is, we should all support him."

"I'm not supporting that, Eden."

"Why? Don't you want Daddy to be happy?"

"Do you really think some other woman can make Daddy as happy as our mother did?"

Eden blew a deep sigh. "I think Daddy has the right to decide that for himself. I also think that he should be able to trust that his daughters are going to let him decide what's best for him."

"I'm sure she's a very nice person, Eden. But I don't need a new mother. And neither do you and Marla. I bet this plan to sell our home is all her idea. She's probably scheming Daddy along with the rest of them."

"Just try to be nice, Marah. Okay?"

Marah shrugged her shoulders, pushing her thin frame skyward. "Whatever. I don't want to discuss this anymore," she said, no longer pouting for pretend.

"Fine. So, what's first on the agenda today?" Eden asked

Looking down to her watch, Marah took a swift inhale. "You're going to be late if you don't get a move on it. You're doing the Marvin Wheeler Show this afternoon so you need to get over to the radio station."

"Me? Why me?"

"You're better at that sort of thing than I am."

Eden looked stunned, her mouth hung open. She stared at her sister. "I swear!" she finally exclaimed, rising from her seat. "Do you know the failure rate for businesses that aren't organized?"

"We're organized. And I made the executive decision that you're doing promotion this week. So get moving. I'm meeting with John Stallion at three."

Eden raised a curious eyebrow. "So what's that about?"

"I just want him to get a taste of the ranch from my perspective."

Her sister shook her head. "You're not going to let this go, are you, Marah?"

"No, and I'm thinking that a distraction or two might

be all we need to get them Stallions looking for land elsewhere. Besides, what do they want ours for? Like Dallas
needs another skyscraper," Marah said facetiously.

Eden grabbed for her leather handbag off the top of
the desk, her head waving from side to side. "Just try
not to hurt the man, Marah."

Marah feigned ignorance. "Whatever do you mean,
sister dear?"

"You know exactly what I mean. Don't make Daddy
mad, Marah."

Marah sucked her teeth. "I'm just going to run a little
interference that's all, Eden." She glanced at her watch
a second time. "You better run or you're definitely
going to be late."

Heading for the door, Eden tossed her sister a look
over her shoulder. "Just for the record, I get to be the
executive next week. You just remember that," she said
with a soft chuckle.

Marah winked. "That's a deal. Go get 'em!" she
said, laughing. She watched as Eden swept out of the
small office, muttering under her breath the whole time.

Following Eden into the interior of the club's
intimate front lounge, Marah's gaze swept around the
room, admiring the newly renovated space. The Post
Club had been their brainchild. The concept had come
when the two of them were mulling over the fact that
neither had a man or even the prospect of a man in her
life. Marah remembered the moment as if it had
happened just last night instead of four years ago. Marla
had just married Michael Baron, her high school honey.
Marah and Eden had been sitting in the den of their
family home, bedecked in emerald-green satin brides-

maid's gowns bemoaning their woes into flutes of very expensive 1995 Dom Pérignon Rosé.

Eden had just come out of a bad relationship. Marah hadn't had a relationship for so long it was as if she'd not known what one was. The two had laughed and cried, happy about Marla's joy and dismayed by their own situations.

"We should start our own dating consulting service," Marah had said in jest.

"We could do that," Eden had responded. "Maybe it would solve our own personal problems and help a few other women out along the way."

From that moment on the idea had evolved, starting with the letter-writing service—where they offered men and women help in reviving the ancient art of penning love letters—and then expanding into a service that connected letter writers, one with the other. Before either of them knew it, with some hundred-plus love connections made, twenty-seven marriages and twelve babies produced from the unions, they'd outgrown Eden's dining room table and were in need of larger space to expand their services. It hadn't helped that during that time Eden had met Jack Waller. When the two married, Eden and Jack were happy to run the business out of their new house.

That's when Marah came up with The Post Club, a private lounge where the privileged few could meet, greet and take their seduction skills to a whole new level. Leasing the pricey loft space in downtown Dallas had been their father's idea, Edward Briscoe's many business connections affording them first dibs on the prime real estate. Located on the twenty-fourth floor, the plush accommodations gave them an expansive view of shiny, new Dallas, with upscale restaurants, shops and one gorgeous glass-and-steel tower after another. Marah loved that she could stand in the center of the room and see the Fairmont Hotel, the Dallas Museum of Art, Lincoln Plaza and the Trammell Crow Center through the expanse of glass that walled the interior space. What she loved more was being just minutes away from the family ranch with its rustic down-home feel. For her there was great beauty in being able to leave one world for a whole other as the moment moved her.

However, with everything they'd been able to accomplish, Marah herself had not made a love connection of her own. Four years later and she still rarely had a date worth talking about. A fact that her sisters and father were fond of reminding her of.

The telephone ringing pulled at her attention as she engaged the Bluetooth headset she had clipped behind her ear.

"Thank you for calling The Post Club! This is Marah."

A man's deep voice resonated on the other end. "Marah, hello. This is Victor Tomes. How are you?"

Marah bristled, a chill rolling up her spin. She forced herself to smile. "Very well, thank you, Victor. How about yourself?"

"I need some help, Marah. I'm taking a close friend to Paris with me for the weekend and I want to send her something special."

"How special is special?" Marah asked, an annoyed expression crossing her face.

"Just enough to pique her interest for the weekend, but not too over-the-top in case I get tired of her by Monday," the man replied nonchalantly.

Marah shook her head. Some men made her sick, she thought to herself. "Do you want a full-fledged letter or just a simple note card?" she asked, trying to hide the annoyance that had risen in her tone.

"Do you have something in between?"

"I think I can come up with something for you. And I think a bouquet of fresh flowers would be appropriate, as well."

"I can do roses."

"No, definitely not roses. Roses are very personal. They signify long-term relationship."

"Oh, heck no!" the man exclaimed. "That is surely not the message I want to send."

"Well, I suggest something exotic, instead. Birds of paradise, I think. They'll show intrigue and seduction."

Marah could sense the man nodding over the other end. "You know best," he said, his enthusiasm seeping over the phone line. "You have my credit card number on file. Just charge me, please. And send the card and flowers to my office. They're for my secretary, Pamela."

"Pamela?" Marah shook her head. Just last month Pamela had been calling on Victor's behalf. Calling to order love letters for some woman in London and another in Memphis. The man clearly got around. "I'll take care of everything," she concluded, her head waving from side to side in disgust.

"You're my girl, Marah," the man responded before ending the call.

"Thank the good Lord I'm not close to being your girl," she said out loud as the call clicked off in her ear.

Marah heaved a deep sigh. She still had errands to run before her meeting with John Stallion. There were also a million things she needed to do to prep for the week. There was the Art of Fellatio class she was expected to teach, then later in the week they were hosting a speed dating night—forty men and forty women had already signed up to do three-minute, round-robin dates in hopes of meeting the perfect partner. There were two letter-writing seminars and a weekend retreat on the Nuances of Seduction as well. It was a good thing she was going to be busy, Marah thought as she headed for the exit, because she needed anything and everything she could find to keep her mind off her father, his new girlfriend and that man.

Edward was giving instructions to one of the ranch hands when Marah sauntered to his side in the middle of a regulation-sized dressage arena. The needed repairs on the stadium fences in the jumping arena were finally being completed and Marah blew a sigh of relief that she didn't have to make a complaint about it again. Her father winked in her direction as he finished his conversation and sent the hired help on his way.

"What brings you out here this afternoon?" Edward asked as they made their way in the direction of the stables.

"I'm meeting John Stallion."

He cut an eye in her direction, then nodded slowly. "He's a good man, John is."

"So you've said before."

"Have I?"

Marah chuckled. "You know you have."

Her father laughed with her. "So what are you two meeting about?"

"The ranch."

Her father paused and Marah took advantage of the moment to try and plead her case.

"Daddy, he's coming here because I'm hoping to convince him not to buy this ranch. We don't need a new mall down here and this is our home. I don't think you realize just yet what you'll be losing."

Edward stopped short, tossing Marah a look she couldn't read, his expression one she'd not seen before. He studied her momentarily before he opened his mouth to speak.

"Your mother loved this ranch. She devoted her whole life to this place. I loved your mother and so I devoted my whole life to her and what she wanted." The man blew a deep sigh before continuing. "I'm tired, munchkin. I don't want to do this anymore. I don't have any more of myself to give to this ranch and I don't feel like I have to do it anymore now that your mother is gone."

"But, Daddy…"

"But nothing. This part of my life is over. You might not like it but you're going to have to accept it. I'm selling this ranch and if it's not to the Stallions, then it will be to someone else. This place was your mother's dream, Marah. I'm ready to go live my own dreams."

"And do your dreams include that woman?" Marah asked, snapping unnecessarily.

"Watch you tone, young lady," Edward admonished. "You ain't that grown."

Marah dropped her gaze to the ground, contrition spreading across her face. "I'm sorry. I didn't mean…"

"I know what you meant. And yes, my dreams now include Juanita. She's very special to me. And I hope that you and your sisters will make a genuine effort to get to know her."

Marah suddenly felt like she wanted to cry but she didn't, willing the flush of saline not to fall from her eyes. Her father reached out a callused palm and lightly caressed the side of her face.

"Munchkin, your mother would be proud of you and she would want you to make your own dreams. Your mother loved life. She lived a good one. She would want you to do the same thing."

Without another word, Edward left her standing alone. From his stall, Brutus whinnied for her attention, moving to nuzzle her arm with his nose as she drew closer to him. Reaching into her pocket, Marah pulled out a small red apple and passed it to the animal, brushing her palm against his head as she did. "This isn't right," she whispered out loud, thinking only the horse would hear her. "This just isn't right, Brutus."

"What's not right?" John interrupted, easing his way inside.

Marah jumped, startled by his arrival. He was a few minutes early and she hadn't been prepared to see him so soon. She shook her head. "Nothing. How are you?" she asked, fighting to put a smile on her face.

The man nodded. "I'm well, thank you."

Marah nodded with him as she appraised his attire. "I should have forewarned you," she said casually as she admired the designer suit and expensive shoes that blessed his broad frame. "We don't usually wear our dress suits out here in the yard."

John laughed. "I guess I am a little overdressed," he said, admiring the fit of her tight jeans and plaid shirt. "I wasn't expecting to get my hands dirty, though."

"You have to get your hands dirty to appreciate this place," Marah said, passing him a five-prong pitchfork as she grabbed another for herself.

The man grinned. "Is this some kind of test, Marah?"

"Not at all," she said pointing him in the direction of an end stall. "The stables need cleaning and I figured we could get the job done and talk at the same time."

John looked down to his leather shoes, his head still waving from side to side as he shrugged his broad shoulders. "Whatever it takes," he said easily, moving to the area she'd pointed him to. "So, how often do you have to do this?" he asked.

"If you don't clean a stall daily, it makes for a longer, harder, smellier job later. It's also harder on the back," Marah advised, adding that it was wise to strip the stall down to the bare floor once a week and let it air-dry for the day before adding new bedding.

John listened intently as she detailed what needed to be done and how to do it. Following her lead he mucked the stalls as best he could, laughing with her when she made fun of his facial expressions, the pungent aroma of horse burning his nostrils. Only once did he miss the large wheelbarrow used to cart off the soiled bedding, Marah teasing him brutally about his aim.

When the stall was cleaned to her satisfaction and fresh hay laid out for the animals, Marah guided him back outside to take in the landscape. Only once had she actually thought about giving him a swift kick into a pile of dirty hay, but the impulse had passed as quickly as she had formed the thought and lifted her boot. She smiled, wondering if he would have been as good a sport had he been knee-deep in dirty hay.

Standing at the edge of one of four paddocks, John admired the horses that grazed lazily about. There were seven, most a chestnut brown in color, one black horse and one a sandy yellow color with a wild golden mane.

"How many horses do you have?" he asked, genuine interest in his voice.

"We can board up to fifty at a time. Twenty-one of them are ours, though. We have eight stallions that we use for breeding and the others we use for teaching. Three of them were gifts from our parents and then there's old Bess," she said pointing to the gold-toned horse. "Bess was my mother's horse."

"Stallions, huh?" John said, his tone teasing. "Like that one there?" he asked pointing to a spotted pony grazing on the grass.

Marah chuckled. "Yes, stallions, but she's not one. You don't know very much about horses, do you, John?" she asked, laughter brightening her eyes.

The man shook his head. "Actually, I don't know anything about them. Matthew is the horseman in the family. But I'm learning. So tell me about your stallions."

Marah leaned back against the fence, turning to face him. "A stallion is a male horse that has not been castrated."

"That's a good thing," John said with a quick laugh.

Marah rolled her eyes. "They usually have a thicker

neck compared to a mare or a gelding. They also have very muscular physiques and fiery temperaments."

"Very interesting," John said, his gaze locked with hers.

"Stallions can be more unpredictable than the other horses. But that fire can give them a competitive edge."

"Oh, you don't say." John stepped in closer to her, reaching to brush a stray hair from her forehead.

Marah found herself shivering from his touch and so she took a step to the side as she continued, pretending not to be distracted by the overt gesture. "Typically, they can exhibit sex-driven dominance behaviors and they might bite, or square up and rear. Only experienced handlers should ride a stallion."

"And you're experienced, I hope?"

Marah chuckled softly. "I haven't met a stallion yet that I haven't been able to tame," she said, falling into the wave of his seductive gaze. "Not a one."

The two stood staring at each other for some time, neither saying a word. Marah enjoyed the quiet of the moment, the semblance of understanding seeming to pass between them. When John moved to her side, resting his crossed arms against the fence as his shoulder pressed next to hers, she didn't move, allowing herself to enjoy the innocence of his touch.

"You love this place," he stated casually, his gaze sweeping out over the landscape.

"Everything that I am and know is here," Marah responded. "That's why I'm so against my father selling it."

John nodded ever so slightly. "I know you don't believe this, but we have good intentions for this place."

"No, I don't believe it. Isn't your company in the business of acquiring and demolishing small businesses?"

The man chuckled. "Not quite. We have a number of interests. There's our shipping company, the real estate investments, the entertainment ventures—"

"And now a ranch?" Marah interrupted. "My, my, and you wonder why I would be concerned," she said sarcastically. "Are we building condos on this property or do you plan to somehow bring the Gulf of Mexico farther inland for your tankers to get in and out of more easily?"

John laughed heartily. "You are dramatic, aren't you?"

Marah rolled her eyes. "I'm serious," she said her tone softening. "Why do you want this place? What are you going to do with it?"

John studied her, his gaze caressing the serious lines that creased her face, noting the solemn stare that penetrated his. "Come to my offices in the morning. Eleven o'clock," he said, his deep voice commanding.

"Why?"

"You need to understand why we want to buy this ranch," he said. "Maybe if you understand you'll feel better about this deal."

Marah paused just briefly before nodding her assent. She turned to face where he stared as she leaned against him. "Maybe, and maybe not," she said softly, allowing her head to drop lightly against his shoulder.

Edward Briscoe cradled baby Michael in his arms, the infant snoozing comfortably against his chest. He stood with the infant on the rear balcony of his antebellum-style home, reflecting back on all the times that he and his late wife Hazel had stood arm in arm taking in the beauty of the landscape. Those days had long since passed and Edward blew a heavy sigh. He had never imagined that he would be at this point, without Hazel and alone, giving up the many dreams they had worked so hard for.

He nuzzled his cheek against the baby's forehead, cooing softly under his breath. He hadn't wanted to admit it, but he was beginning to question if he'd made the right decision. If selling the ranch was what he needed to do. He'd been blessed to find Juanita, to be given a second chance at love with a woman who loved him as much as he loved her. And though he looked forward to the time they could spend together in retirement, he couldn't help but think that maybe Marah was right.

Marah. Edward chuckled softly. From the moment she'd come into the world she'd been hell on wheels, a spitball of pure fire. As a little girl she'd been a hurricane of energy, always challenging the status quo. Marla had been the quiet twin, the baby girl who rarely fussed or made a noise. Big sister Eden had been their confidante and protector. But Marah had been all thunder and lighting with Marla the calm before her sister's storms.

Marah was very much her mother's child, the duo like two sweet peas in a pod. Both kept him on his toes and he could almost imagine that Marah's insistence they keep the ranch was being channeled across some heavenly pipeline from her mother.

The baby shifted against his torso as Edward braced a protective palm against his grandson's back. Edward blew a gentle sigh, nudging his lips against the baby's forehead.

He had always thought his one and only legacy to the world would be the magnificence of his children and grandchildren. Now it would seem his children and the world were asking for more from him than that. Whether or not he had more to give was a whole other story.

Chapter 7

As Mark Stallion entered the Oak Cliff barbershop he and his brothers had frequented since they'd been boys, John and Luke were in a heated debate with two other patrons over the forthcoming presidential election. While like most elections this one had folks arguing over trivial matters of no consequence, it held more interest and was made more relevant by the presence of a black Democratic candidate who was giving the Republican candidate a serious run for his money. In another corner a line of old soldiers were arguing the assets of Lena Horne and Beyoncé with Matthew Stallion, Lena's holdings garnering more favor with the old-school crowd.

Mark laughed as Luke tossed his hands up in frustration, his point completely ignored by the old-timer who just wasn't interested in considering an opposing view.

"Give it up, bro! You know you can't change Mr. Baker's mind!"

"Dat right!" Mr. Baker exclaimed, a toothless grin filling his dark face. "I knows what I'm talking about. That 'Bama boy can't win this election. Folks wouldn't know how to act."

"He can win if you vote for him," Luke reiterated for the umpteenth time. "Not voting is what will keep folks from making any progress."

The old man waved a dismissive hand in the man's direction, changing the subject from politics to sports without blinking an eye.

Mark moved from brother to brother, the men punching fists in greeting.

"What have you been up to?" John asked, his head tilted forward as the shop's owner, old Eddy Branton, moved to give him his weekly haircut. The old man held a pair of barber's clippers in his weathered hand. As always, the tips of a comb and a pair of scissors protruded from his shirt pocket.

Mark paused before responding, standing and watching as old Eddy whisked a barber's wrap around John and proceeded, with clippers and scissors, to crop and trim his crisp black hair. Eddy worked quickly, his touch light and sure, the delicate operation seeming odd coming from the old man's thick fingers.

"Just planning a road trip," he said finally. "I plan on heading to Myrtle Beach, South Carolina, for the Atlantic Bike Festival."

Luke reached out to give his brother a high five.

"Hot damn! Now that sounds like a trip. I can smell the barbecue grilling already!" the man exclaimed.

Old Eddy shook his head of gray curls. "You young fellas gonna hurt yourselves on them motorcycles."

"You've just got to know how to ride, Mr. Eddy," Mark said, dropping into the empty chair his brother Luke had just vacated.

John shook his head, admiring his reflection in the glass mirror that adorned the wall. "I agree with Mr. Eddy," he said, tilting his head from side to side as he checked out the line of his freshly cut head. "'Cause you ride like a fool, little brother."

"No, I don't," Mark said grinning in his brother's direction. "Why don't you come with me?"

John waved a flat hand from side to side. "Not me. I've got work to do. And, if I remember correctly, you have some of your own to do as well."

"Man's got to take a vacation some time," Mark responded.

"I want a vacation, too," Luke said, chuckling lightly.

"You just had a vacation. Four years' worth of vacation," John stated.

"And from the looks of your grades you did spend most of that time on vacation," Matthew interjected.

Luke grinned. "But I graduated. That's all that matters. Got my college degree just so John could leave me alone."

"Like that was gonna keep John off your back," Mark laughed.

"I know that's right," Matthew agreed.

John rolled his eyes, his gaze moving from brother to brother.

Old Eddy interjected, "When you gone let me do somethin' with that head of yours," the man asked, his eyes meeting Mark's.

Mark brushed the palm of his hand against the length of cornrows that ran from the front of his skull down to his shoulders. "I can't cotton to what you want to do, Mr. Eddy. I like my hair."

John shook his head. "He's lucky I don't enforce a stricter dress code," he said, rising from the seat.

"Like I'd follow it," Mark said, stretching his long legs outward. "As it is, you're lucky I'm wearing a suit every day. You know this is me through and through," he said, gesturing a hand down his body. "So you know I'm not cutting my hair."

The brothers turned to admire his new Rocawear sweatshirt, baggy jeans and Timberland boots.

John pulled two twenty-dollar bills from the billfold in his pocket, passing the crisp green bills to the old man. "Thank you, Mr. Eddy. I'll see you next week same time," he said, moving toward the door.

Matthew called out to him just as he reached the door. "You coming to the house for dinner tonight?" the man asked, all three brothers waiting for a response.

John shook his head no. "I've got plans."

"Anyone we know?" Luke asked curiously.

John smirked. "Stay out of trouble, little brother."

Mark laughed. "Tell Ms. Briscoe we said hello," he said warmly.

John shook his head. "Stay out of my business," he said, laughing with them.

As the door closed behind him, Mark turned his attention to Luke and Matthew. "So what's the deal with them two? John hasn't been this interested in one woman since…"

"Since never," Matthew finished for him.

Luke nodded. "That woman is *foine!* He'd be a fool not to give her some attention."

"John doesn't mix business and pleasure," Mark said, contemplating the prospect of John and Marah Briscoe together as a couple. "I can't see it working out. You know John will always choose business over pleasure."

"What are you thinking?" Matthew asked, noting the rise of concern in his brother's comment.

Mark shrugged. "Let's just see. Maybe it's nothing."

"And if it's something?" Luke asked.

Matthew cut his eye to Mark and back. "Then we make sure we've got our brother's back."

The door to John Stallion's modest ranch-style home was slightly ajar when Marah rang the bell to announce her arrival. When no one answered she eased it open all the way, calling out his name as she made her way inside. "Hello? John?"

Silence greeted her as she stepped into the immaculate and sparsely decorated family room. Looking around Marah was taken aback by the home's simplicity and charm. After the experience of the Preston Hollow estate, she wasn't quite sure what she was expecting, but this clearly wasn't it. Nothing about the space was indicative of the John Stallion she'd come to know. It lacked the grandiose bravado that appeared to be the man's trademark. In fact, Marah thought as she made her way from room to room, poking about curiously, the house was warm and inviting, feeling very much like home.

Turning the knob to a closed door at the end of the hallway, Marah called his name again, just in case, before peeking inside. A wall of windows looked out to a heavily treed lot, the view eerily reminiscent of the scene Marah could see from the upper porches at the ranch. She inhaled swiftly, taken aback by the sight. The smell of wet paint filled her nostrils. Looking around quickly, Marah realized that she'd wandered right into the man's studio.

An easel sat room center, a small stool poised in front facing outside. A large table sat against a side wall, the top spilling over with piles of unfinished sketches and tube after tube of oil color. Several blank canvases were leaning against each other, propped up by the desk. Three paintings hung side by side on the opposite wall, compositions in varying stages of completion. As Marah stared at the imagery, the artwork reminiscent of the classics she'd seen in an exhibit of works by Claude Monet and Edgar Degas, she was duly impressed. The man was good. Much better than he gave himself credit for. His impressionist style had captured the images of children at play. They were bright and vibrant and Marah found herself smiling as she stood evaluating each one.

Easing back in the opposite direction, she peered into what was clearly the master bedroom. A king-size bed sat imposingly, the largess of it occupying most of the space. The room was pristine, the decor simple with nothing out of place. One framed photograph sat on the center of a large bureau and Marah couldn't resist moving inside to take a closer look.

As she lifted the picture to examine the image she was suddenly aware of John's scent filling the room, the aroma of his cologne teasing her senses. For a brief moment she lost herself in the revelry of sensations that swept across her spine, out into her limbs and exploded in the pit of her stomach. Her body quivered ever so slightly and she struggled to shift her focus back to the picture in her hand.

The black-and-white image had faded ever so slightly. The mother and father standing with full grins were almost haunting as Marah could see the Stallion lines detailed in their facial features. The sons were the spitting image of their father, the man's stern demeanor and handsome good looks staring back at her. But John had his mother's smile in the shy bend to his mouth.

Resting the photo back onto the dresser, Marah moved to the side of the bed, noting the alarm clock, well-worn bible and copy of *Fortune* magazine that rested on the nightstand. Taking a quick glance over her shoulder, Marah couldn't resist pulling open the nightstand drawer and peeking inside.

A box of condoms sat discreetly in the corner of the drawer and Marah found herself smiling as she read the label, the Trojan Magnums proclaiming themselves a comfortable fit for men who felt the standard and large-size condoms were too small.

"Were you looking for something in particular?" John asked, the boom of his voice startling her.

Marah jumped, pressing a palm over her heart as she turned to find him standing in the doorway, leaning against the frame with his arms crossed over his chest. She could feel a rush of color heating her cheeks as she hurriedly closed the drawer behind her.

"The door was open. You weren't..." she stammered, embarrassment sweeping through her. "I'm sorry. I didn't mean to..."

John smiled sweetly. "I'm glad you made yourself at home. I forgot to get something for dessert so I had to make a quick run back to the market."

Marah wrapped her arms around her torso. "I was just looking around. You have a very nice home. Not what I expected."

He nodded. "I like this place much better. The other one suits the public image of Stallion Enterprises, though." He gestured with his head. "Why don't we take this back into the den," he said as he turned an about-face, leading her out the room.

Marah followed behind him, noting his casual attire. Tight jeans hugged his thick behind and firm thighs, a cotton T-shirt nicely fitting his broad back. He was barefoot and Marah noted a pair of sandals resting at the entrance by the front door. Moving comfortably in his kitchen, he opened a bottle of wine and poured two glasses. Passing one to Marah he held it briefly, his fingers brushing against hers before he let it slide into her hand.

"I'm glad you came," he said softly, meeting her gaze evenly.

Marah nodded her head. She hadn't been sure she should and he knew it. When he'd asked, just before leaving her atop her horse in the stables, she'd said no. He'd asked again, his tone commanding. She'd given in to his insistence and now that she was here, with him, Marah couldn't remember why she'd been so hesitant.

As much as she wanted to dislike the man, Marah

found herself drawn to him. She liked him. She liked everything about him and she liked that he was clearly feeling the same way about her. He was also sexy as hell, she thought, his gaze piercing as he stood staring at her. He had the body of a warrior, his imposing stature taking her breath away. He was cool and confident, but so down-to-earth that Marah sometimes found it difficult to reconcile John Stallion CEO with John Stallion regular guy.

Realizing that he'd asked her a question, Marah shook the clouds of thought from her mind. "I'm sorry, what were you saying?"

"I said I hope you like salmon."

"I do. Very much."

"That's good. I'm making my famous honey-almond salmon with a salad of baby greens and slices of sour-dough bread."

"That sounds good."

John nodded. "So, what did you think about my artwork?'

"Your artwork?"

"You mean you didn't go into my studio?"

Marah laughed. "Okay. I did, but I was looking for the bathroom."

John laughed with her. "I can see how you might have gotten the two confused."

"Yeah," Marah said nodding her head vigorously. "That happens when a woman is being nosy."

"I don't mind you being nosy. Not every woman could get away with that, though," John said, tossing her a wink of his eye.

Marah grinned. "I guess that makes me special."

"Very."

Marah was suddenly overwhelmed by the gaze that passed between them. His stare was intoxicating and she could feel herself becoming inebriated by its intensity. She took a quick step away from him, spinning in the opposite direction to take a seat in an oversize lounge chair. It was suddenly too warm for comfort and she imagined that if they spent one more moment together she'd be buck naked on the kitchen counter top without his even asking.

"You're artwork is quite spectacular," she said trying to divert her attention elsewhere. "I was very impressed."

"Your father said you were an avid collector."

"I have a small collection and it's growing. I would definitely love to add one of your pieces to the mix."

He smiled. "Maybe we can work something out."

"So how long have you been painting?"

"Since high school. I took an art class, loved it, and I've been hooked ever since."

"Why not make it a career?"

"It couldn't feed three growing boys. I had to do what I thought would take care of my brothers."

"That was a huge responsibility to take on. And you were so young."

"I did what I had to," he said matter-of-factly. Then, changing the subject, he continued, "I thought we'd eat out on the patio. It's a beautiful evening."

Marah nodded her assent as she watched him skill-fully prepare the meal, engaging her in casual conversation about her sisters, college life and their mutual interests. Marah was excited to discover his passion for foreign films equaled her own as they debated the merits of French cinematography.

Out on the large patio, both sat back full and content. John watched her, enamored by her exquisite beauty. There was something about the woman that made him feel comfortable. More comfortable than he'd felt with any woman. He found himself sharing things about his past and his family that he had never volunteered to share with anyone else. Things not even his brothers knew about him.

"I can't believe you're scared of heights," Marah said with a deep chuckle.

He nodded, sipping the last drop from his wineglass. "Believe it. I turn into a complete mess when I fly."

"I'll have to see that to believe it, John Stallion."

The man shook his head. "I don't think so. I think you'd get a kick out of teasing me unmercifully if you did."

Marah grinned. "Yes, I would."

He looked down to the watch. "Wow. I didn't realize it's so late."

Marah stared at her own wristwatch. "You're right. I should be leaving."

"I don't mean for you to rush off it's just that I have some things I need to take care of before I go into the office tomorrow. I need to be ready when you get there."

She waved a palm in the air. "No. I understand. I appreciate the invitation. Dinner was great. I had a very nice time."

"So did I," John said, looking at her again with his stare edged in pure, unadulterated longing. "We have to do it again soon."

"I'd like that," Marah said, rising from her seat.

The moment suddenly felt awkward and Marah found

herself twisting her hands together nervously. "So, thank you," she said, as he stood, moving easily to her side.

John pulled her hands into his, leaning to kiss the back of her fingers. He winked an eye, that beguiling smile washing over her. "I'll walk you to your car," he said politely. And he did, leaving Marah to wonder what might have happened if she had just stayed.

As she pulled her car out of his driveway, John was tempted to call out to her, to invite her back to languish with him just a little longer. He'd enjoyed the evening more than he'd imagined, Marah having challenged everything he knew about himself and the opposite sex. He'd been open and honest with her and unnerved by the magnitude of his longing. He'd wanted to touch her and it had taken every ounce of his reserve not to see how far he could push for her attention. But he hadn't wanted to rush anything between them. Fearing that if he pushed too fast, he might push her interest away.

But he couldn't help himself from imagining the moment he might make love to her for the first time and just the thought brought a smile to his face, sending his heart racing. And he couldn't help wondering if maybe Marah had thoughts like that about him.

Chapter 8

When Marah entered the room, the Stallion Enterprises' conference room was filled to capacity, the table surrounded by a representative from every department in the organization. Juanita greeted her warmly, guiding her to an empty seat at the front of the room, dropping a stack of documents and charts down on the tabletop in front of her.

No one seemed concerned about her being there and the fact that they were conducting themselves as if business were usual was slightly unnerving to Marah. She inhaled deeply, pulling at the front of her navy blue blazer. Her attire was business conservative, the tailored suit fitting her neatly and even John Stallion didn't miss the fact that Marah had come with her game face on.

He began the meeting abruptly, interrupting the flow of conversation that was being held around the table. "Let's get down to business," he said gruffly, moving toward the large screen that dropped from the ceiling. He moved swiftly, clicking the remote to a digital pointer in his hand.

"Marah Briscoe is here with us this morning to assess our acquisition of Briscoe Ranch. I've asked you all here to ensure that we can answer any questions she may have."

A small man with blond hair lifted his hand as if seeking permission to speak.

"Yes, Paul?"

"I thought the Briscoe acquisition was a done deal?" he said with a slight lisp.

"Mr. Briscoe's family have some concerns. It will be a done deal when those concerns have been alleviated," John answered.

The blond man nodded.

Mark Stallion rose from his seat, moving to the front of the room to stand with his brother. "Marah, allow me to give you a brief overview on why we want the property and what we plan to do with it."

"Thank you," Marah said softly.

An hour later Marah sat in awe of all she had heard. Stallion Enterprises had bigger plans for Briscoe Ranch than she would have ever begun to imagine. The presentation was extensive, with the staff reviewing every minute detail from the financial forecasts to their proposed marketing plans. There had been an answer for every question she posed and when all was said and done, Marah knew that her father's decision had not been made in haste. The proposed purchase price was well above market value and as Marah sat absorbing the significance of it all, John Stallion raised the stakes by sweetening their original offer by an additional thirty thousand dollars. Marah sensed the financial director wanted to balk, but the man held his tongue, knowing better than to go up against his employer.

"As you can see," Mark concluded, "Stallion Enterprises has no interest in sabotaging the current infrastructure at Briscoe Ranch. Your father has built a viable operation that we only want to expand upon." He was smiling in her direction.

"Do you have any other questions, Ms. Briscoe?" John asked, his face void of any emotion.

Marah shook her head. "No."

He nodded. "Thank you, everyone," he said, dismissing them.

Mark gave Marah a quick wink of his eye as he patted his brother against the back. "I'll have the revised contracts ready before the end of the day," he said as he moved toward the door.

John nodded, his gaze studying Marah's face. When they were finally alone, the door closed behind the group of business suits and pocket protectors, he dropped down into the seat beside Marah. Neither said anything as they sat staring at each other, neither knowing what else there was to say.

"I guess I should talk with my father," Marah finally whispered.

John nodded. "It's a good deal. Your family has been well taken care of. I have great respect for your father. I would not have taken advantage of him."

Marah could feel a hot rush of tears pressing against the back of her eyelids. "But it's our family home. We…my mother…"

"Your mother would want you all to do what will make you happy."

"I don't believe this will make my father happy."

"He believes it will and that's all that matters."

"You really don't get it, do you?"

"Get what? That you're not ready to let go? That my buying that ranch is going to force you to face the fact that this part of your life is done and finished and you have already moved on?"

Marah met the man's intense gaze, the first tears beginning to fall over her cheeks. John reached out a tender hand, his thumb brushing lightly against the round of her cheek. Marah pulled away from his touch, rising swiftly from her seat.

"I should be going," she said, rushing toward the door.

John called after her. "Marah?"

She paused, not bothering to turn back to face him, her hand reaching for the conference room door. "Yes?"

"I'd like to take you to dinner tonight. Will six o'clock work for you?"

As she swept into the club's interior, heading straight for her office, Marah was greeted by her sister, who was setting up the workspace for the evening's class. Tossing up her hand in a quick greeting she sauntered quickly past, not bothering to stop to ask what else might need to be done. By the time Eden eased into the room behind her, Marah's breathing had returned to normal, her head and heart in a far better state than it had been earlier.

"How'd it go?" Eden asked, concern painting her expression.

Marah shrugged. "He had me beat before we even got started."

Eden reached out to wrap Marah in a warm hug. "It wasn't a fight, Marah."

Marah rolled her eyes. "Is it just me?" she asked. "Don't you and Marla think this is wrong?"

"It doesn't matter what we think, Marah. It's what Daddy wants."

"Daddy doesn't know what he wants, Eden. Since Mommy died…"

"Since Mommy died you are the only one who hasn't tried to move on. Daddy is worried about that. So are me and Marla."

Marah stared at her sister, then shook her head, not wanting to discuss the matter any further. She glanced at the watch on her wrist noting that time had gotten well away from her.

"I'm having dinner with John Stallion," she said, still surprised that she had agreed to spend the evening with him again.

"What about your class?" Eden asked. "I don't do fellatio," she said in Marah's ear with a low chuckle. "At least not in public."

Marah couldn't help but to laugh with her. "He's picking me up here after the class," she said.

Eden nodded. "You had me nervous for a second there," she said with a warm smile. "I blush when I say the words *blow job*. Imagine what could happen if I tried to explain to someone how to do one." Both women laughed warmly.

"So," Marah said, finally moving out of her sister's embrace. "What else do we need to do to get ready?"

No one noticed when John Stallion entered the room; all attention was focused on Marah and the row of artificial penises lined up in front of them. There were eight women in the class, ranging in age from a very young twentysomething to a mature sixty-plus-year-old. Giggles rippled through the room as the women were laughing over some comment Marah had just made, her casual attitude moving them to relax and enjoy the experience.

John leaned back against the wall, his arms crossed over his chest, and watched. He was early. Much earlier than Marah was expecting him, but that was his nature. As he watched, he couldn't help but smile, a full grin blessing the lines of his face.

"Fellatio is a great way to give pleasure, regardless of whether it's foreplay, after play or the main event," Marah was saying matter-of-factly. "And, like all other sexual skills, it must be learned, so communication with your partner is highly recommended. Finding out what he likes will invariably go a long way toward you performing mind-blowing oral sex."

The elderly woman waved her hand excitedly.

"Yes, Gladys?"

"What if it's something you really don't want to do?"

"Then don't do it," Marah answered. "You're doing this because you really want to please your man. If he feels like you're not into it or that you think of it as a chore, then that's going to take away from his experience as well as yours. If you have fun with it, chances are it will be over faster and then you two can turn the tables and you'll be on the receiving end."

Gladys giggled. "Now, I like that!"

The other women echoed her sentiments.

"Everyone grab a penis," Marah said.

"Oh, I want the big one," Gladys exclaimed.

The table of women laughed and John couldn't help but smile. He continued to watch as Marah demonstrated the subtle nuances of teasing one's partner.

"At this point," Marah continued, "he should be hard as a rock and supersensitive to everything that you do. You can continue teasing if you like, but we don't recommend teasing too long, as this can become frustrating for the receiver.

"And don't just use your mouth," she added cheerily, "you don't want to get a sore jaw. Mix it up a bit by stroking him with your hand and exploring his testicles and thighs."

John tossed his head back, fighting not to laugh out loud as each of the participants practiced her technique. The enthusiasm was admirable as Marah walked from person to person to dole out advice.

"Once you're comfortable with the basics," Marah said, "increase your options to increase the pleasure. Try a flavored lubricant on his shaft. They also have some that heat up when blown on or rubbed. And then of course you can use whipped cream, spreads and other foods to make the experience more erotic for both of you.

"As well," Marah added, "always remember to use a

condom if you're not sure of your partner's sexual history. They do have flavored condoms. Stay away from the lubricated variety, though. That stuff tastes horrible!"

"Do you recommend sex toys?" someone else asked.

Marah nodded. "Highly. If your man is game then I say why not."

At that moment Marah caught sight of him out of the corner of her eye and a rush of color flooded her face. She didn't know how long he'd been standing there but she was certain that it had been minutes longer than she would have liked.

"Excuse me, ladies," she said. "Keep doing what you're doing. I'll be right back."

Making her way to where he stood, she grabbed him by the arm and pulled him into her office as she closed the door firmly behind them.

"You're early."

"You're good."

"That's not funny."

"It wasn't meant to be," he said, laughter shining in his eyes.

Marah heaved a deep sigh. "The class is almost over. I'll be ready in a few minutes. I'd appreciate it if you would stay in here, please. I don't want my clients to be upset about there being a man in the room."

"Yes, ma'am. Whatever you say," he answered, holding both his hands up as if he were surrendering.

Marah found herself staring at his palms and the length of his fingers. He had beautiful hands, firm appendages that seemed to tease her sensibilities. She met his stare for a second time, lingering as they both fell headfirst into the moment.

Marah suddenly felt out of sorts, disconcerted. From out of nowhere she could see the two of them stripped naked, their bodies sprawled across the top of her new desk making love like there was no tomorrow. She could feel her heartbeat quicken, her breathing suddenly coming in short gasps. The expression on her face must have conveyed the rise of discomfort.

Without realizing it, John had taken a step in her direction, concern seeping past his thick lashes. The nearness of his body to hers only seemed to magnify her wanting. Marah couldn't remember the last time a man had her feeling so vulnerable. She blushed profusely, then turned to make her way out of the room.

"Don't forget to warn them," John said, stalling her exit.

She took a deep inhale of air before responding. "Warn them about what?"

"Teeth. We don't like teeth."

Marah found herself smiling. "I'll make sure I mention it," she said and then she turned, closing the door behind her.

"So, just what is it you do for a living?" John asked later, the two having just finished a shared plate of shrimp appetizers. "That seemed like it went well above your average dating service."

"Actually the dating service is an adjunct part of our business. Connecting people with mutual interests is only one facet of what we do. We specialize in helping couples create and find intimacy. The classes like the one you just saw are for women, and men, as well, who want to take their sexual skills to another level and want a safe environment to ask questions and alleviate their anxiety about it."

"Interesting."

"It is, actually. Because romance isn't all about sex. Some folks don't seem to understand that."

John nodded, leaning in her direction. "And business is good?"

"Business is very good."

The man smirked and Marah sensed there was something on the tip of his tongue that he wanted to say. The moment passed as he swallowed hard, shaking his head lightly.

"What?"

"Nothing. I just…"

"Just what?"

"I was going to make a bad joke but I caught myself."

Marah chuckled. "Sure you were. Trust me, though, I've heard them all. You should think about taking one of my classes," Marah said.

John laughed. "What do you think you could teach me?"

Marah smiled. "You never know. We know you're skilled in the boardroom, but typically men like that are always lacking something in the bedroom," Marah said, meeting his gaze evenly.

John studied her momentarily, pausing before he responded. He leaned closer, his voice dropping an octave. "I guess I'll just have to prove you wrong then. You see, I'm not like most men, Marah. If I set my mind to it, there's nothing that I can't accomplish. In or out of bed."

Marah propped her elbows on the table and rested her chin against the back of her hands. "Just how skilled are you?"

John leaned even closer. "Guess you'll just have to let me show you," he said, his seductive tone caressing the open invitation.

Marah could feel the blush coloring her face. The waiter delivering their meals interrupted the moment. The rest of the evening was uneventful as John asked her question after question about her life, her family, her dreams and her goals. Marah answered as many as she in turn asked and by the end of the meal both were certain that they knew quite a bit about each other, adding to what they'd learned the night before.

A band was playing a set of soft jazz in the background and suddenly the room lights dimmed ever so slightly, the mood in the restaurant shifting into something warm and seductive.

"Would you like to dance?" John asked, gesturing with his head toward the dance floor. Without waiting for a response, he lifted his large body from his seat and held out his hand for her to take.

Moving on its own accord, her body followed behind him. The music was organic, an assemblage of deep, harsh drums and unsettling, soaring strings. The tones were seductive, vibrating through every nerve ending in her body. It felt tactile, as if it had wrapped itself around her, spreading through her and him.

John pulled her to the center of the room and turned, pulling her into his arms. He curled his left arm around her waist, the spread of his hand and fingers pressing against the curve of her lower back. He entwined his right hand into her left, lifting both their arms upright as he dipped her ever so slightly toward the floor. The cusp of her pelvis pressed into his and she could feel him hard and wanting as his manhood strained against the material of his slacks.

The feel of him seemed to turn a switch on inside her and Marah's eyes widened as she felt a shiver of want rush the length of her body and back again. They moved in sync with the music. The room was hot, perspiration rising in the valley of cleavage that peeked past her silk blouse.

Marah was lost in the moment, barely able to contain herself as they moved from one side of the floor to the other. She could feel his moist breath hot against her neck as he nuzzled his face against hers, his mouth drawing a slow trail along her profile. Marah clutched his broad back tightly, her nails digging into the muscular flesh. She heard herself purr, a low hum rising from somewhere deep in her midsection and John answered with his own low moan that enlisted a rise of heat from the core of her femininity.

"So what about that kiss?" John whispered into her ear. "Any urges lately?"

Marah could feel herself smiling. "Kissing is a delicate art and must be taken slowly with a new partner. A good kisser knows how to pace himself. He has an active imagination and understands what his partner likes or may not expect, but will enjoy."

"Do you teach that class as well?" John asked, his hand gliding across her back.

She nodded, his cheek brushing lightly against her check. "I do."

"So what else should I know about kissing you?"

"There's no such thing as too slow," Marah answered as John lifted her chin to stare into her eyes. "A girl doesn't like to rush these things," she said with a soft whisper.

Marah closed her eyes as their lips touched for the first time. John slowly kissed her top lip and then her bottom before his mouth met hers evenly. It was an easy caress, so soft and gentle as they both eased into the intimate contact. John worked his mouth over hers, teasing her with the tip of his tongue as he brushed it lightly across her lips, easing it slowly past the line of her teeth until he touched hers. Their tongues did a slow dance inside the warm cavity of her mouth and, as he pulled her closer, his hands skating across the curves of her buttocks and waist, Marah almost forgot that she was standing in the center of a room crowded with diners.

Her arms moved up and around his neck as she kissed him back, suddenly hungry for more of him. A roar of maddening pleasure surged through them both as she pushed her tongue past his, lightly teasing the roof of his mouth. John felt her heat enter and then flood him, fill him, the wealth of it a soothing effluence. Several times Marah moaned into his mouth as his lips moved against hers. John inhaled the moans like he was inhaling her soul, never once breaking the kiss.

When he finally lifted his mouth from hers, Marah could barely remember her own name. Her mind had gone blank, all thought having melted with the moment.

"How was that?" he asked, his breath blowing like warm mist against her neck.

Marah nodded. "You done good."

"I'm sure I could teach you a thing or two if you let me," he said teasingly.

"I'll bet you could," Marah answered, a wide smile filling her face. "I'll just bet you could."

Chapter 9

The morning sun washing over her face pulled her out of a deep sleep. Marah rolled halfheartedly over in her bed, pulling at the tangled mess of sheets and covers around her feet. She'd slept later than she'd planned, but then her evening had ended much later than she'd anticipated.

She and John had danced the night away. The club had closed around them. Its owner, deferring to an extremely generous tip, had allowed them to stay after everyone else had gone. John had kept her laughing until her sides and face had ached and just when she'd been ready and willing to move their party to somewhere more private, their date had ended abruptly, John sending her on her way.

Marah had been certain that he'd been feeling her as

much as she'd been feeling him and then, without an explanation, his interest seemed to have waned. Marah didn't have a clue what, or who, had turned the tide of their moment together, but something had shifted his mood straight to cool.

Marah heaved a deep sigh. She couldn't remember the last time a man had her feeling as out of sorts as this man had her feeling. In fact, no man had ever had her feeling the way John Stallion made her feel. Any plot she may have fathomed to turn his attention from the purchase of Briscoe Ranch had gone by the wayside when she'd been in his presence. With him, Marah lost all sense of thought, falling headlong into the moment they were sharing together. So much for her control, she thought, chuckling to herself.

The telephone ringing on her nightstand pulled at her attention. Reaching for the receiver she answered it cheerily. "Good morning!"

"Good morning to you," her father answered back. "You're in a good mood this morning."

"I am," Marah said. "How are you doing, Daddy?"

"All's well here, munchkin. The reason I was calling is I want to see all you girls before we have dinner tonight. Do you think you can stop by a few minutes early? I want to talk with you all before Juanita gets here."

Marah nodded into the receiver. "Sure. What's up?" she asked curiosity pulling at her.

She could feel her father nodding his own gray head on the other end. "Not over the phone. We'll talk when you get here. Love you!"

"I love you too, Daddy," she said as he disconnected.

Marah sat upright in her bed. *The day has already begun on an interesting note,* she thought. She could only imagine what the rest of it had to hold.

As John entered his office, Juanita greeted him with a hot cup of black coffee and his itinerary for the day.

"Good morning, John!" she exclaimed warmly. "How are you this morning?"

John smiled, leaning to kiss the woman's cheek. "Just fine, Aunt Juanita."

"Well, you have a full schedule today," the woman said, organizing a stack of folders atop the large mahogany desk. "You've got meetings booked back-to-back starting at eleven and you're giving a presentation at the community college this afternoon. Luke also needs some of your time to discuss an acquisition he thinks you might be interested in and Mark called in sick. Seems he needs extra time to get things organized for his vacation," she said, an annoyed expression crossing her face.

John laughed. "My little brother's dropping the ball again, I see."

"Not really. He's just so excited to be going away on that motorcycle trip that he can't stay focused."

John nodded. "Not to worry, Aunt Juanita. He needs the time. In fact, we could all use a break if you ask me."

The woman dropped her hands to her hips. "My, my, my! This from the man who hasn't taken a vacation in almost five years? What's gotten into you?"

John shrugged, a coy smirk pulling at his mouth. "Nothing. I'm just being more sensitive to other people's needs, is all."

Juanita stood eyeing him curiously. She nodded her head slowly. "I hear you had dinner with Miss Marah last night. I take it things went well between you two?"

"Yes, ma'am. They went okay," John answered, dropping his gaze to a stack of papers labeled Urgent. He could feel Juanita still staring at him, her gaze boring a hole straight through him.

"Nothing happened between you two, did it?"

"No, Aunt Juanita. Our relationship isn't like that."

He could tell from the woman's expression that she didn't believe him. "It isn't," he reiterated. "We're just friends."

"Well, there's nothing wrong with that. Just…" she said, hesitating.

"Just what?"

"Just be careful. I don't want you to get in over your head."

"I'm a big boy, Aunt Juanita. "I know what I'm doing," he said firmly.

Juanita nodded again, moving back toward the office door. "Let me know if you need anything," she said, her professional air returning. "I'll be at my desk." With that, she made her way out of the room and straight to the telephone to give Edward Briscoe a call.

John settled down against the leather executive's chair. Juanita's questioning had left him just a touch unnerved. He wasn't use to his family questioning him about any woman he was dating and the questions had started earlier that morning with a telephone call from his brother Matthew.

John had still been in bed, having slept straight through his alarm when the ringing phone startled him out of a sound sleep. He wasn't quite sure who was more surprised, him or Matthew.

"You're still in bed?" Matthew had asked, concern seeping into his tone. "You okay?"

The last remnants of sleep still clung to John's eyes as he struggled to open them and focus. "I overslept. It was a long night."

"Were you working?"

He'd shaken his head, still trying to shake himself awake. "No. Marah and I were out late."

There was a brief pause as Matthew had registered what he'd said. "She's not still there with you, is she?"

"No. We didn't leave the club until four o'clock then I took her right home. It wasn't like that. We didn't spend the night together. At least we didn't sleep together."

"Oh."

John could hear the question in Matthew's voice. "What oh? We didn't."

"So, what's going on with you two? This is the second night in a row you two have spent together, isn't it?"

"It's the second night that we had dinner together. What's wrong with that?"

"Nothing. I was just asking."

"You were asking for a reason."

"Well, I was just wondering if you're breaking your rule about mixing business with pleasure. It's bad for business, isn't that what you use to say?"

"It is. But I'm not doing business with Marah."

"You're doing business with her father."

"And he's not Marah."

"Like hell he isn't. He didn't ask for a meeting to renegotiate what he'd already negotiated. His daughter did and you gave it to her. Sounds like business to me."

John said nothing, silence his only response.

Matthew could almost see the wheels spinning in his brother's brain. "You really like this woman, don't you?" he asked after the brief pause.

John could feel his head bobbing against his shoulders as he nodded slowly. "I do. I like her a lot."

"There's nothing wrong with that, John," Matthew said. "It's about time you gave your personal life some attention."

"Look," John said, not use to his younger sibling being the one to give him advice. "Let me get going. I need to get into the office. I'll catch up with you later."

"Do that," Matthew said firmly. "We should talk more."

Dropping the telephone back onto the hook, John had pulled himself up and out of the bed. A warm shower had been calling his name and when the first spray of water hit his chest and face, he felt invigorated. Ready to take on the world. And as he'd soaped his body, his hands gliding against the rock-hard muscles that he spent hours in the gym training, he had thought about Marah Briscoe.

John leaned back in his chair, spinning around to stare out the window to the view outside. Marah had his full attention like no other woman before her. He'd been ready to take her home to his bed last night. He'd been acutely aware that she wanted him as much as he wanted her, but he'd resisted the temptation that had been pulling at him. It had taken every ounce of fortitude he'd possessed not to try and move their relationship to the next level. But he hadn't because he'd known instinctively that if he had, there would have been no turning back. Marah had his nose wide open and he couldn't get enough of her. And though he would never admit it to anyone else, traveling that path of no return scared him to death. And John Stallion had never been frightened of anything a day in his life.

Edward Briscoe stood in deep thought when Eden and Marla entered the family home. The women were in deep conversation, mulling over fabric samples for the chairs they wanted to reupholster in the bed and breakfast rooms. Both seemed to sense the seriousness of his mood at the same time, stopping in mid-conversation to stare in his direction.

"Daddy, is everything okay?" Eden asked.

"Are you feeling okay, Daddy?" Marla echoed.

He nodded, his gaze skating from one face to the other. "What do you girls know about Marah and John Stallion? Has she said anything about him to you two?"

Marla chuckled. "Just that she couldn't stand him. It just burns her up that he's interested in buying the ranch."

Eden nodded. "I think she feels like he got the best of her and you know how much Marah hates when someone gets one over on her."

Edward nodded his own head. "Do you think she likes him at all? I mean they did have dinner together, didn't they?"

Eden shrugged, her narrow shoulders jutting skyward. "You know how Marah is, Daddy. If she does like him, she's not going to let us know."

Marla chuckled. "And she might not even let him know."

"I hope she's not playing games with that young man. I would sure hate to see that happen," Edward said, blowing a loud sigh past his full lips.

The two sisters cut an eye toward each other. "It's hard to say what Marah's up to, Daddy," Marla said.

Eden agreed. "She's so focused on not losing this ranch that she would probably do almost anything to get you or Stallion to change your minds."

Edward sighed again. "That's what I'm afraid of."

When Juanita arrived for dinner with the family she wasn't quite prepared for the reflective mood she found Edward and his daughters in. The three young women had greeted her warmly, even Marah went out of her way to be polite.

"It's nice to finally meet you all," Juanita said sweetly, looking from one curious face to the other.

"It's nice to meet you" Eden had echoed as her husband, Jake, had taken the woman's wrap and handbag.

"It's nice to see you again, Juanita," Marah had said nicely. "Welcome to our home."

Despite their show of Southern hospitality, Juanita sensed that something wasn't quite right and when she had an opportunity to, she pulled Edward aside and asked what was wrong.

The man took a deep inhale of air before answering, his gaze skipping from Juanita's face to the door of the family room where everyone was gathered.

"I told the girls I'm reconsidering the sale. I'm not sure if I'm going to sell the ranch."

Juanita was taken aback by the comment. "Reconsidering? Edward, why? I thought you'd made up your mind?"

"I thought I had, too, but Marah's been so insistent that I had to rethink it. I don't want to make a mistake, Juanita."

"But what about all of your plans? What about our plans? If you decide to keep the ranch where does that leave things? What about your retirement?"

The man shrugged. "I'm not sure. I've asked the girls to think about how much responsibility they're going to be willing to take on and then we'll see from there. I know we wanted to travel and just go explore the world, but if I keep the ranch we might not be able to do all of that. How would that make you feel?"

Juanita leaned to kiss his lips, pressing herself against his torso. "Edward, whatever you decide, you know I'll support you. I just want you to be happy. But I don't want you to feel pressured into doing something that you don't want to do, either. I want you to be sure that this is right for you."

"It's important that this is right for my family, Juanita. I can't do it if it isn't. My girls mean the world to me and if they're not happy, I'm not happy."

The woman nodded her head. "I understand, darling. You know best."

The moment was interrupted as Marah poked her head into the room. "Excuse me," she said softly, her eyes focused everywhere but on the couple in front of her. "Eden says your hot fudge sundaes are ready when you two are."

Her father chuckled. "Now that sounds like a plan. I love me some hot fudge now."

The two women laughed as Edward moved toward the door.

"I'll be right there," Juanita said, smiling after him. Her gaze met Marah's. "Thank you for making me feel so welcome tonight, Marah. I have really had a nice time."

Marah nodded. "We're glad."

Juanita paused for just a brief moment. "Your father was just telling me that he's thinking about not selling the ranch."

Marah's smile widened. "So it seems."

The older woman nodded her head slowly. "John will be disappointed."

Marah shrugged. "He's a big boy. I'm sure he'll get over it."

"Perhaps. Perhaps not."

Marah crossed her arms over her chest, her weight shifting to her right hip. "Is there something you want to say to me, Juanita?"

The woman stood staring, then she turned, slowly easing her way to stare out the large bay window to the land outside. "I get the feeling that John cares for you very much, but I wouldn't want him to get hurt if you didn't feel the same way about him," she said. "You two really don't know each other that well. And if all this attention you've been showing him is just about the ranch and nothing more…" Her voice trailed off, her concern not fully verbalized.

Marah said nothing.

"You do like John, don't you, Marah?" the woman persisted.

"Of course I like him. We've become friends," she answered, her tone edged in a hint of attitude at the woman's motherly concern.

"Is there anything you wouldn't do to stop your father from selling this land, Marah?" Juanita asked point blank.

"No," Marah said without pausing. "I'd do anything to save this land. This is our home."

Their names being called from the other room interrupted the moment. Edward peered through the entranceway.

"You two gals okay in here?" he asked.

Marah nodded. "Just fine, Daddy. We were just finishing our conversation."

"Juanita? Everything all right?" the man asked again, his gaze resting on the other woman.

Juanita tossed Marah one last look, then nodded and smiled. "All's well, Edward," she said, the words sounding more convincing than she had thought she would be able to muster.

Marah was kicking herself as she pulled out of the driveway of her family's home, headed in the direction of her downtown apartment. She couldn't begin to understand why she'd allowed that woman to get under her skin, but she had, finding herself angry at Juanita's mere presence. Everyone else had warmed up to the woman almost immediately, but Marah had built a mile-high wall between them. It was bad enough that Juanita had stolen her father's affections, but questioning her about John was something else altogether.

Marah could feel the rise of warm saline pressing at her eyeballs. She'd always imagined that when she fell in love for the first time that her mother would have been the first person she could have told. Her sisters would have been second. But her mother wasn't there to share Marah's news and Marah resented Juanita for being there instead. Marah couldn't begin to tell Juanita that what she was feeling for John had far surpassed her simply liking him. She didn't have the words for Juanita to explain that John Stallion actually had her imagining what forever might be like with him at her side. And she resented the woman having the audacity to question what Marah's feelings were for the man as if Marah's couldn't possibly be coming from a place of genuine affection.

Hazel Briscoe had been there for Marla and her tribulations before she'd walked down the aisle with her husband Michael. Now that Marah had her own stories to tell, her mother was gone and there were no words she could find to express the level of hurt she felt about that.

Without realizing it, Marah had turned left instead of right, her car headed in the direction of John's home. As if something else were guiding her, she made her way to his driveway, parking beneath a tall oak tree that sat in the front yard. The home was dark with the exception of a faint light that glowed softly from a rear window. Marah sucked in air, filling her lungs. Her heart was beating a mile a minute and she couldn't begin to fathom why she'd driven herself here instead of home. And then she remembered that being with John felt as warm and as inviting as any other home she'd ever known.

Moving to the front stoop, she stood poised to knock when the door swung open unexpectedly. John eyed her curiously from the other side.

"Hey," Marah said softly, the word catching in her throat.

"Hey yourself," he answered, still staring at her intently.

Marah stared into his eyes, losing herself beneath the intense gaze he'd wrapped around her. In that moment she knew that he was as lost in her and that they had found themselves in each other. As he pushed the screen door open, stepping aside to welcome her in, Marah knew there would be no turning back from whatever was going to happen between them.

As she made her way inside, John stopped her in her tracks, pressing a warm palm against her abdomen as she moved to step past him. Turning to look him in the face, she smiled as he lowered his mouth to hers and kissed her softly. It was a sweet caress, like none Marah had ever experienced before; the wealth of it soothed her soul.

Saying nothing, John eased the door closed behind them, then grabbed her hand beneath his and led her down the hall to the studio at the end. Inside, Marah saw that he had been working, a new painting taking form against his easel. She stepped in closer to admire the beginning lines of a couple in a sweet embrace.

"I'm interrupting," Marah said, her voice barely a whisper.

"So why did you come?" he asked, meeting her gaze evenly.

Marah hesitated for just a split second, pondering the question before she answered. "I wanted to be with you," she said, her voice coming louder, her tone controlled and even. "I wanted you."

The man nodded and smiled, the bend to his mouth confirming what Marah saw in his eyes. He wanted her as well. She smiled back, the fullness of it spreading her face with sheer joy.

John's gaze raced the length of her body, admiring the fit of her tank top and denim skirt. Her legs were bare, a pair of slip-on sneakers covering her feet. When Marah saw him looking, she kicked the shoes off into the corner and stood barefoot, her newly manicured toes peeking up from the floor.

John moved to her side and brushed the length of his fingers against her forearm. He stood staring at her, saying nothing as his fingers danced a slow drag up and down the length of her arm.

"Say something," Marah commanded.

John laughed. "I want to paint you. Will you let me paint you?"

Marah giggled. "Is that all you want to do to me?"

He nodded, chuckling with her. "It's a start."

She nodded, her head waving up and down slowly. "Where do you want me?" she asked, looking over her shoulder.

John pointed to the worktable, moving past her to push the clutter on top to the floor. "Here," he said, patting the tabletop. "Climb up here."

Hiking her skirt past her knees, Marah climbed up onto the table and made herself comfortable. She watched as John moved to the other side of the room to adjust the lights, dimming them noticeably. He stopped, lost in thought, then excused himself, exiting the room.

"I'll be right back," he said tossing her a wink.

As he disappeared, Marah lay back against the table, her arms crossed behind her head, one leg bent at the knee, the other hanging off the table's edge. She was lost in thought when John came back into the room, pulling his stool up to the tabletop beside her.

"What are you doing?" she asked, eyeing the objects he held in his hand.

The man smiled. "Do you trust me, Marah?" he asked, staring her in the eye.

She nodded her head without hesitation. "I do."

"Then relax and let me paint you," he said, his seductive tone mesmerizing.

Marah nodded her head again and lay back down, still eyeing him curiously. She watched as he removed a plastic wrapper from a brand-new paintbrush. When he passed the soft bristles lightly across the top of her foot, a small shiver of electricity shot through her body and she felt herself jump ever so slightly. John grinned.

Moving quickly, John uncapped the top from a tube of what appeared to be an intimate moisturizer and she watched as he squeezed the gelatinous liquid into the palm of his left hand. "Now, I'm going to paint you," he said as he dipped his brush into the goo then drew a light line along the length of her calve.

Marah giggled, the bristles and cool moisture tickling her flesh. John continued to tease her, the paintbrush gliding back and forth across her thighs as he eased her skirt farther up her body. She knew her pale peach G-string was on complete display but didn't care, giving in to the erotic sensations the man was eliciting from her body.

Stroke for stroke the man was teasing her senseless

and when she reached out for him, wanting to pull him close, John had only cooed in her ear, easing her hands back above her head, holding her back from taking charge. He kissed her mouth, the connection urgent and hot, sucking on her lower lip as his teeth lightly scraped the sensitive skin. Her tongue met his and danced frantically inside his mouth, searching for the back of his throat. And then he moved his mouth from hers, his lips dancing against the line of her cheek, down the length of her neck, nuzzling in the soft spot beneath her chin.

Marah felt he was playing her like a delicate instrument. With each stroke of his paintbrush he was hitting high notes and low notes. She could feel her breathing take on a rhythm of its own and she could feel his follow in sync. Soft noises that she couldn't hold back escaped past her lips, dancing against the walls of the room.

With no memory of how or when, Marah was suddenly aware of the paintbrush gently caressing the lines of her secret treasure, lavishing bold strokes over each crevice and fold. There was no sign of her G-string to be found, all of her glory open to him. Marah desperately ran her fingers through the length of her hair. She was panting and heaving and all at once she bit her lip to suppress her sobs as she closed the length of her legs, trapping his hand, his paintbrush still dancing like silk against the swollen nub of her womanhood.

His other hand was caressing every other part of her body, strong solid fingers sweeping against the skin on her arms, over her shoulders, across her abdomen. Marah imagined that there had to be more than one of

him for her to be feeling so many delicious sensations
at one time.

John watched as Marah gave herself over to him. He
was enjoying his exploration, delighting in being able
to take her to a place of no return. Heat danced the
length of hers arm as he drew a pattern of intricate
designs against her skin. She was warm and wet and he
grew hard, the length of a heavy erection straining for
release.

Marah opened her eyes and stared at him briefly. As
she stared, John realized that everything behind her
eyes was his, her gaze meant only for him. Her eyes
rolled back as she savored his touch. Her breath was
coming in shorter, harsher bouts, each breath coming
faster than the one before as she struggled to retain the
last of her composure. And then she muttered his name
over and over again, the lilt of it warming his soul as
she rode down the last of her orgasm, her body trembling, her heart beating rapidly. When it was over, everything was a blur but the satisfied smile on John's face
as he looked into Marah's eyes.

He let her linger there until her breathing had
returned to a semblance of normal. As she lay trying to
compose herself, he kissed a path of damp kisses across
her cheek, his mouth finding hers again. His kiss was
passionate, consuming, moving Marah to scream his
name for a second time, but the sound was lost to her
as she struggled to speak.

Then, lifting her from the tabletop, John carried her
from the studio into his bedroom, resting her gently
against the cotton sheets on his bed. She reached her
arms around his neck and kissed him again, hungry for

more of him as her mouth danced a jig over his. She
was free from her clothes in seconds, the garments
tossed to the floor on the other side of the room. They
struggled with his, both of them suddenly frantic to get
him out of his jeans and T-shirt.

When he was naked, towering above her, Marah was
mesmerized by the sheer beauty of him. He was a solid
foundation of black marble, the dark of his skin the
perfect complement to her own warm complexion.
Marah imagined he tasted like dark chocolate and she
pressed her mouth to his chest, savoring the salt and
sweet of him. With exquisite skill, his knowing fingers
plucked at her nipples, the responsive buds already
achingly erect. Dropping his head to her, he suckled one
breast and then the other, his tongue sweeping the rock-
hard candy against his lips.

Marah reached her hand between them, her fingers
wrapping around the pulsating steel of his manhood.
John moaned at the first sensation of her touch, leaning
his forehead into her shoulder as she stroked him
brazenly, the tips of her fingers doing their own dance
up and down the length of him.

Marah pushed against him with the palm of one
hand, easing him gently from her. As he lifted himself
upward, she reached for the nightstand and the prophy-
lactic she knew to be hidden inside. John watched as
Marah ripped the cover from the condom and slowly
sheathed the length of him, her fingers teasing and
stroking him with complete abandonment.

With her eyes half-lidded, Marah pulled him back to
her, dropping down against the bed, the weight of him
warm and embracing. She parted her thighs in invita-

tion and John whispered his appreciation against her neck. Their mouths met in a tongue-delving kiss as he entered her slowly, her body yielding easily to his. She met him stroke for stroke as they danced across the mattress, the duo two-stepping as if they might never dance again. Bliss came once and then again and again, John moving her body to heights Marah had never imagined. When the sun rose the next morning, Marah was still sleeping soundly against him, his naked body curved protectively around hers.

Chapter 10

John had never called in sick a day in his life and even he couldn't explain what had gotten into him when he called Juanita and told her to cancel his day, that he wasn't going to be coming to work.

"What's wrong?" Juanita had asked, concern spilling over the telephone lines.

"Everything's fine, Aunt Juanita. I just need to take some time off. I'll give you a call later," he'd said, dismissing her offer to come by the house to nurse him well.

After hanging up the line, he rolled back beneath the sheets, curling his body back against the heat of Marah's naked frame.

"Mmm," she purred softly, her eyes still closed to the sunlight peeking through the closed blinds.

"Good morning," John said, the warmth of his breath blowing against her ear.

"It is a good morning," Marah answered, turning to press her face into his chest. She pressed a kiss against his skin, allowing her lips to linger where they rested.

"Wanna play hooky with me?" John asked, brushing the loose strands of her hair against the side of her face. "We could spend the whole day right here in this bed."

Marah smiled, her eyes still closed as she snuggled up to him. "I can certainly do that," she exclaimed softly. "Pass me your telephone," she said, extending her arm in the direction of the receiver.

Minutes later, with her sister pacified that she wasn't clinging to death's door, Marah relished the sensation of John's touch as he massaged her gently, his hands lightly caressing the length of her body.

"Where did you learn to do that?" she asked, passing her own palms across his broad chest.

"Do I need more practice?" John responded, his mouth brushing a kiss against her forehead.

Marah shook her head from side to side, her cheek knocking against the soft pillow. "Not at all. You've mastered that perfectly," she said. "Two gold stars for you, Mr. Stallion."

The man chuckled. He flinched, a shiver running up his spine as Marah drew a soft palm down his back, pausing as she cupped his buttock in her hand. She laughed softly as she felt him harden against her leg, her knee stroking him brazenly.

"Glad you're standing at attention this morning," she said coyly, shifting her body against him.

"Two gold stars for you," John murmured under his breath, his breathing quickening with each caress.

Marah suddenly lifted herself up and out of the bed, moving in the direction of the bathroom. "I like my eggs scrambled," she said, tossing him a look over her shoulder. "With buttered toast and bacon, please."

John laughed. "Woman, if you don't…"

Marah waved a finger in his direction. "A girl needs her nourishment. I perform much better when I've been refueled," she said, mischief shimmering in her eyes. "Hop to it, Mr. Stallion."

He leaned back against the pillows, a large palm cupping the bulge of flesh between his legs. "And what do I get in return," he asked, rising up on his elbow.

Marah turned to stare at him, leaning her body against the doorframe leading into the master bathroom. She smiled sweetly. "Do me right, Mr. Stallion, and I might take you for a ride," she said, her tone teasing.

"Can you ride a stallion?" John asked smugly.

Marah laughed. "Haven't met one yet I couldn't," she said closing the bathroom door behind her.

Later, laughter rang through the small house as Marah raced naked from one room to the other, John chasing behind her. They'd played like kids most of the morning, teasing and taunting each other unmercifully. John couldn't remember the last time he'd had such a great time. The telephone had finally stopped ringing, each of his brothers having called to inquire what was up with him. Each grinning knowingly upon discovering their big brother wasn't alone, his "sick day" not a day of illness at all.

He'd fixed Marah's requisite scrambled eggs and

bacon, the two of them sharing breakfast in bed. Then they'd lain side by side in deep conversation, sharing intimate secrets neither had ever ventured to share with anyone else. They'd traded easy caresses back and forth, dozing off and on through the morning game shows and John found himself surprised by how easy it was to just let himself go and relax without the stress of work and responsibilities weighing him down.

When Marah had sprayed him with a shaken bottle of soda, it had been on. They'd been racing through the house since, both determined to up the other, giggling as if they didn't have a care in the world.

Back in the bedroom, Marah jumped atop the bed and John lunged, grabbing her by the ankle. A quick tug and she fell face forward against the mattress, dropping with a loud thud into the mound of pillows and sheets. Crawling up and over her, he covered her body with his, holding her hostage by her wrists as he nuzzled her neck, leaving a trail of kisses across her shoulders and back.

Marah allowed herself to enjoy the moment. Her breath came in short gasps from all the excitement. She suddenly wiggled beneath him. "Stop, stop, stop!"

John lifted himself up, suddenly concerned that he had done something to hurt her. "What's wrong? Are your okay?"

Marah giggled. "I'm fine. But it's my turn," she said, her eyes shimmering.

He eyed her curiously as she continued.

"Last night I trusted you, now I want you to trust me," she said, her eyebrows raised in mischief.

John shook his head. "I'm scared."

Marah grinned. "You should be. Now, you wanna play my game or not?"

The man paused, pretending to give the thought serious consideration. "I guess…" he said, pretending to be skeptical.

Marah giggled, jumping from the bed and out the room. She came back moments later with a large bowl covered with a dishtowel. She dropped the container on the nightstand and pushed John back against the bed. She took his hand and brought it to her mouth, kissing the back of it before slowly sucking each of his fingers into her mouth and out again. John purred as he watched her, a low hum of appreciation rising from his midsection.

Moving away from him, Marah went searching through his walk-in closet returning with four silk neckties snatched off a hanger.

"Do you trust me, John Stallion?" she asked as she took his right arm and tied it to the bedpost.

John's eyes widened but he shook his head yes, saying nothing out loud. Marah's smile spread as she blew him a kiss, moving to secure his left hand to the other post. She swung her body around to the foot of the bed and secured both of his feet to the footposts, leaving him spread eagle on the mattress. The man shook his head slowly, beginning to wonder what he'd gotten himself into.

Marah stood at the foot of the bed and gave a little whistle. From where she stood, the view was spectacular. From his muscular legs to the protrusion of manhood that was standing at attention, past the taut muscles of his abdomen, he was simply breathtaking. Every sinew was hard and tight, yearning for her attention. Even his little nipples begged to be kissed and, with methodic precision, Marah paid homage to every ounce of him.

She started kissing her way up his legs first, paying attention to each toe and making sure she kissed, licked or bit every square inch of the journey. She blew warm breath against his manhood, teasing him with her mouth and when he moaned and pushed his hips up to her face, she left him hanging, begging her for more. Marah licked his belly button and made goose bumps rise against his flesh. Then she eased her way slowly up to his chest. The sensations were so incredible that John felt like his entire body was about to explode, his erection stretched to the maximum, solid as steel. She took his left nipple into her mouth and gently sucked on it, rolling the little pebble as she teased it with the tip of her tongue. She sucked it into her warm mouth and held it there, allowing him to savor each delicious sensation. Pulling back she looked to his face, watching him revel in the moment, his head pressed back against the bed, eyes closed, mouth open as he gasped for air. Reaching across him, Marah slipped her hand into the bowl and took out an ice cube. She popped it into her mouth and sucked it slowly for a few moments, her hands still dancing easily across his chest. When she dropped her mouth back down to his nipple, John gasped from the shock of the sudden cold, his body jerking beneath her.

"Whoa," the man exclaimed excitedly, a low chuckle caught in his throat. "You promised to be nice."

Marah giggled. "I am being nice.

She moved to his other nipple, suckling it warm and

hot, teasingly. The second time she teased him with an
ice cube, she could feel his body tighten from the cold
sensation and the accompanying moan let her know
that he was enjoying every moment of it. Marah continued to tease him, hot and cold, gliding back down
until she was settled between his legs. His organ
twitched in anticipation and Marah grinned up at him
as he lifted his head to watch what she might do.

"Close your eyes," she commanded, shaking her
index finger at him. "Close them now or I won't play
anymore."

John laughed, then settled back against the pillow,
closing his eyes excitedly. When she licked him, his
hips jumped off the bed and he groaned her name.
Marah curled her lips around him, slowing demonstrat-
ing everything she'd ever taught in her fellatio class.
She could feel him harden even more, his hips moving
in sync with her ministrations.

Lifting herself above him, Marah quickly drew a
condom over his member and dropped her body down
against his, easing him slowly into her secret box. Every
muscle in his body tensed as she danced against him,
pleasuring him like he'd never been pleasured before. Air
suddenly seemed nonexistent and his heart beat like it was
about to burst and then his whole body exploded, sound
and sight leaving him a second away from unconscious.

As Marah fell against him, her own orgasm convulsing her body against his, the man couldn't imagine
ever sharing his bed with any other woman again. As
he gasped for air, he heard her laugh, her warm breath
a sweet mist against his ear. She kissed his face, her lips
brushing lightly against his cheek.

"Are you okay?" she asked softly.

John could only nod, words failing him.

"That's good," Marah said. "'Cause I might just keep you like this for the rest of the day."

John nodded again, totally unconcerned, everything feeling as right in his world as it could be.

"Thank you," he finally muttered, turning to nuzzle his cheek against hers.

"For what?"

John laughed. "My ride."

Chapter 11

"John has lost his damn mind!" Mark exclaimed, throwing a punch into the air in front of him.

Matthew shook his head, saying nothing as Luke sat looking from one to the other, his hands clasped together as if in prayer in his lap.

Juanita paced the length of the room, back and forth. "This is the fifth time he's cancelled his schedule in the last three weeks. I don't know what to tell people."

"I can't believe he missed the meeting with the mayor about that revitalization project. He knew we needed that contract."

"He said he has it under control," Juanita said, her voice not sounding too confident.

"And why haven't we gone to contract yet with the

Briscoe project?" Mark asked. "He had that deal closed weeks ago."

Juanita heaved a deep sigh. "Edward has changed his mind."

"Like hell," Mark shouted. "I thought John had pacified the Briscoe daughters?"

"Marah convinced her father to reconsider."

"And what, now she's working on John losing the rest of his business?" Matthew asked. "What's going on with those two?"

"Your brother says he's in love," Juanita said.

"What do you think, Aunt Juanita?" Luke asked.

The old woman shrugged. "I think that woman has his heart and I'm worried that she might not be as interested in him. That's what I think."

"Did she say something?" Mark asked.

"Did her father say something?" Matthew questioned.

Juanita sighed. "I just didn't get any warm and fuzzy feelings from Marah. I asked her again about the two of them last night and her responses were just…I don't know…not what I would have expected from a woman in love with John. She didn't show me any excitement.

"Even her father has expressed his concerns that Marah might not be in this relationship for the right reasons," Juanita concluded.

"So what do we do?" Luke questioned, his gaze moving from one brother to the other.

"Whatever we have to do to make sure John doesn't get hurt," Matthew answered.

Mark nodded. "Any suggestions?"

The room went quiet, all of them contemplating

what was just said. Juanita suddenly waved her head up and down, nodding excitedly. "I say we nip this in the bud, right now," she said.

An hour later, Juanita was cleaning the top of John's desk, the man very much on her mind. She hated that they would have to interfere in his life so blatantly, but she refused to see him hurt if there was anything at all they could do about it. She understood she was being meddlesome, but the boys were like the children she had never had. She was fiercely protective of them and at the moment she was scared to death one of her cubs was in the path of some serious heartbreak. The conversation she'd had with Marah the night before played repeatedly in her mind.

Edward's daughters had been gathered together in the home's family room, laughing and joking about their daily mishaps. Juanita had been invited to dinner and she'd come bearing a lemon pound cake for dessert. Eden and Marla had welcomed her warmly, but Marah's bright smile had dimmed considerably with her arrival. Edward had told her not to make anything of it.

"She'll come around," he'd intoned, his broad hand gently caressing her back.

Juanita had nodded her head, hopeful that he knew what he was talking about. The other girls had welcomed her to their conversation, allowing her to interject, seemingly pleased to be able to share with her. But Marah had withdrawn.

Eden had been the first to ask about John, both sisters wanting to know more about the man who was occupying so much of Marah's time. Marah had shrugged the questions off, deferring her answers with other questions and so Juanita herself had tried to learn more about Marah and John.

"John's been right off his schedule lately. You two must be having a grand time together."

Marah had shrugged. "It's been okay."

"I think he likes you a lot."

Again, her shoulders had pushed skyward, seeming to skim the lobes of her ears. "We're just friends," Marah had said, reaching for a glass of iced tea that sat atop the table.

Eden and Marla had exchanged a look between them, both seeming to understand something that Juanita wasn't aware of. Then Marah had changed the conversation, asking her father something about the horses and the stables.

Juanita blew warm breath past her lips. Marah's hesitancy had given her cause for concern. She seemed nonchalant and disinterested in the stories Juanita had shared about her life with the Stallion men when they'd been boys. Put off by the behavior, Juanita was convinced Marah wasn't enamored with John as he was with her. And that wasn't a good thing because the man was making too many drastic changes to his life to have her be so blasé about the relationship.

Marah instinctively knew that Marla and Eden were talking about her when she entered the room. The conversation was clearly about her because they both stopped talking mid-sentence and looked like they'd been caught with their hands in the cookie jar. She shook her head and rolled her eyes, dropping down into the seat beside her look-alike.

"What?" she said, her gaze moving from one to the other.

"You tell us what," Eden answered. "You're the one being all secretive. Sneaking around with that man like people weren't going to find out."

Marah heaved a deep sigh. "I'm not sneaking and I'm not being secretive."

"So how come you didn't tell us what's going on with you two when we asked last night? You got all defensive and hostile. You'd think Eden and I had done something to you the way you were behaving," Marla said.

Marah rolled her eyes a second time. "I don't need to share all of my business with strangers."

Marla cut her eye toward Eden. "Are you talking about Juanita?"

"She's so nosy! Every time I see her she's asking me questions about John. I don't know what her problem is."

"Did you stop to think that maybe she just wanted to make conversation with you, Marah?" Eden asked.

Marah didn't answer. She cut her eyes around the room, purposely avoiding her sister's stare.

"Why are you acting like this, Marah?" her twin asked. "Why don't you like Juanita?"

"I don't dislike her, but I don't have to be buddy-buddy with her."

"No, you don't, but you need to be a little more respectful. She and Daddy have become very close."

"And what about that? Don't you two think it's a little fishy that she became cozy with Daddy just before they convinced him to sell the ranch?"

"No fishier than you becoming cozy with John Stallion just before Daddy decided to change his mind," Marla countered.

"That's not fair," Marah said, her tone defensive. "One has nothing to do with the other."

"How can anyone be sure? It's not like this thing with you and John is serious—at least that's what you keep saying," Eden stated.

Marah crossed her arms over her chest, attitude dropping like a vapor over her disposition. She understood that her sisters only had her best interests at heart. And though they were annoying nuisances, they loved her and that love was always channeled in such a way that they each knew when another was in need. Until that moment, Marah hadn't realized how much she needed her sisters. She paused momentarily to let the ugly in her disposition subside.

Her voice dropped an octave as she finally responded. "I said it's not like that. That's how you can be sure. Both of you know me better than that."

"What I know is that you're acting like a spoiled brat," Marla said. "And we just want to know why. What's going on with you?"

Marah heaved a deep sigh. "Why can't you two understand that I don't need a new mother. Neither do you. Why does that woman have to—" she stopped suddenly as she realized just how childish she actually sounded. Tears sprang to her eyes and she brushed the moisture against the back of her hand.

Marla reached out to hug her, wrapping her in a warm embrace, Eden wrapping her arms around them both. That sat quietly together, neither saying anything as Marah cried softly against her sister's shoulder. When she was all cried out, Eden wiped her face with a tissue, leaning to kiss the round of her cheek.

"Juanita isn't trying to replace Mommy, Marah. You know that. She makes Daddy happy. If you're half as concerned about Daddy being happy as you claim to be, then you would support his relationship."

Marla echoed their older sibling's sentiments. "You know Mommy would have a fit if she saw you acting like this," she said. "And what about that man? Does he have anything to say about all this? I mean, Juanita adores him. He's like a son to her and that's why she's concerned about him. So tell us the truth. What's up with you two?"

Marah sighed, taking a deep breath of air as she collected her thoughts. "John and I….we…." She paused, her joy suddenly glistening in the wet that filled her eyes. "I think John loves me. And I love him," she said, her gaze dropping shyly. "He's everything I've ever wanted in a man."

Marla hugged her again, kissing her cheek. "Marah, we're so happy for you. Why didn't you just say so?"

Marah shrugged. "I would have told you but when Juanita started to ask all her questions, all I could think of was Mommy not being here for me to tell and I just…"

"You just acted a fool!" Eden exclaimed, swatting at her head with a flat palm. "You should know better, Marah. Mommy and Daddy didn't raise us like that."

"Oh, stop lecturing me, Eden! You can be such a drip sometimes," Marah responded, breaking out into laughter.

Marla grinned. "So, tell us," she said, leaning in as if they were conspiring amongst themselves. "What have you and your man been up to?"

The brothers knew that John could see right through them, so trying to get anything over on him wasn't going to be easy.

"That's ridiculous," Matthew said, squashing Luke's most recent suggestion to discredit Marah with their brother.

"Do you have a better suggestion?" the youngest Stallion queried.

"No, but I'm sure we can come up with something that doesn't involve duct tape and a camera."

Mark chuckled, shaking his head. "Look, if the girl isn't on the up and up that shouldn't be at all hard to prove. I'm sure if we give her enough rope she'll hang herself. All we have to do is get her to say the wrong thing at the right time. In the right situation I'm sure her true colors will show."

Matthew nodded his agreement.

Luke was more wary. "Maybe we should just be straight with John. Tell him what we know and let him decide for himself."

Both of his brothers shrugged. "I tried," Mark said, sinking down lower in the cushioned chair he occupied. "He wouldn't even discuss her with me. But the boy is sprung. I've never seen him so wound up over a female."

"Just that girl in high school."

"What girl?"

"Sarah Brevard."

"Big-booty Brevard?"

"Busty big-booty Brevard!"

"John wasn't interested in that girl. That was you."

A blank expression crossed Matthew's face as he reflected back. "Oh," he said a stupid grin filling his face. "I did have it hard for her, didn't I?"

Mark shook his head. "I declare, if I didn't know better I'd swear you had a substance abuse problem. You need to stop doing whatever you're doing though that's burning your brain cells."

Luke laughed as the two men bantered back and forth.

Minutes later Operation Marah was set into motion. Mark made the first telephone call, dialing the Briscoe residence. When Marah came to the phone, there was no turning back.

Chapter 12

John had gone riding with her, mounting a horse for the first time. The moment had been comical, John Stallion, man of steel, not as staid as he would have liked. The horse, one of Marah's favorites, had bested him a few times before he got the hang of handling her, but by the end of the afternoon he'd come to appreciate why Marah enjoyed horseback riding as much as she did.

A picnic lunch down by a small stream had been the perfect accompaniment to the afternoon, the duo enjoying the light banter that had become a trademark of their relationship. Marah made him laugh, allowed him moments that transposed his boardroom demeanor. When he was with her he was reminded of those youthful moments before his parents' accident when he'd been carefree and unconcerned with anything serious.

Marah marveled at the ease with which the two inter-acted. Her time with him felt as right as rain in a desert storm. They were a perfect complement to each other, her carefree spirit and impulsive nature a nice match for his controlling, take-no-prisoners deportment.

After the horses had been groomed and bedded for the evening, Marah had invited him to dinner with her father and sisters, the family welcoming him warmly. John had been impressed with the familial bond they shared, the wealth of it much like what he and his brothers enjoyed together.

Back in his home, Marah had left a trail of her clothing from the living room into his bedroom, dropping shoes, T-shirt, jeans, bra and panties one at a time. By the time he'd locked the front door, securing it for the night, she was blissfully naked in his bed, posed seductively across the duvet cover as she waited for him.

Only the light from a full moon illuminated the bedroom, the bright rays shining boldly. He stood staring, in awe of her incredible beauty, at a loss for words. The moment was even more stalling when Marah eased up onto her knees and beckoned him to her, pure unadulterated lust gleaning in her eyes. He felt himself grow hard at the thought of what they might ex-perience before the night was over.

Deft fingers slowly undid the buttons of his cotton shirt, exposing his broad chest. Marah ran her out-stretched hand across his warm brown skin, leaving a faint impression to mark her passage. It was a bold touch that sent a shiver of excitement through John's body, the wealth of it converging through his groin. With each pass of her fingers, the shiver grew to a shudder that had his muscles convulsing with pleasure.

John leaned forward and kissed the center of Marah's back, then the base of her neck. She let out a soft moan as he pulled his fingers through her hair and tilted her head back. Realizing his intent, Marah leaned back even further and closed her eyes just as their lips met. The crush of John's mouth against her own was even sweeter than Marah knew it to be. It was filled with a passion so strong that it stirred a low flame through her, warming her down to her toes. The intensity of it made the playful kisses they'd shared earlier seem like child's play.

John continued to caress her mouth with his. His tongue pressed hard against her lips, plying them apart easily. Marah responded in turn, opening her mouth wide to accept the taste of him, teasing him with her own. The exchange seemed to continue forever, both focused on the exquisite sensations sweeping over them.

John drew his hands along the lines of Marah's shoulders, drawing a slow path that burned hot against her skin until they came to rest against the round of her breasts. His palms were like fire against the nipples that had bloomed full and hard. Marah's breath caught in her throat as he slowly caressed her, kneading each mound of flesh with the gentlest touch.

Reluctantly, Marah let their lips part, John relaxing his embrace just long enough to slip out of his clothes. As he stood naked before her, she felt a surge of exhilaration that seemed to sweep from her to him and back again. John felt himself being drawn deep into the look she gave him as their gazes met. A gasp spilled from his lips as Marah pressed her lips against his abdomen, her tongue flicking lightly over the taut muscles. John was filled with delight and a soft moan eased out of his mouth, a long cry that evoked murmurs of joy from Marah.

As Marah reached up to wrap her arms around his neck, drawing him to her, it heralded a rising need that John could no long ignore. The feel of her body against his incited his hunger, a lust too urgent for him to neglect. Easing her down to the mattress, he wrapped himself around her, his mouth latched to hers. Marah's heart raced and she felt light-headed and breathless as John drew every ounce of her sensibilities from her. She was drunk with wanting, her own needs suddenly consuming.

Sweet kisses were followed by even sweeter caresses, gentle touches that sent escalating sparks of electricity through the two of them. John brushed light fingers across the mound between her legs and those tiny sparks exploded into bolts of lightning. Marah writhed beneath him, opening herself widely to welcome him to her. The rising heat between them merged, forming a single soul-shattering inferno. Every motion was transformed into pure joy. The rapture that gripped them both could not be described and, when it was over, John holding her sweetly in his arms, both their bodies satiated, he whispered that he loved her and both relished the moment that Marah whispered it back.

"Eden will skin me alive if I call in sick one more time," Marah said as she stepped out of John's large double-headed shower. "We're not being very responsible, Mr. Stallion."

John chuckled, allowing the last of the hot water to rinse the suds from his body. "You've got a lot of nerve, Marah Briscoe. Wasn't it your idea for us to play hooky the last three times that we did? I think so!"

Marah laughed with him. "A mere technicality. But we need to be more disciplined now. Folks are starting to talk."

"What folks?"

"My sisters for sure and I don't doubt your brothers have had a word or two to say about us."

The man grinned as he accepted the large white towel Marah was passing to him, using it to swipe the moisture that graced his skin. "So they've had a thing or two to say. They can't fire me so I don't worry about it."

Marah shook her head. "You're a bad influence on me."

"Who?"

"You are. I've never been so....so..."

John laughed heartily. "The nerve. I doubt that would ever stand up under any serious scrutiny. If anyone has been a bad influence on anyone, it's been you on me."

Marah rolled her eyes. "You wish!"

He pressed his nakedness against hers, hugging her warmly. "We'll play hooky next week?"

"I promise."

The man winked. "I'm sure you'll be able to convince me," he said, pressing a warm kiss to her cheek.

As they dressed, Marah got a brief view of what his day entailed and she didn't envy him. John thrived on the brokering his job required of him, the hard and fast wheeling and dealing that had driven him to the top. Her job was more laid-back, requiring creative energy and an open-minded spirit. As they kissed goodbye, they made plans to meet later for dinner, both anxious to get back to each other even before they were out of the driveway.

Mark Stallion was waiting in her office for her when Marah arrived at work. He and Eden were discussing politics and Eden was offering her opinion about the female candidate that had folks flapping their jaws over who said what about whom. The political climate was too ugly for Marah, the backstabbing antics of exposing every personal ill an opponent could pull from nowhere taking precedence over the real issues that needed to be addressed. Eden was in her element, though, she and Mark seeming to enjoy their friendly debate.

"Good morning," Marah exclaimed, greeting them cheerily as she made her way into the room. "How's everyone doing this morning?"

Mark came to his feet, drawing his suit jacket closed as he extended a hand in her direction. "It's good to see you, Marah," he said politely.

"You as well, Mark," she responded, moving to the leather executive's chair behind the desk. She dropped her handbag on the desk and seated herself comfortably.

Eden moved toward the door. "I enjoyed our conversation, Mark. You and my husband have a lot in common. We'd love for you to join us for dinner sometime."

Mark nodded. "I'd like that. Just give me a call and say when," he answered as Eden moved out the room, tossing her sister a smile as she reached the door. "Oh, Marah," Eden said, stopping short. "Victor Tomes would like you to call him as soon as possible. Something about him wanting to propose and needing you to help him make that happen."

Marah winced. "I think I'm going to be sick."

Eden laughed. "Not as sick as you're going to be when you find out who he's proposing to."

Marah shook her head, racing a flat palm to stall her sister's comments. "Don't tell me," she said. "I don't think I could take it."

Eden shrugged. "Yup! Seems like Pamela had the juice to tame him all this time," she said with a laugh.

Marah chuckled. "My, my, my," she said as Eden closed the door behind her. Marah turned her attention back to Mark.

"So, Mark, what was so urgent that you needed to speak with me this morning?" she asked.

"I appreciate you taking the time to see me, Marah. And thank you for not saying anything to John. I understand that you two have become very close."

Marah eyed the man curiously. "I care about your brother, if that's what you want to know."

"I'm sure," Mark smiled. He continued. "I understand that your father is reconsidering the sale of the Briscoe Ranch. I was hoping you'd speak to him for us and maybe convince him that the sale of the ranch is a good thing. After our presentation the other week I think you have a good understanding for what John would like to do with the property. I would hate to see him disappointed."

Marah could feel herself bristle. "My father's whole life has been committed to that ranch. Why would I want to help take that from him?"

Mark nodded. "And I understand that, but John sees great promise in that ranch for the children's programs that we're looking to initiate. You saw that. You have to agree that we could do so much for the community with that property. More than your father can probably do under the circumstances."

"What circumstances?"

"The financial burden and his age to name two, but the list is extensive."

Marah nodded. "Mark, I appreciate your interest, but I'm not talking to my father. John understands why I don't think my father should sell that land. I plan to support whatever he decides."

"Like you supported his decision to sell in the first place?"

Marah met the man's gaze and held it. "Thank you for stopping by, Mark."

The man came to his feet. "My brother will be disappointed, Marah. I'm sorry that you don't care enough to want what's best for all of us, especially John."

Marah could feel a slow rage starting to simmer. She bit her tongue, afraid of the words that wanted to spill past her lips. Mark did an about-face before she could form a retort that didn't border on the edge of hostility. When the door closed behind the man she was tempted to pick up the telephone to call John. But as she reached for the receiver, determined to set him and the rest of the Stallions straight, Victor Tomes was knocking excitedly on her door.

Chapter 13

John could feel the tension weighing heavily on his shoulders. He and Marah had battled again, the same argument repeated for no reason whatsoever. He'd tried to make Marah understand that the company's decision to still pursue Briscoe Ranch wasn't all his doing. The other members of the board had outvoted him and not even he could override his brothers' determination to do what he knew in his heart was good for business.

Marah and Mark had butted heads first. Then Marah and Matthew. And each time each of his brothers had tried with methodic precision to convince him that Marah's interest in him was more about saving her father's homestead than any genuine feelings for him. John had balked at the insinuation at first but with each swipe, each question, he found himself starting to doubt his own judgment.

"Her timing just seems too convenient," Mark had said, shrugging his shoulders.

"Why would she be opposed if it would serve you both well?" Matthew had questioned.

Luke has simply shaken his head. "Should have taken your own advice," he'd said thoughtfully. "Never mix business with pleasure."

Of course Marah had gone on the defensive, angry that any of them would question her motives, furious that John would seem to.

It would have to come to a head soon, John thought to himself. They'd finally turned it over to the attorneys, allowing their respective legal teams to hash out the details. Mark was insisting on holding Edward Briscoe to the original agreement, the one he'd agreed to verbally. John had hoped to persuade him to accept the other, the one Marah and he had hammered out when Marah had been seemingly amenable to the idea. John would hate to see them heading to court, but if something didn't give sooner rather than later, they were all liable to break from the pressure.

John heaved a deep sigh, his thoughts interrupted by the buzz of his intercom. He reached to depress the talk button. "Yes, Juanita?"

"They're looking for you in the conference room, John."

The man nodded. "Thank you," he said. "Tell them I'm on my way."

Marah, too, was through. She'd been summoned to the Stallion offices one time too many and she'd had more than enough. She had no idea why Juanita wanted to see her this time and why it was so important that she be there at the stroke of three o'clock. She'd been with her twin sister when the call came and Marla had convinced her to go, to give the woman a chance. "For Daddy's sake," Marla had said beseechingly. "Just try to be nice, Marah," she'd intoned.

A faint smile pulled at her mouth as she took the elevator up to the executive suites. The memory of her and John in that elevator that first day was on her mind as she reminisced over all they'd shared since then. The smile fell to a slight frown as she remembered the words that had spilled between them that morning, Marah fuming that their quest to buy Briscoe Ranch still hadn't come to an end and John annoyed at being caught between their rock and her hard place.

Juanita was waiting in John's office for her when she arrived, the woman standing at the expanse of window that looked out on the city below.

"Dallas really is something, isn't it?" Juanita said, greeting her with a slight smile. "How are you, Marah?"

Marah smiled back. "Well, thank you. How about yourself?"

Juanita gestured for her to take a seat. "I have no complaints," she said. "No one pays much attention to you when you do, so why bother, right?"

Marah chuckled with her, more from nervous energy than anything she said having been funny. "So, what's this about?" Marah asked, curiosity pulling at her. "Why did you want to see me, Juanita?"

The woman nodded, taking the seat beside Marah. "I was hoping that you and I could talk about John."

Marah barely nodded, the gesture with her head ever so slight. "What about him?"

"I'm worried about him," Juanita said. "I don't want him to get hurt."

"Why would John get hurt?"

"Sooner or later he's going to realize that you don't care for him as much as he cares for you. I imagine that will probably break his heart."

Marah felt her body stiffen and tense. She couldn't begin to believe the woman's audacity. "Where do you get off telling me how I feel about John?" Marah said, her voice rising.

Juanita stared at her, studying her carefully. "I'm sorry, Marah, if I misjudged you, but I just haven't gotten the impression that you're serious about him. What I have gotten the impression of is that you'll do anything to save your father's ranch. Even use John if it will get you what you want. Am I wrong?"

Marah's anger answered for her, the words flying out of her mouth before she could catch them. "No, you're not. I will do anything to save it."

"And if John gets hurt, then what?"

"John's a big boy, Juanita. I'm sure he'll get over it."

The woman shook her head. "What if the ranch can't be saved? What if the sale inevitably goes through?'

"It won't."

"And you're sure of this?"

Marah shook her head. "Why are you so concerned, Juanita? Don't you want my father to be happy?"

"Your father was happy. He was looking forward to his retirement. We were planning our wedding…."

"Wedding? What wedding?"

Juanita paused, realizing her slip. "I'm sure your father was going to tell you soon, Marah. We're very excited. And I'm looking forward to getting closer to you and your sisters. I really want to be a good stepmother to you all."

Marah suddenly felt like her head was about to explode. Stepmother? How could her father do this to her? How could he even think about replacing her mother? She wanted to rage, but she couldn't. Her mind was suddenly an accumulation of thoughts, most of which didn't make an ounce of sense to her.

She jumped to her feet, her body shaking with emotion. Juanita was still talking, her words seeming to spill one into the other until they sounded like nothing but static in Marah's ears.

"Please know that you can come to me anytime, Marah. I'm here for you, just like I'm here for John. And I'm glad that you care about him. That really makes me happy."

Marah snapped. "I don't care if you're happy or not. You think you can just snap your fingers and turn my family inside out. Well, that's not going to happen. This is all your fault. My father would never have thought about selling his home if it wasn't for you. You don't fool me. So don't think I'm going to let you or John or anyone else just think they can come in and take what's ours. It will never happen."

"But Marah, you care about John."

"You'd like that wouldn't you. You'd like it if we could all be one big happy family. But that's not going to happen." Frustration fueled the last words out of Marah's mouth. "You and all the rest of the Stallions can go straight to hell. I don't need you. I don't need any of you."

John's voice coming from the doorway startled her. "Is that really how you feel, Marah?"

She bristled, a wealth of unhappy fueling her anger. John's appearance only served to broaden her confusion. "I…John…I…"

The man nodded. "I'm sorry to hear you feel that way," he said, his expression hard as rock. "But I'm glad I found out before it was too late."

The man moved behind his desk, his stare colder than Marah could have ever imagined it being. He turned to Juanita.

"Juanita, I'm flying to New York tonight. Tell my pilot to be ready."

Juanita nodded. "How long will you be gone?"

The man let his eyes rest on Marah's face one last time. "Indefinitely," he said, and then he marched back out the room, leaving the two women staring after him.

Marah couldn't stop crying. Every time she tried to pull herself together, the tears would start to flow all over again. John hadn't answered any of her calls. Her father had been furious with her and even her sisters hadn't been able to make her feel better about what had happened. And as she replayed it over and over again in her mind she couldn't begin to understand what had happened or even why she'd said half the things she'd said.

How that woman had managed to goad her into saying the ugly things that spilled out of her mouth was beyond her. She hadn't meant to curse John and certainly it had not been her intentions to declare that she wouldn't ever need him. But that woman! Marah fought back a new wave of sobs that had thickened in her chest.

She'd been trying for days to try to explain to him what happened. How hearing the news of her father's impending nuptials and Juanita once again questioning her sincerity had pushed her to a point of no return. But he'd been unreachable.

She couldn't believe this was happening. Nor could she understand how they had all gotten to this place. When had John begun to question her sincerity? She could understand the others not understanding her need to keep what was between them to herself. But John had to have known that her need to just not share that part of their relationship with others was just about her wanting the two of them to simply enjoy the beauty of it without everyone else interfering. He had to have known.

She swiped the back of her hand against her swollen eyes, curling up into a fetal position in her bed. Sooner or later she would have to figure out a way to make this all better. She would have to make amends and was hopeful that he would understand because he knew her like no one else did. She just had to make him understand how much she truly loved him.

John sat alone in his hotel suite, nursing the last drops of a glass of scotch. He still couldn't understand how he'd been so wrong. He had thought he'd known Marah, had understood her, and he'd been wrong. He thought back to the last time that they had seen each other.

His meeting had lasted all of ten minutes, the staff

just needing his approval and signature on a series of documents to initiate their next deal. He should have done it all from his office, he remembered thinking to himself.

He'd been surprised to hear Marah's voice coming from his office. More surprised by her harsh tone and the bitter words she was spewing. As he'd stood listening, suddenly everything his brothers and Juanita had been trying to tell him seemed valid and there he was questioning whether or not he'd really known Marah at all.

He took a deep breath and then a second, holding it long enough to calm his weathered nerves. Had he focused on the business and the business alone he wouldn't be going through this right now. He'd always been able to maintain full control when doing a deal and he had purposely avoided relationships and all the complications associated with them because in matters of the heart, there was no control. But Marah had struck a nerve—or two or three—and she'd gotten under his skin, occupying a huge chunk of his heart. And now here he was, missing her like hell, wondering where it had all gone wrong. Why hadn't he been able to see what his brothers had seen? What had happened to his judgment? More importantly, how had he convinced himself that Marah had actually loved him as much as he thought he loved her?

Chapter 14

Ten women sat on the floor in a circle around a low oak table, each finishing the last segment of a two-page questionnaire Marah had prepared for them. The ensuing discussion would revolve around the dynamics of relationships, past, present and future, with the direction of the discourse being determined by who was willing to be the most open about her concerns and dilemmas. As Marah sat waiting for them to finish, she felt just a touch hypercritical about giving others sage advice when she didn't have an ounce of it for herself.

When all were done, Marah began to review the questions one by one. Every so often there was a low titter or a muffled giggle, someone finding something asked or something answered humorous.

"If your sexual relationship were a symphony orchestra, which musical instrument would you be?" Marah asked, her gaze sweeping the table. "Would you be a string instrument, a percussion such as a drum or tambourine, a woodwind, part of the brass section or the keyboard?"

Linda Carter, a newlywed, answered first. "I'd be a string instrument. A violin."

"Definitely, a wind instrument," someone else answered as they went around the table.

One woman paused, still pondering the question. The woman beside her nudged her gently. "You have been to the orchestra before, haven't you, Gertie?"

The woman named Gertie laughed, her head waving from side to side. "Oh, I've definitely been to the orchestra. Been so many times I fancy myself to be a conductor, of sorts."

The group laughed, amused by the woman's response.

"Sorry, Gertie," Marah said. "Orchestra conductor isn't one of our choices this go round. Do you have another answer?"

Gertie nodded. "I think I'd probably be a flute. So what's that?"

Marah smiled. "That would make you a woodwind."

After all the women had answered, Marah continued. "Well, all you string instruments, you enjoy being played. You like to be touched and handled and if you're played well, then you respond with soft expressive sound."

The four women who'd considered themselves string instruments laughed.

"Now, you percussions like your loving with a little

more oomph," Marah exclaimed. "The word *percussion* means the hitting of one body against the other and you percussions like your contact straight to the point. You're more adventurous in your bedroom activities and a few of you even like it a little rough."

Gertie laughed heartily. "Oh, yes!" she hissed glee-fully. "I change my mind. I'll be a drum."

The women laughed as Marah shook her head.

"What about you, Marah? What are you?"

Marah chuckled softly. "I'd probably be a woodwind instrument," she said. "To play a woodwind you have to use your hands and your mouth," she said, her eyebrows raised. "Woodwinds enjoy the occasional oral fixations."

Gertie clapped her hands together. "Heaven help us," she said chuckling warmly. "I can be one of them, too."

The women were all laughing heartily. It didn't go un-noticed that Marah wasn't as cheerful as the rest of them.

Gertie leaned back in her seat. "So what's wrong, Marah?" she asked, concern washing over her expression. "You're not yourself tonight. What's going on with your love life?"

Marah shrugged. "It's nothing, Gertie. I appreciate you asking, though."

The woman raised an eyebrow. "Now you know there is nobody here who believes that. Since I'm older than most of you here, I know a broken heart when I see one."

Marah could feel the tension in her chest tighten, her eyes glazing with moisture.

"Isn't that why we're here, Marah, to help each other

get through our relationship issues?" someone else asked. "If you won't participate how can you expect us to?"

The others nodded, their gazes locked on her.

Marah blew breath past her lips, her defenses deflating. She did need to talk, she realized. She needed an impartial opinion from someone who wasn't caught in the middle of her mess. The group gathered had been meeting for months and they'd grown comfortable with her and her with them. And so she talked, sharing every detail that had gotten her to this point, even disclosing her unhappiness with her father and his new relationship.

"My, my, my," Gertie said when she'd finished spilling her heart out.

"I hear that," the woman beside her said.

Marah waited as they all sat pondering her options.

"You need to do some apologizing first," one woman said, her head bobbing up and down like a loose hinge. "Starting with your father and then your man."

"And your father's friend," someone else interjected.

Marah rolled her eyes. "Why?"

"Because you're a grown woman acting like a two-year-old child. Fine, you might not like the woman your father is dating, but that's his right. And that doesn't give you the right to be rude and nasty."

"That's what I'm saying," someone added.

"Why do you think she had doubts about how you felt about your man?" Linda asked.

Marah shrugged. "I don't know."

"Yes, you do."

Marah sighed. "I went out of my way not to let her see how I was feeling about anything. I guess I would have questioned my behavior as well."

"So you fix that mess and then you move on to your man."

"He won't even talk to me," Marah whined.

"His feelings are hurt."

"Just like a man."

"What is it you told us once, Miss Marah? If the mountain won't come to Mohammed, then Mohammed needs to go to the mountain."

Marah laughed. "I hear you."

Gertie waved her head from side to side. "Girl, you know how to do this. Pack you a bag of toys, throw on some lace and go get your man."

"Stroke him first," Linda chimed. "You know how fragile their egos are. If you don't stroke him and get him feeling good, he'll just keep digging his heels in and that's only going to make your job harder."

Marah grinned. "Thank you," she said, her eyes meeting each woman in turn. "You all have learned a lot these past few weeks. And I appreciate you all teaching me a thing or two tonight."

Edward was pacing the floor of Juanita's small bedroom as if he were an animal locked in a cage. He couldn't begin to believe what the woman had just shared and he didn't know if he wanted to be angry with her or furious with her.

"What were you thinking, Juanita?" he finally managed to say, pausing just long enough to stare down to where she lay on the bed. His jaw was clenched so tight that veins protruded from his neck, a rush of red coloring his cheeks.

"I was worried about John," the woman answered,

contrition painting her expression. "It felt like the right thing to do at the time. Even you didn't think your daughter was being sincere."

He resumed his pacing, his bare feet slapping against the hard wood floors. Disappointment was clearly written in every square inch of his face. "Do you know how hurt my child is right now? I can't believe you caused that."

Tears ran down Juanita's face. "I'm so sorry, Edward. I didn't think it would end up like this. I didn't. You just have to believe me. I'll do anything to make things right between them."

The man finally dropped down to the bedside, his back to her as he sat in thought. "Have you talked to John?" he asked.

She nodded. "I tried to tell him that we did what we did on purpose. He was angry at first, but he thinks we did him a favor. He refuses to consider that we might have actually made a mistake."

The two sat in silence, both waiting for the other to say something. Neither knowing what, if anything, there was to say. Juanita couldn't believe she'd gotten herself into this mess. What had she been thinking? She knew what she'd been thinking. She had just wanted to save John from any hurt that threatened him. She'd been protecting him and his brothers for so long that she didn't have a clue how to stop.

John's mother had been her dearest friend in the world. The two had grown up together, best friends since they'd both been singing in the children's choir of the Baptist church they'd been raised in. They'd gone through every imaginable trial and tribulation with each

˙other, from bad hair days to bad boy days. There wasn't a secret Juanita hadn't shared with Irene or Irene with her. The two had been inseparable, even after marriage, moving in sync as if they were joined at the hip. Juanita had not been able to have children, fertility issues negating every effort to try. Irene's babies had become hers by default and she'd loved each and every one of them from the moment their mother had birthed them into the world.

The day Irene and James Stallion had been killed had been the worse day of Juanita's life. She'd been the first to get the news about the accident and, truth be told, she'd wished many a time that it had been her instead of them. As their godmother, Juanita had promised to care of the boys as if they were her own and she had stayed true to her word. The Stallion children had been everything to their parents and when they were gone they'd become everything to Juanita.

John had been the stoic older brother, assuming responsibilities a teenager had no business assuming. Juanita imagined the guardian angels sitting on his shoulder would definitely have been proud of his many accomplishments. He'd stepped in to parent his younger siblings despite Juanita assuring him that it wasn't necessary with her there to take command. John had adamantly refused to let go of the reins, feeling in his heart that it was something he just had to do. Juanita hadn't given him a fight. Instead, she'd been there to support his efforts and lend a helping hand.

She sat upright in the bed, her small palm gently caressing Edward's shoulder. Edward flinched ever so slightly but didn't pull away. He hated to admit it, but if the situation had been in reverse he probably would have done something equally drastic. He also imagined that he might not have been as forthcoming about his actions as Juanita had just been with him. He heaved a deep sigh.

"First thing tomorrow," he said finally, "we get our two families together and we fix this mess. Neither one of our children should be this miserable and they are both miserable. Let's see if everyone can help get them back together as easily as we all tore them apart."

Juanita nodded her agreement, her gaze meeting his as he turned to face her. He pressed his lips to her forehead as he wrapped his arms around her torso, hugging her to him.

"I'm still mad with you, woman," he said softly.

Juanita nodded, raising her face to plant kisses on his chin. "I'll make it up to you, Edward. I promise," she answered, nuzzling her face into his. "I sincerely do."

Marah was pulling clothes from her closet, shoving them, hangers included, into a suitcase. Eden and Marla sat on the side of her queen-size bed watching her.

"I don't know about this, Marah," her twin said, cutting an eye toward Eden for support. "Maybe you should just let it go."

"I can't believe you just said that," Marah said, spinning in her sister's direction. She settled her hands against her hips, her feet braced shoulder-width apart as she eyed her sisters.

"We just don't want to see you get hurt again," Eden said. "We just…"

"Just nothing," Marah said, her vision blurring with

a sudden rush of tears. "I love him like you love Jack and Marah loves Michael. What would you two do?"

The two women gave each other a look, then both stood up. Eden pulled undergarments from the top drawer of Marah's bureau and Marla tossed toiletries into an overnight bag. Marah swiped at her eyes with the back of her hand, then reached out to hug both of her sisters. They all sniffled, fighting not to cry, then burst out laughing as they finished Marah's packing.

"What time's your flight?"

"Eleven o'clock," she answered, looking about the room to insure she'd not forgotten anything.

Marla leaned to kiss her cheek. "Good luck," she said, smiling brightly.

Marah shook her head. "Luck doesn't have anything to do with this. I'm playing smart. I'm playing for keeps."

Eden grinned. "She's definitely her father's daughter," she said chuckling. "Briscoe through and through."

It would be the first of many family gatherings where the Briscoes came face-to-face with the Stallions. The brothers were as curious about the meeting Edward and Juanita had called together as the sisters and their husbands were. When everyone had been offered food and drink, comfortably seated around the formal dining room table in the Briscoe home, the older couple got right to the point.

"That was a lousy thing you boys did to your brother and my daughter," Edward said, looking at each one. "A lousy thing."

The men eyed each other quickly, then turned their focus to Juanita.

"I take full responsibility," Juanita said, looking from Marla to Eden and back. "I thought we were doing what was best."

Eden shook her head as Juanita told them exactly what the Stallion clan had done to drive a wedge between the couple and mar their developing relationship.

"I told you we should have stayed out of it," Luke said, his head waving about.

"Shut up, Luke," both Mark and Matthew said at the same time. "You're as guilty as the rest of us."

"So you mean Marah really is in love with our brother?" Mark asked, his gaze flowing between the sisters.

Marla nodded. "Head over heels in love."

Matthew rolled his eyes. "That really bites," he said.

"Especially because John loves her, too," Mark said.

Michael and Jack both chuckled. "I'm glad we didn't have it this hard," Jack said teasingly.

Michael echoed his sentiments as he rocked his infant son against his chest. "Getting past Edward there was bad enough," he said

"Actually, you two didn't have it that easy," Eden said with a chuckle.

"No, you didn't," Marla agreed. "You just don't want to remember some of the stuff we put you through."

"We need to fix this," Edward said, resting against the arm of the chair Juanita sat in.

The woman drew a warm hand against his thigh. "And we need to fix it quick," she said thoughtfully, looking from one to the other. "Any suggestions?"

"I suggest we stay out of it," Luke said.

"I'm with him," Marla said. "We could just make this thing worse."

"Marah's going to New York to see him. Maybe they'll patch things up and we won't have to get involved," Eden interjected.

Juanita sat upright in her seat. "New York? When? When did Marah leave for New York?"

The two sisters tossed a look between them. "She left last night," Eden answered.

All the Stallion men let out a soft groan at the same time.

"Why?" Marla asked, concern washing over her expression. "What's wrong?"

Juanita shook her head, not believing how things seemed to be going from bad to worse. "John flew back last night," she said. "I imagine the two of them probably passed each other in the sky."

Edward shook his head. "Isn't this just a fine mess," he exclaimed. "Have either of you talked to your sister," he said, turning toward his daughters.

Eden and Marla shook their heads no.

"She probably doesn't even know yet," Marla said thoughtfully.

Eden leaned into her husband, who'd wrapped his arms tenderly around her. "Poor Marah," she said, voicing what everyone else was thinking.

"What about John?" Juanita asked, looking at her surrogate sons.

Mark answered. "He got in late, but he's here. I expect we'll see him at the office sometime tomorrow."

"Fine," Edward said firmly. "Once Marah gets back

here, we need to do whatever we have to do. Until then," he said, turning toward Matthew and Mark, "I have a few ideas. And the first thing we need to do is finalize the sale of this ranch."

Both Eden and Marla looked at each other, startled by their father's statement.

"Are you sure about that?" Eden asked him.

The man nodded. "Absolutely. As long as you boys can agree to my terms."

Mark came to his feet. "I'm sure we can do this, Mr. Briscoe. Shall we take this to your office?"

Edward nodded, tossing a look over his shoulder as the two men made their way toward the door. "Eat up," he said, looking at them eagerly. "When we get back, I'll tell you all what we need to do."

Chapter 15

"All you Stallions can go straight to hell. I don't need any of you," she'd said.

John tossed and turned as he lay supine against his living room sofa, trying to forget Marah's lingering presence in his home and in his heart. He couldn't seem to avoid thinking about her, though. Thoughts of the woman invaded his mind continually.

He hadn't slept well since that day, a peaceful night's sleep as elusive as the search for a unicorn might be. Turning onto his side, he faced the back of the chenille couch and closed his eyes tightly. He understood that this couldn't go on for much longer, its effect having paralyzed his ability to function while he'd been away on business. He could only imagine what the client today had thought of him as he'd fumbled his way through the presentation. No matter how he'd tried to throw himself into his work, hurt had festered until it took full control and rendered him incompetent.

John groaned, the crux of it rising from deep in his midsection. God, he missed that woman. He hadn't missed anyone this much since his mother and father had been killed. He suddenly became reflective, thinking about the couple that had given him and his brothers life, both sacrificing everything they had to afford them a wealth of opportunity.

Their father, James Stallion, had called their mother *Sug* for as long as he could remember. Sug, short for sugar, his sweet and honey, he use to say. John remembered thinking that he wanted to be just like his mom and dad when he grew up and found a wife. Their love was so magnanimous that he and his brothers used to look at them with awe. He had wanted a woman just like his mother who would love him as hard as Irene Stallion had loved her man.

There had been little the couple hadn't shared or done together. John had vivid memories of the two bowling together, camping together, just enjoying the beauty of each other's company. They'd been the perfect complement to each other. His father had been stern and commanding, with only one weakness. John's mother. Irene had been the epitome of soft, a woman with a huge heart of pure gold. She'd been the most giving person John had ever known, devoting her time and energy to more causes than any of them could ever begin to count. But not once did she sacrifice her children or her family, the Stallion boys always front and center in her mind and her heart. John smiled as he remembered the many kisses and hugs that passed between them when neither thought anyone was paying attention. The two had loved a lifetime in a short time and John couldn't help but be envious and want that for himself.

John had honestly believed he'd found such a union with Marah, a woman who possessed many of the qualities he'd seen in his mother. He flipped onto his other side and stared at the diamond engagement ring that sat on the edge of the tabletop. He'd been ready to ask her to marry him, to become his wife. The first Mrs. Stallion to be welcomed into a house ruled by Stallion men. He'd had no doubts that Marah would have soon been ruling them all, her beguiling personality ever so persuasive. And despite her butting heads with his Aunt Juanita, he'd been convinced that the two women would have eventually grown to adore each other as much as he adored them both. And now he was missing her so hard that it felt like a physical pain; ruthless, unbearable, almost moving him to tears.

Hours later John was still staring into the space that surrounded that black velvet box and the gift it held inside. Nowhere close to being ready to fall asleep, he was remembering her touch, her scent, the essence of her presence when she was near and close. He wanted to hold Marah against him, to hear her tell him all of this had just been a bad dream, that nothing at all had changed between them. But he couldn't sleep, knowing that when he did and he woke up, Marah would still be gone and he would still be alone.

The telephone ringing pulled at his attention and as he answered, hearing his brother call out his name, John suddenly wished he'd just pretended to not be home.

"Hey, Mark, what's up?" John said, pulling the receiver into his ear.

"What's up with you? We were starting to get worried. No one's heard from you."

John shrugged, his shoulders jutting against he sofa's cushions. "I'm just a little jet-lagged. I haven't been sleeping well lately."

"Maybe if you called Marah and talked to her you could cure that problem."

"Advice from a man who hasn't dated the same woman twice in two years?"

"Unfortunately, I wasn't as lucky as you were. I haven't found the woman I want to spend the rest of my life with yet."

"Doesn't seem like I have, either, at least that's what you boys believed last week. Didn't I get that right? You were so sure that Marah was the wrong woman for me that you went out of your way to prove it. You did a good job, Mark. I'm impressed."

Mark chuckled, just a touch embarrassed to be called on his behavior. "Well, we all make mistakes, big brother. This one was just a real whopper. So how can we make this right?"

"There's nothing to make right. It just is what it is. Marah wasn't the one. I'm sure I'll get over it."

"A few of us beg to differ."

John grunted, lifting his body upright on the couch. "So, what did you really call for? I highly doubt my love life, or lack thereof, is the amusement you were looking for."

"You're right. It isn't. We have a new business prospect coming in at the airport in a few hours. I hate to put this on you, but one of us executives needs to pick him up and make him feel welcome."

"I'm not in the mood for this, Mark."

"Tough. We need you on this. No one else is available."

John shook his head as if his brother could see him over the telephone line. "I really don't think—" he started.

His brother interrupted. "The service will pick you up in one hour. Be dressed. The driver will have the flight information and pickup details. I'm not quite sure who the company is sending, but when you make contact just do what you do best. This is good business for us. I know we can depend on you."

Before John could respond, his brother disconnected the line. Great, he thought to himself. Now he had to go make nice with some stranger and he didn't have a clue about the business deal. It was bad enough he couldn't pull himself together, but it was starting to look like the whole company had lost their minds.

Marah couldn't begin to believe that it had all been for nothing. She'd flown hours from Dallas to New York's Kennedy Airport to try and make things right between them. She'd been on pins and needles the entire taxi ride to the Waldorf-Astoria hotel, checking into a room and readying herself to surprise him.

She'd worn a new silk and lace teddy set beneath a classic Diane Von Furstenberg wrap dress, figuring she could be in his arms and out of her clothes within minutes of their making up. But the surprise had been on her when the front desk clerk politely advised her that

John Stallion had checked out of the hotel the night before.

Marah heaved a deep sigh—one of many—and she could feel the man in the first-class seat across the row from her lift his eyes to see if all was well. Marah turned her face to the window, eyeing the skyline. She refused to cry, tired of drying her eyes, so she turned every ounce of emotion inside, pushing it deep beneath her heart to let it churn like bile in the pit of her stomach.

She still couldn't fathom how they'd gotten to this place, how so much unhappiness had made its way into their lives to haunt them. Everything she'd thought she'd wanted in a man she'd found in John and more. She'd seen her future in his eyes and she had liked every bit of what she'd seen. John completed her, made her whole and without him she was feeling lost and lonely. Marah couldn't ever remember feeling this way and definitely not over the loss of some man.

She suddenly wished for her mother. Her mother would have had the answers Marah couldn't quite seem to find for herself. Had Hazel been there she would have steered Marah in the right direction long before Marah had gotten herself caught up in such a wealth of a mess. Marah would have given anything to have had her mother's shoulder to cry on, to be able to tell her mother about her love for John.

Marah hugged herself tightly. She couldn't believe how much she missed him. She missed everything about him: his smile, his touch, the way he curled his toes when he stretched, the look that crossed his face when she would gently massage the back of his neck.

She missed the looks and gestures that held so much love. She missed the way that when they were together all was well in their little world. She missed him dearly.

She shook her head, still not believing that while she'd been primping and pampering herself, getting ready to fall down to her knees to beg for his forgiveness, he'd already been back in Dallas without her. If she didn't have bad luck, she wouldn't have any luck at all.

She didn't want to think about it anymore. The hurt was lingering and it was all she could do to hold herself together. She reached for the sky phone, plugging in her credit card information and her sister's cell phone number. When Eden answered, Marah was grateful to hear a familiar voice.

"Hey, how are you?" Eden asked, concern spilling over the phone. "Where are you?"

"Who knows," Marah answered. "Somewhere over the big blue yonder. I'm flying home."

"Marla told me what happened. I'm so sorry, Marah. But you can still talk to John when you get home."

"I don't think so," Marah answered, resolve voicing her thoughts. "I think I should just leave things as they are. This happened for a reason. I'm taking it as sign of divine intervention."

"Sounds like you're throwing yourself a pity party," Eden said. "Why would you even think about giving up now?"

"I don't know if I can do this," Marah answered. "I don't know what I'm supposed to say."

"You knew what you were going to say when you went to New York. Say that."

Marah sighed again. "I don't know…."

"Look, I'm sending a car to pick you up. Look for the driver with the big sign that has your name on it. Once you get home, me, you and Marla will sit down with a bag of M&M's and cups of hot chocolate and figure it out. Okay?"

Marah nodded into the receiver. "Thank you. I don't know what I'd do without you two."

Eden chuckled. "Don't we know it."

Chapter 16

It had been a long while since Edward had last ridden around the ranch to appreciate the expanse of property. It was at an easy gallop that Edward took in the scenery, reminded of all the great times he and his family had shared together.

Over the years, he had ridden these paths many times with his late wife and each of his children. He couldn't help but remember the first time he'd put each of his daughters onto a horse for their first ride. It had been a family ritual, each of the girls designating her own time and place to ride with their father. As they'd transitioned into their teens, Eden and Marla had both given up riding with him, but Marah had persisted, engaging him to continue even when he'd thought them both well past their time. As he thought about it, he'd turned her down the last few times she'd asked, the timing never seeming quite right. He would have to make up for that when Marah came home. He would definitely have to ride the trails with his daughter sometime soon.

As the black stallion strode into the acreage of standing timber Edward had to marvel at all he'd accomplished over the years. Reflecting back, he knew he couldn't have done it without his late wife. They had started with sixty acres of land he'd inherited from his father. Sixty acres of land that had exhausted every dime of their life savings to maintain and each year Hazel had insisted they purchase additional acreage, sometimes mortgaging themselves beyond reason. The woman had dreamed a big dream and he'd become enamored with her enthusiasm. They had only continued to thrive and Edward's only regret was that Hazel wasn't there to bear witness to it.

Losing his precious Hazel had devastated his family. The first year after her death he'd been consumed by his grief, unable to imagine a life without her. Time had slowly assuaged the hurt of it and then, one day, while visiting her grave he'd come face-to-face with Juanita paying her respects to her dear friends. That had been the first of many encounters, then one day, out of the blue, he'd asked her out for a cup of coffee and some conversation. Their friendship had begun slowly, both taking their time as they learned to enjoy each other's company. But, the more time they spent together, the more time they wanted to spend together. And the rest, Edward thought to himself as he felt himself smiling, was history.

His girls had suffered in silence, their grief overshadowed by his own. Marla had found comfort in Michael and the girls, of course, had each other. In the end, he hadn't given any thought to how his children might still be missing their mother and he wanted to give himself one swift kick for being so blind.

He maneuvered the horse down to the back pastures, the space where they hosted the annual Black Rodeo. The event had become a staple of the community, black cowboys coming together in one place to pay tribute to their history and show off their skills. And that land was rich with history.

Stories about African-American cowhands who worked side by side with the vaqueros of New Spain and Texas when it was the northern territory of Mexico were not as well known as those of their white counterparts. But the black cowboy had many a story to be told.

Most had been slaves who'd found freedom the hard way. Theirs hadn't been a glamorous life by any means. They were men who had been poorly fed, overworked, deprived of sleep and prone to boredom and loneliness. During the day they choked on dust and at night suffered through the cold. Many suffered broken bones from falls and spills from horses that had been spooked by snakes or tripped by prairie dog holes. Work centered on the fall and spring roundups when scattered cattle were collected and driven for branding, sorting for market and castration.

And the black cowboy also had to survive discrimination and bigotry. They were men who epitomized true grit and skill, doing what was necessary to be the best at roping, busting broncos and taming mustangs.

Their stories had been long omitted from the history books. Briscoe Ranch had become a place for those stories to be shared with a generation of young people who didn't have a clue. And now as he thought of the plans the Stallions had for the property, promising to maintain the integrity of everything they'd built, he couldn't help but think how thrilled Hazel would have been. He couldn't help but to imagine her excitement at the prospect. She would have gotten one heck of a kick out of all this, he thought, his gaze sweeping over the fields.

He heaved a deep sigh. He'd made the right choice. He'd known it the minute he'd written his signature across the stack of legal documents that passed all of it on to its new owners. The ink had barely dried on the bright white paper when he felt the first ripples of relief flush over his body. The Stallion brothers had made him some big promises. Now, there was only one thing standing in the way of the deal being finalized. One last compromise to ensure the Briscoe legacy would continue as destined.

Edward felt himself smiling, a broad grin stretching across his face. Hazel would have approved, he thought. He didn't doubt that she would have probably thought of it herself had she been given the opportunity. He'd known he was on the right track when Eden and Marla had expressed their excitement, confident that he'd done the right thing.

He stalled the horse briefly, maneuvering across the low stream that divided the northern end of the ranch from the southern. Taking a glance down to his watch he knew that it was only a matter of time before the last details of the family's maneuverings would take place. Only then, when all was said and done, would he know that this had truly been worth it.

"We should have put a hidden camera in the car," Luke said just before spooning a forkful of pasta salad into his mouth.

Marla shook her head, passing baby Michael to his father. "I'd give anything to be a fly on the wall for just a minute.

Matthew pulled a knife through the grilled steak that filled his plate. "I imagine John's going to be some sort of angry."

"At least for the first five minutes," Mark agreed.

"Let's hope they get over it quick," Eden interjected. "If it lasts too long Marah's liable to spill some blood."

They all chuckled, content and pleased with themselves as they imagined the possibilities of what they'd managed to arrange for John and Marah.

"You guys eat like this often?" Luke asked. "'Cause this food is good!"

The Briscoe women chuckled. "We can cook now," Marla said, passing a bowl of mashed potatoes to her husband.

"They can definitely do that," Jack said, tossing his wife a wink.

"What's for dessert?" Mark asked, glancing over his shoulder as the assortment of sweets that lined the countertops.

Juanita shook her head. "You're worrying about dessert and you haven't even finished your meal."

Mark chuckled. "I hear a chocolate cake calling my name. I can't help myself," he said with a wide grin.

Marla laughed with him. "Mississippi-mud cake. It's decadent."

"That's like dark, dark, dark chocolate, right?"

She nodded. "With chocolate icing and a marshmallow and nut filling. It's to die for."

Mark shook his head. "Lord, have mercy. I can't wait!" he exclaimed, licking his lips excitedly.

Laughter rang around the room.

"So, Mark, tell us about this trip you're taking?" Michael asked, shifting a bottle in his son's mouth. "Sounds like a good time to me."

Mark nodded. "I'm riding my bike to Myrtle Beach for Black Bike Week."

"I declare he's trying to hurt his fool self," Juanita exclaimed, her head waving from side to side. "I'm going to be a nervous wreck the entire time he's gone."

Mark leaned to give the woman a big hug. "Not to fear, Auntie. I promise I'll be careful."

"Who are you riding with?" Eden asked curiously.

"A couple of friends from my bike club. But anyone's welcome to tag along. We're going to have a great time."

"I should go," Michael said, tossing Marla a quick glance.

"Oh, no you shouldn't," his wife answered. "Not unless you can strap that baby onto your chest and me on your back for the ride."

Michael chuckled. "We could do that. Couldn't we, son?" he said nuzzling the infant under his chin. "My boy would like to ride a motorcycle, wouldn't you, junior?"

"Not before he rides a horse," Edward said, coming into the room, injecting himself into the conversation with a soft chuckle.

Everyone turned to look in his direction. Juanita stood, moving to his side.

"How was your ride, Edward? Did you enjoy yourself?" she asked, concern tinting her tone.

He nodded, guiding her back to the table to take the seat beside him. "I did enjoy myself. More than I realized. So," he said, his gaze moving from one face to another, "have we heard anything yet?"

Matthew Stallion grinned widely, giving the man a thumbs-up. "We're right on schedule. Whatever's going to happen is going down right now."

The patriarch nodded, lifting a full glass of sweet tea into the air. "Here's to a successful merger," he said, making a toast. "Let's hope that all goes well."

Juanita smiled. "And it probably wouldn't hurt if we all said a prayer or two as well."

Chapter 17

John had just about had enough. They'd been parked in front of the airport for almost an hour, the flight delayed due to high winds out of Chicago. He still didn't have a clue who he was meeting and no one was answering a cell phone or a telephone at the office or the house. The driver had departed the vehicle some time earlier and now John sat waiting, his patience beginning to wear extremely thin.

And he couldn't stop himself from thinking about that woman. Thoughts of Marah kept intruding into his mind, numbing his spirit. He missed her terribly and he wanted to call her, to hear her voice, but something he couldn't name kept holding him back.

He was suddenly distracted by voices outside the air-conditioned vehicle, the driver finally returning with his passenger. John leaned forward in his seat, collecting his thoughts, just as the door swung open to usher in their guest. His eyes were drawn first to the stiletto heel of a Jimmy Choo shoe and the length of bare leg that stepped inside. As his gaze glided up past a short skirt and silk blouse, he could feel himself stiffen and then his eyes rested on Marah's face, her surprise as visible as his. Before either of them could say anything, the limousine's door closed and, with an obvious click of the locks, they were trapped inside.

"What are you…" Marah started.

"What's going on?" John asked, both talking over each other.

The front panel to the driver's seat opened and a white envelope was pushed through, falling to the floor. Both John and Marah stared at it and then each other, neither quite sure what it was they were supposed to do and why they were suddenly being thrown together.

John finally shook the clouds of confusion from his head and reached for the envelope, tearing it open quickly. The note was short and sweet, typed neatly on Stallion Enterprises letterhead.

Since you two can't seem to get it together, we've decided to give you a helping hand. Talk. It's the first step to reconciliation. The driver has been instructed to not let either of you out of the car until he's told. His salary is dependent on him completing this task and since he's got three kids to feed we doubt that you'll be able to change his mind. You'll be driven to a neutral location of our choosing. When we

think you're ready, someone will come let you
out. We love you both. Now deal with each
other.

The letter was signed by each of his brothers, her sisters
and Edward and Juanita. John read it three times before
passing it to Marah so that she could read it for herself.
As her eyes skated across the paper, John tried unsuccess-
fully to open the car door. Sitting back onto the leather
seat, he stared at her, waiting to see what she had to say.

Marah couldn't believe this was happening to them.
She read the note over and over again, then lifted her
eyes to meet his. His efforts to open the door had failed,
so she didn't even bother to try. Instead she knocked
against the partition window that separated them from
the driver. She knocked with a closed fist first and when
the driver didn't answer, she pulled off her shoe and
hammered the heel against the shatterproof glass.

John sat watching her, his amused expression grating
right on Marah's nerves. Settling back against the cushioned seat, she crossed her arms over her chest and one
leg over the other. The gesture caused her skirt to rise
up against her thigh and she didn't miss John's apparent
interest as his eyes widened. His stare was obvious.

She shook her head. "Well, isn't this one fine
mess," she said.

John didn't answer, turning to stare out the darkened
windows. "Where are you coming from?" he suddenly
asked, his gaze moving back toward her.

She eyed him before answering, unsure whether she
wanted to tell him the truth or not. She decided on the
truth. "New York."

"What were you doing in New York?"

Marah paused again before responding, weighing the options of her response. "I went looking for you."

Her answer threw him off guard for just a brief moment. He felt his head bobbing slowly up and down against his thick neck. "Why?" he asked, his deep gaze meeting hers. John felt as if he was suddenly being swallowed whole by her stare, the wealth of it so mesmerizing that he was finding it difficult to stay focused.

Marah was feeling it as well as she leaned forward in her seat, leaning toward him as if some sort of magnetic pull was drawing her to him. "To apologize. To try and explain what you heard. And to tell you I love you," she said, her voice dropping an octave with her last three words. "I love you," she repeated a second time, allowing the magnitude of the statement to swell full in the space between them.

For one of the first times in his life, John was speechless. He opened his mouth to speak but no words came out, his lips flapping closed, open, closed again as though he were a guppy sucking in air. Marah, though, had a mouthful of words that suddenly spilled past her full lips.

"John, I never meant to hurt you," Marah said, her hands clasped nervously in her lap. "And I didn't mean what I said. In fact, what I said didn't come out like I meant for it to. I was angry and I was hurt. Juanita had just told me she and my father were getting married and I didn't take it well. I lashed out. I was wrong to do what I did but at the time I couldn't help myself."

A pregnant paused filled the space, seeming to swell thick and stagnant between them. When John still hadn't said anything in response, Marah continued talking.

"I don't know what I can do to make it up to you, John, but I'll do anything. And I am sorry. I'm so, so sorry." Marah took a deep breath, blowing it slowly out of her mouth. Cocking her head ever so slightly, she suddenly found herself angry all over again. Before either realized what was happening, Marah turned on him. "You know, John Stallion, you've got some nerve. I don't believe you."

"What did I do?" John said, a slight smile pulling at his mouth.

"I can't believe you wouldn't even talk to me about it. How dare you! What kind of relationship do we have if you won't talk to me when something goes wrong? You wouldn't even return my telephone calls. That really makes me mad." Marah sat back against the seat, crossing her arms back over her chest.

"I was hurt. You hurt my feelings," he said pouting ever so slightly.

"So you don't even talk about it? If our relationship were strictly business and you were offended by something I did or said, I bet you'd have something to say then. Wouldn't you?"

John nodded. "You're right. Had it been business I would have said something."

"So what, you have a double standard for your personal relationships or just for me?"

"I don't know what I have. I've never felt like this about any woman before you. With you I can't seem to think about anything at all except how much I love you."

Marah's eyes widened at John's admission. She took another deep breath and held it, allowing it to fill her lungs with warm air. "So now what?" she finally asked. "Where do we go from here?"

"Let's start over. Insult me again and this time neither one of us is going to just let it go."

"I'm not going to insult you," Marah said, fighting not to giggle. "That's just ridiculous."

"Now I'm ridiculous?"

"Yes. I mean no. I mean, your suggestion is ridiculous."

John threw up his hands. "Well, if you have all the answers, why ask me the questions?"

"You are so pigheaded, "Marah chimed.

"Look who's talking!"

Marah watched as John sat back in his seat, still appraising her. To ensure she had his attention, she uncrossed and crossed her legs slowly, affording him the opportunity to sneak a quick peek beneath her skirt. His gaze followed the motion with casual ease and Marah couldn't keep herself from smiling.

"And for the record," she stated, "I didn't insult you. I just said that I didn't need you. And I don't."

"If that was supposed to be an apology, I think you missed the point."

Marah rolled her eyes. "Don't patronize me."

"I wasn't. I was just saying that wasn't a very good apology. There is nothing flattering about you saying you don't need me."

"Well, you should be flattered."

"Why?"

"Because I want you. I want you in my life and that is far more important that my ever needing you could ever be."

"A man likes to feel needed. I would have thought

you of all people would know that. Don't you teach folks about relationships? Isn't that what you do?"

Marah rolled her eyes skyward, ignoring his comment. "You should have trusted that you knew my heart. Because you know my heart, John Stallion. You know it just like I know yours."

The two sat staring at each other, both suddenly aware that the vehicle was traveling. Marah was mesmerized by the sheer beauty of his eyes. As he stared at her she could feel his love caressing her gently, gliding over her as he took her in. And so she caressed him back, allowing her gaze to show him exactly how she was feeling for him. John smiled. He'd forgotten how exquisite she was. He suddenly had an overwhelming urge to kiss her and he said so.

"I really want to kiss you right now."

Marah smiled, the wealth of it warming the delicate lines of her face. "What's stopping you?" she asked.

He moved to take the seat beside her, wrapping his arms around her torso. "I need to apologize first. I'm sorry I didn't take the time to hear you out."

"You should be," Marah said, leaning gently into his chest. "You made me crazy when I thought I'd lost you."

John tightened the grip he had around her shoulders. "You drive me crazy, too, do you know that?"

Marah smiled, lifting her mouth to his. "The feeling is mutual," she said and then she kissed him. Hard. Her mouth moving against his as if she might never have an opportunity to kiss him again. Heat flooded through her veins. As they broke the connection, Marah was consumed by a flood of emotions like nothing she'd ever experienced before. She suddenly felt as if she would cry and she pressed her face into John's chest, tears dampening his pale blue dress shirt.

Concern washed over John as he lifted her chin gently in the cusp of his hand, tilting her head to look at him. "What's the matter, baby?" he asked softly, his gaze skating over her face.

Marah nodded. "I'm just being silly," she said, her voice barely a whisper. "I just realized how much I missed being in your arms. How safe I feel when I'm with you."

John caught her hand beneath his and lifted it to his mouth. He kissed the center of her open palm, then blew butterfly kisses down the length of each finger. Marah felt herself melting beneath the sweetness of his touch. Suddenly they both became aware of the music playing softly from the speakers set in the limousine doors. Norah Jones was singing about feeling the same way all over again and they both smiled, the lyrics seeming to send them a message that they both understood.

John pulled Marah onto his lap as he curved his arms around her waist. Leaning against him, Marah felt more relaxed than she'd felt since that awful day in his office. They talked for another hour, both finally finding the words to explain what had been going on in her head and in his. Both shared more of themselves than they had shared before and when the limo finally came to an abrupt stop, the time they'd spent apart and angry felt as if it were a faint memory both could barely remember.

After sitting for an extended period, Marah leaned up to peek out the window. "Do you think they'll ever let us out of here?" she asked.

John chuckled. "Do you really want to leave me?'

Marah smiled, her mouth curving into a slow grin. "Not at all, but I just flew from New York back to Dallas and jumped right into this car. I could use me a restroom right about now."

John shook his head, reaching for the cell phone in his breast pocket. "Let's see if we can get one of them on the phone."

As John dialed, Marah reached for the door handle and pushed at the door. Both were surprised when it opened, Marah almost tripping out the entrance onto the ground.

"Well, I'll be…" she started, a harsh cuss threatening to cross her lips.

"Perfect timing," John said, stepping out, too.

They both looked around, realizing they'd stopped in front of John's home, the car stopped at the end of the driveway. The driver was standing sheepishly by the door, looking from one to the other with apprehension.

"Will that be all, Mr. Stallion, sir?" he said an edge of fear lifting his tone.

John chuckled. "Yes, thank you."

Marah shook her head. "I sure hope they paid you well," she said to the man, her head waving from side to side.

The tall Hispanic man smiled. "Yes, ma'am," he said as he pulled another envelope from his pocket. He passed the letter to Marah, then moved to remove her bags from the vehicle's trunk.

Marah tore at the seal, lifting the paper from inside. The message was short and sweet. Welcome home, printed in large letters. She smiled and as she did, John wrapped his arm around her shoulders. They both eased onto the front stoop and he unlocked the door.

Balloons in every color of the rainbow filled the living space. Someone had gone to great pains to decorate the room with joy. Both John and Marah were awed by the sight, the decor moving them both to grin widely.

"This is too much fun," Marah said, moving into the living room.

John nodded. "I use to love balloons when I was little. I forgot how much fun they could be," he said, punching one lightly and watching as it rose higher toward the ceiling.

The dining room table was set for two and, before either could comment, the front doorbell was ringing loudly for attention. On the other side of the closed door stood a deliveryman from Marah's favorite Thai restaurant with orders of chicken satay, spring rolls, hot and sour shrimp soup and mussaman curry for their supper. John laughed out loud as Marah skipped to the table with the bags, excitement filling her face.

When the deliveryman had made his exit, a large tip burning his pocket, Marah grabbed John's hand and pulled him toward the bedroom.

"What?" John said curiously. "Don't you want to eat before the food gets cold?"

"I'm just thinking that if Eden or Marla had anything to do with this, then there's definitely more waiting for us on the other side of this door," she said as she turned the knob to open the bedroom door.

Easing in behind her, John's grin broadened. Rose petals across the room, leading into the master bath and back to the large bed. The bed linens had been turned down, silk and lace sheets tempting the senses. A bottle of champagne sat chilling in an ice bucket and two glasses sat on top of the dresser. A number of candles had been placed around the room, waiting to be lit, and the delicate scent of almonds and honey wafted through the air.

Marah took a deep inhale and giggled softly, her gaze resting on the nightstand. "They are too funny," she said, taking note of the bottles of massage oils and naughty novelties that had been left for them to explore. Her giggles turned to a deep laugh when John picked up a vibrator that looked like it would do more harm than good, giving her a *don't even think about it* glare.

"What, Mr. Stallion? Not challenging enough for you?"

The man chuckled. "That's not challenging. That's just too over the top for my blood."

"You never know," Marah said coyly.

The man shook his head from side to side. "Oh, I know, girl. I know."

He leaned to kiss her lips, allowing his to slowly explore hers. When he pulled away, breaking the connection, Marah stood with her eyes closed, her head tilted back against her neck and the sweetest sensations sweeping down her spine.

"What's that?" John asked, pulling her back to the moment.

Marah turned to stare where he stared, taking note of the television set and DVD player sitting in the corner of the room. A pale yellow sticky note sat against the center of the television screen, play me was printed in bold letters. She shrugged her shoulders as she moved to depress the On buttons. As she moved back to where John stood, both taking a seat on the edge of the bed, she was suddenly shocked when the movie credits introduced the two of them.

John suddenly laughed out loud as images of him and his brothers when they'd been boys danced across the screen. Even then, John was bossy, dictating to his siblings how to move in front of the camera as they were obviously entertaining their parents.

"You were so cute!" Marah exclaimed excitedly.

John scowled. "That was Matthew, not me."

Marah gave him a light punch to his arm. "No, it wasn't. I know you when I see you."

The man chuckled, pulling her to him as he wrapped his arms tightly around her torso. "That's my mother," he said softly, pointing out the woman who was leaning to kiss all of their cheeks.

Their visual suddenly changed and toddler twins were sitting atop a small pony, a robust woman with a wide smile holding onto them tightly.

"That's my mother," Marah whispered back, tears rising to her eyes.

John gave her a warm squeeze as they sat watching their lives play out across the screen, old home movies having been burnt onto a DVD. There were moments when both laughed out loud and a few when one or the other was wiping at the moisture that suddenly pooled beneath their eyelids.

The closing credits moved them both to smile, the movie dedicated to their future. John rose from where he sat to turn off the machine. He turned and stared at her, marveling at the natural beauty that embraced her.

"Do you want children?" he suddenly asked, realizing that they'd never discussed the subject.

Marah nodded. "I do. How about you?"

"Twins. Two sets. Boy and girls."

Marah laughed. "I don't know if I want that many!"

John laughed with her. "Okay, that's fair. But we have to have at least two."

Marah rolled her eyes teasingly. "If you insist."

"I do."

Moving slowly toward her, John was suddenly consumed with desire, the wealth of it pouring out of his eyes as he stared at her. Marah found herself squeezing her thighs together, a shiver of excitement rushing through her body. It was suddenly hot, the temperature in the room seeming to have risen twenty degrees. Smiling mischievously, John pressed his palms to hers, pushing her back against the bed, and Marah felt her heart leap as he dropped his mouth to hers. Kissing her hungrily, his tongue danced in the moist cavity as if he were kissing her for the very first time.

Marah's body was suddenly on fire, heat burning from her head to her toes. Her nipples stood up full and stiff beneath her blouse and all she could think of was releasing them from the confines of the fabric. Leaning over her, John eased himself between her thighs, Marah opening her legs. He eased his body downward, his large hands cupped around her face as he continued to work his mouth over hers, Marah bearing the full weight of him above her.

When he paused to catch his breath, Marah regarded him tenderly. With the tips of her fingers she traced the line of his profile. An inner chill consumed her as she suddenly realized the magnitude of just how much she loved him.

John seemed to read her mind as he looked down at her. Her adorable face was both shy and impudent, the promise in her eyes beguiling. She was so sweet, so deliciously desirable that he couldn't begin to imagine how he'd gotten so lucky. He bit down against his lip, fighting back the sudden urge to cry.

Color had risen in Marah's face, her cheeks and eyelids flushed beautifully. Her mouth seemed to be begging for his attention and so John obliged, allowing his lips to roam back over hers. He slipped a hand between them, slowly undoing the buttons on her blouse as Marah released him from his dress shirt at the same time. Urgently he began to work the closures of her bra, reaching hungrily for the naked flesh beneath. Marah gasped as his hands touched her bare flesh, sending a current of electricity through her. He fondled her gently, then sucked her engorged nipples into the hollow of his mouth, his tongue lashing back and forth against one and then the other. She shuddered beneath the attention and perspiration suddenly beaded against Marah's brow.

Pushing himself up and away from her John pulled at his clothes, undoing his necktie and throwing his dress shirt and pants to the floor beneath his feet. In no time at all, he stood naked, every muscle in his body hard with desire. As Marah watched him, she pulled at her own clothes, sliding her skirt and panties off her hips. Rising up, she pulled her arms out of her blouse and tossed it and her bra to the floor with John's clothes.

John smiled seductively, the beauty of it inciting

desire like Marah had never felt before. The man slowly crawled above her, drawing a trail of kisses up the length of her body as he eased himself against her. When they were finally lying side by side, Marah whispered his name against the side of his face, snaking her tongue into his ear. She smoothed her palms along his neck and shoulders, kneading the firm flesh tenderly and John reveled beneath her soft touch.

Marah was fascinated as she stroked his dark skin so salaciously, delighting in the familiarity of his body. He shivered beneath her touch and Marah smiled, her inquisitive fingertips dancing with abandonment against him. John marveled at the sensations, his body tingling with anticipation. His open mouth sucked hungrily at hers as they met in a passionate kiss. She moaned into his mouth, exulting in the exquisite sensations he was drawing from her as his hands traveled slowly up and down her body.

A finger slid from her rock-candy nipples across her taut breasts, down to her belly and navel. When John teased the silky hairs of her pubis, Marah couldn't take it anymore. She pushed herself against him, thrilled by his touch, her center throbbing with desire. Moisture puddled in every crack and crevice as he stroked her boldly, his hand slowly massaging the taut pearl at the door to her womanhood.

Marah's tongue danced eagerly in his mouth, loving and uninhibited. And then she screamed out her delight, her body quivering uncontrollably as his name rolled past her lips. Leaning upward again she kissed her way along his jaw to his ear. John shuddered as Marah nipped delicately at his earlobe, caressing the sensitive skin with the tip of her tongue. Opening herself widely, she pulled him to her, reaching for the pulsating rod of steel that swung blatantly between them. Her fingers wrapped tightly around him and John was suddenly overcome with emotion, wanting to drop his body deeply into hers.

Pausing to pull a condom out of the drawer, he sheathed himself quickly, then plunged his body against hers, entering her easily. The sensations were glorious as he danced inside her, their connection seamless as she met him thrust for thrust. The slicked interior of her body felt as though it had been designed exclusively for him and John marveled at the mystery of such a phenomenon.

Marah shuddered as he sank even deeper into her. She felt herself gasp for air, the heat swelling between them feeling as if it were about to combust. Gasping in delight, she buried her face in the crevice of his neck, suckling the soft flesh beneath his chin, her fingernails digging into the flesh along the length of his broad back.

Their loving was ravenous as familiar pleasures throbbed between them. Indescribable sensations coursed up his spine and hers, the delight of it reverberating back and forth along their trembling limbs. They made love wildly, tenderly, hips bucking against each other, quivering to a natural rhythm that was all their own. John suddenly shuddered convulsively, muttering Marah's name over and over as if he were chanting in prayer. Marah felt as if she were being transported skyward, a mounting pinnacle of rapture spiraling joy straight through her. As she clung to him,

holding as tightly to him as she could manage, she
vowed to never let him go again, and John promised to
hold her to it.

Edward hung up the telephone, a wide grin filling his
face. The crowd that gathered in his family room looked
on curiously, waiting for details. When he nodded his
head, waving his hands above his head as if he'd just won
a prizefight, the Stallion brothers let out a loud whoop
and Eden and Marla both jumped up to hug each other.

"John says they are doing very well," Edward said.
"And Marah sounded happy. I haven't heard her so
happy in a long time!" the man exclaimed.

Juanita moved to his side, wrapping her arms around
his neck. She leaned to give him a kiss, hugging him
tightly. "That's wonderful," she said, smiling widely.

Edward hugged her back. "Yes, it is," he said
thoughtfully. "Yes, it is."

Chapter 18

Her father was in the barn when Marah came through the double doors intent on riding her horse. His own horse was saddled and waiting patiently and when she saw them, a broad grin filled the young woman's face.

"Daddy! What are you doing?" Marah asked excitedly.

Edward grinned back. "I thought you and I might go riding together. We haven't done it in a long while and I miss our time together. Do you think your old man can tag along with you today?"

Marah nodded excitedly. "I'd really like that, Daddy."

Minutes later the duo was crossing across the fields, headed toward the narrow bridle paths that bordered the perimeter of the property. They crossed one end of the vast acreage to the other, stopping periodically to take stock of the views. As both enjoyed the experience, Marah marveled at how easily she could zone out, forgetting everything as she merged with her horse. When riding she never felt like she was thinking about what she was doing, but instead was simply moving in time with the animal as they soared together over the ground. The sensation was amazing. Knowing her father's love for the sport had been the catalyst for her own only made it sweeter.

Edward sidled up beside her as she and Brutus came to a standstill down by the large pond. The man dismounted, tying the mammoth creature he'd been riding up to a nearby tree. Marah did as he did, joining him as he took a seat at the water's edge. Sitting side by the side the two said nothing, enjoying the quiet of the moment. Minutes later Edward broke the silence.

"Are you happy, Marah?" he asked casually, cutting a quick eye in her direction before focusing his gaze back over the water.

Marah nodded, a smile filling her face. "I am, Daddy. I am. If you'd asked me that a few weeks ago I don't know that I would have had the same answer, but I feel really good right now."

"And I reckon John Stallion has something to do with that?"

"A little something."

The man nodded. "He's a good man, Marah. A damn good man. A father couldn't ask for a better man to love his daughter. I consider this a blessing for us both."

"I love him, Daddy. I love him very much."

"I know you do, munchkin. And I know he loves you. He told me so."

Marah turned to stare at her father, a curious expression crossing her face. "He did? When? What else did he say to you?" she asked, curiosity pulling at her.

Edward shrugged his shoulders, a broad smile filling his dark face. "Now, that's none of your business. But John and I had a nice long chat. I asked some hard questions and he gave me some honest answers."

"What did you ask him?"

"What his intentions were with my baby girl, first of all. Then the usual stuff a father asks about—his credit report, prior relationships, whether or not he's a NASCAR fan…."

Marah laughed. "No, you didn't."

"Yes, I did."

"And John passed the inquisition?"

"He scored in the high nineties. I'll give him an A."

Marah shook her head with a low giggle. She leaned her head on her father's shoulder, leaning in to him as he kissed her forehead, an arm wrapping around her shoulders.

"I miss Mommy," Marah said softly.

Edward nodded his understanding. "So do I, precious."

There was a moment of silence that spread between them. Neither said anything, the horses neighing lightly in the distance, the sounds of nature spinning around them.

"Do you love Juanita?" Marah suddenly asked, closing her eyes as she waited for her father to respond.

The man paused, taking a deep breath before he

answered. "I do. I didn't think I would ever love another woman after your mother, but I do. Juanita makes me very happy, Marah. She's a special woman."

Marah's head bobbed up and down slowly, but she didn't say anything. Edward waited, listening to the sound of his child's breathing, understanding that the moment would either make or break the two of them. When Marah sniffled softly, he tightened his grip, hugging her tightly to him.

Marah allowed herself to fall into the memories of her mother and her father and the time they'd shared together. She would never have wished this moment on them and now that it was here and undeniable, she knew that she would have to come face-sto-face with her demons.

Juanita had apologized profusely for her actions. Although she'd wanted to resist, the woman's display of emotion and her obvious love for John had moved Marah. The older woman's dedication was endearing, and though she'd not said it out loud, Marah was grateful John had so much love and support from someone looking out for his best interests. She leaned up to kiss her father's cheek.

"I haven't given Juanita a chance, but I promise you that I will, Daddy. If she makes you happy then I'll do everything I can to support that."

Edward smiled, turning to meet his daughter's gaze. "Thank you, Marah," he said softly. "Thank you very much."

Marah smiled. "Ready, old man?" she asked, lifting herself from the ground and extending a hand in his direction.

Edward nodded. "How about a race?" he said, moving toward his horse and climbing into the saddle.

Marah grinned. "Last one to the barn mucks the stables," she said gleefully, laughing as they both took off at a gallop.

John heard voices in the outer office, Juanita greeting someone cheerily. His door was cracked slightly, left open after he'd come inside from his last meeting. The sudden rise of female laughter caught his attention and held it. John instantly recognized the sweet lull of Marah's voice and he found himself smiling broadly as he pushed himself out of his seat and onto his feet.

He paused at the door, his ears perked listening as the two women engaged themselves in conversation.

"That's just too funny!" Juanita was saying, giggling softly. "Edward is just too much!"

"Daddy thinks he's funny," Marah responded.

John felt a blanket of warmth drop against his shoulders. He knew this was a big deal for Marah and he was proud that she'd finally made an effort to break through the barrier she'd put between herself and Juanita. He stood eavesdropping as they chatted casually, both finding a level of comfort with each other that hadn't existed before.

When he heard his name being dropped, followed by a roar of laughter, he pushed his way through the door, his eyes darting from one woman to the other.

"How's a man supposed to get any work done with you two out here talking about him?"

Marah laughed, moving to his side as she leaned up

to kiss his cheek. "Who said we were talking about you?" she asked teasingly.

"Did you have your ear pressed to the door again, John?" Juanita asked, smiling.

John feigned being surprised. "Me? Would I do something like that?"

Juanita cut her eye toward Marah. "When he was little his mama use to tap his bottom for eavesdropping all the time. Use to tap that butt good, she did."

"So, I need to tap his bottom, is that it?" Marah asked.

John laughed, wrapping his arms tightly around her. "Why don't we talk about tapping bottoms later," he said, heat warming his cheeks.

The two women burst out laughing, both shaking their heads.

"So, what brings you here?" he asked Marah, moving to change the subject.

"I actually stopped by to see if Juanita might like to go to lunch with me," Marah said, looking toward the woman, her expression questioning. "I thought we might start all over again."

Juanita smiled, pressing a wrinkled hand atop her heart. "I'd like that, Marah. I'd like that very much," she responded warmly.

John grinned. "What about me?"

Marah leaned to kiss his cheek one last time. "You're on your own, baby. It's ladies only this afternoon."

John pushed his bottom lip out, pouting. "But I'm hungry, too" he said, pretending to be offended.

Marah smiled. "I'm sure you are. I'll tap your bottom later," she said with a sly wink. "Count on it."

* * *

A sudden flash of lightning filled the small home, causing the Bose radio playing on the nightstand to momentarily crackle with static. A few seconds later, the warm night air was filled with a resounding crash as the sound of the thunder caught up with the light. A storm had been raging for most of the evening, alternating between violent clashes in the sky and the steady patter of rain against the windows.

"That one was wicked!" Marah exclaimed, startled by the sudden illumination. She snuggled closer to John, curling her naked body against his. The man wrapped his arms around her, pulling her closer to him as he nuzzled his face into her hair, inhaling the delicate scent of coconut and mango that coated her curls.

"I like a good thunderstorm," John said, caressing the length of her arms with a warm palm. "It's a nice reminder that there are things in this world more powerful than we are."

"I like the morning after a storm, when the whole world feels fresh and new."

John smiled. "So, did you have a good afternoon?"

"I did. I enjoyed having lunch with Juanita and then we both met Eden and Marla for a shopping spree."

"Ohhh. That's why I couldn't find my assistant this afternoon."

"She deserved to play hooky. You've been getting away with it for weeks now."

"I agree. So are you feeling better about Juanita and your father?"

"I'm adjusting to the idea of Juanita and my father," Marah answered, turning to face the man.

They lay side by side, sharing the same pillow as they continued to talk.

"That's a good thing. I think the two of them are good together. And I really am glad to see Aunt Juanita and your father so happy."

Marah took a deep breath, nodding her head slowly. "So am I, actually. It's still hard for me, though."

"What about your sisters?"

"They got past it faster than I did. But then they both swear I'm the one who's always more dramatic about these things."

John brushed a thumb against Marah's cheek, tracing the line of her jaw with his hand. Marah closed her eyes and allowed herself to fall into the sensation of his touch. His hand felt soft and warm against her face and Marah turned to plant a kiss against the inside of his wrist. When his thumb passed across her lips, lightly outlining her mouth, she sucked it slowly into her mouth, rolling her tongue slowly around the length of it. John hummed, a low purr that made Marah open her eyes to see his face.

John's own eyes were closed and Marah was moved by the look of contentment that painted his expression. She felt herself smile, comfort washing over her spirit. John's hands continued to explore her body, the pads of his fingers delving across every inch of her. Another reverberation of thunder rumbled through the house and Marah snuggled closer to the man, a shiver coursing up the length of her spine. She rested her cheek against his chest as John rolled onto his back. His heart was beating strong and steady, the lull of it soothing to Marah's spirit.

John gently kissed the top of her head as he brushed

her hair from her forehead and out of her face. "You should get some rest," he whispered softly. "You've had a long day. I imagine you have to be tired by now."

Marah nodded her head against him. "I am. And I need to be at the ranch early tomorrow."

"What's happening tomorrow?"

"Nothing, really. But with the rain we've had and them predicting warm, dry weather tomorrow, I want to get a good ride in. Brutus needs new shoes on his hoofs as well, so I want to get that taken care of. Then I'm doing a group session on intimacy tomorrow evening."

"That sounds interesting."

"It will be. Care to join me?"

The man shrugged. "I'll give it some thought and let you know."

"Chicken!"

John laughed as he squeezed her gently. "Darn right I'm chicken. Lord knows what you might have me doing," he said as he reached over to turn of the light on the nightstand. Marah giggled softly against him as she snuggled down for the night. Cradling his arms back around her, he relished the moment, having grown accustomed with the routine of Marah falling asleep and waking up beside him. Earlier they had discussed her selling her home since she rarely spent time there and he was more than ready to make their arrangement permanent. He knew Marah was feeling the same way as well.

The diamond he'd purchased was locked away in the safe behind the wall in the walk-in closet and he was past ready to put it on her hand and make their union official. *Tomorrow,* he thought as he hugged her tightly, Marah beginning to snore softly against him. *Tomorrow will be the perfect day to propose.*

Chapter 19

There was a flood of activity going on when Marah arrived at the ranch, brushing by Marla and Michael with a quick hello. Her father had been at the kitchen stove stirring a pot of grits and frying bacon but, though the aromas had been tempting, Marah decided to forgo breakfast until after she'd worked a few of the horses. She was excited to get back onto her own horse and she imagined Brutus was just as anxious for a run.

The stable hands were between the barn and the work track when Marah went down. She waved and greeted the men cheerily, most in the group having been with the ranch since Marah had been a little girl. The elderly Mexican man the girls had nicknamed Papa Chico gave her a warm hug before he led a newly acquired black mustang named Champ to the track.

The horse was impressive, heavy on muscle with plenty of space left to bulk up even more. His legs were long but he didn't look at all out of balance. As he'd sauntered in her direction, the animal had made eye contact with her and Marah was almost tempted to climb on his back herself.

Papa Chico and the mustang headed to the track calmly, both moving as if they did this every day of the week. Marah knew they were putting the horse through his paces to test him, trying to decide if they might race him, breed him or both. Moving down to the fenced field, Marah leaned on the wooded gate to watch. Papa Chico started the horse with a slow trot around once and then a second time. He picked up the pace with the third lap and the horse looked a little awkward through the first furlong. By the time he hit the sixth furlong pole, the mammoth animal was moving like he and not the rider was in full control. As they rounded the back-stretch, Champ's long legs were reaching out for the ground so smoothly that to look at him, it appeared as though he were just a dark breeze blowing in the morning air. Marah was totally enthralled, anxious to find out what plans her father had for the animal.

Marah watched until the end of the workout. The horse wasn't even blowing. Marah had imagined the animal would have been breathing as if he'd just finished running for his life, but Champ sounded like he'd barely been out on a regular gallop. Following the two back into the stalls, Marah moved to help unbridle and unsaddle the animal.

"Papa Chico, he's a beauty. What's Daddy planning to do with him?"

Papa Chico nodded his agreement. "This one's not your papa's horse. This one belongs to Mr. Stallion."

Marah's eyes widened with surprise. "Mr. Stallion? John Stallion?"

The old man shook his head no, the appendage waving anxiously from side to side. "No. No. Mr. Matthew Stallion."

Marah was even more stunned, curious to discover that Matthew even had a love for the animals. "Are they going to breed him?" she asked curiously.

Papa Chico shrugged. "This one's a runner. He loves the track. I will suggest they race him first. He's derby material through and through."

Marah nodded. "What time's the farrier due?" she asked, taking a quick glance down to her watch.

"This afternoon, Miss Marah. He only has three horses to shoe today. Yours, ole Bess and one of the new mares."

"Good," Marah answered. "I don't plan to ride for long. It'll give Brutus a chance to rest. Let me help you with this one first, though."

After cooling the mustang down and giving him a good grooming, Papa Chico turned the animal out into the pastures to graze. Champ had eyed Marah curiously, nuzzling her once before moving off to entertain himself. Papa Chico led Brutus out of his stall, holding him to limit his movement while Marah saddled him up. After a thorough check of her equipment to insure everything was in good working order, Marah moved to the horse's left shoulder and tossed a blanket onto the horse's back. Raising the saddle up over the horse's back she placed it gently into position and secured the rigging.

After ensuring everything was in place, she tightened

the cinch slowly, allowing Brutus to become comfortable with the pressure of it. Papa Chico nodded his approval as Marah bridled the horse just as she'd been taught, duly impressed with her skill. Once she'd check the bit placement, the curb strap, throatlatch and the earpiece, she was ready to ride. Marah led Brutus out of the barn, double-checking her tack and equipment one last time before mounting the animal's back. With a quick wave to Papa Chico, she and Brutus took off jogging.

The air was beginning to warm nicely, the morning sun rising bright and full in a deep blue sky. Marah inhaled deeply and blew it slowly out. As she relaxed the horse relaxed with her, the duo moving as if they were one body. It was a beautiful morning to ride and as Marah led the animal across the trails and through the wooded paths, thoughts of John kept slipping into her mind.

He'd been in a good mood that morning, the early alarm Marah had set barely disturbing him. They'd made love before rising to shower, dress and head in their opposite directions and Marah could still feel the warmth of him covering her body. His touch burned hot, the pressure of his hands felt as though it had never left her skin and Marah was amazed that she was still so aware of him even when they were apart.

They'd been spending every spare minute of their free time with each other. So much so that her father had begun to question her with raised eyebrows. "I won't tolerate a daughter of mine shackin' up with a man she's not married to, Marah Jean," he'd said one time too many. Marah didn't doubt that her daddy had made sure

John knew he didn't approve of Marah spending every night in the man's bed without the benefit of a marriage license.

Marah chuckled softly and Brutus neighed, tossing his head back slightly as if he'd read her thoughts and was laughing with her. She trotted the animal up a low incline, allowing him to stretch his legs before slowing the pace ever so slightly. Her thoughts went back to John.

She was amazed by the level of comfort she had found with him. John felt like home to her and even when she left the ranch to go to his place she was still content and happy. Her own penthouse apartment had literally become a closet from which she retrieved her clothes and even those were slowly starting to fill the empty spaces between John's many business suits and dress shirts.

A thought suddenly crossed Marah's mind and she found herself grinning widely as she spoke the words out loud as if seeking her companion's opinion.

"Brutus, I should propose to John! What do you think? Think he'll marry me?" Marah laughed, the thought of proposing to him taking shape in her mind. Her eyes widened at the prospect, imagining herself getting down on her knees to ask the man to spend the rest of his life with her. The thought was truly intriguing as she fathomed where and when she might accomplish such a thing.

Brutus heard it before Marah did, the familiar rattle startling the horse just as Marah caught sight of it out of the corner of her eye. She recognized the timber rattlesnake immediately, its tail vibrating to announce its annoyance. Startled, Brutus bucked, throwing himself back as he shied away from where the snake lay. As he did, Marah was thrown off balance and she fell backward toward the ground. Before she could catch herself, Brutus pitched forward, breaking out into a full gallop. With her foot tangled in the stirrups she was suddenly being dragged on the ground behind the horse, her body being slammed harshly against the hard earth. It happened so quickly that Marah couldn't form the thought to command the horse to stop and then suddenly everything around her went black.

Edward and the farrier, a man named Joe Titus, were chatting easily as they made their way toward the stables. The two had been good friends since forever and Joe's periodic visits to care for the horses gave them an opportunity to catch up on each other's doings. Both looked up curiously as Papa Chico came rushing out, yelling excitedly in Spanish.

"What's happened?" Edward asked, sensing something was seriously wrong.

The elderly man paused for quick moment to catch his breath. "Miss Marah! Her horse came back without her. I found him down in the north pasture, still in his saddle," the man said, his hands dancing frantically in the afternoon air

Edward bristled, the hairs along the back of his neck and over the length of his arms standing at attention against his skin.

"Miss Marah wouldn't leave him saddled like that," Papa Chico concluded.

Edward moved immediately into action mode,

running to the barn behind Papa Chico. Brutus stood inside, in full horse tack. Marah was nowhere to be found.

"I sent two of the hands out to look already," Papa Chico said. "I'm going now."

Edward nodded. "I'm going with you."

Joe Titus ran a large hand across Brutus' broad chest. "I'll take care of this guy for you. Is there anything else I can do?" The man's concern mirrored Edward's.

"Please, Joe. Call up to the house. Tell Michael and Marla what's going on. Marah could be anywhere and we've got a lot of acreage to cover. Tell Michael to drive down to the southern end and to ring me on my cell phone if he finds her."

"Done," the man exclaimed, helping Edward saddle his own horse.

Papa Chico was out of the barn first, Edward right on his heels, the two men taking off at a full gallop. Both knew that anything could have happened to Marah and that the sooner they found her the better off they would all be. Edward could only begin to imagine which of the trails Marah might have taken, miles of them lying between him and the fenced property line. He did know, though, that something was wrong and finding his daughter was all he wanted to do.

John stood in front of a full boardroom giving a presentation on Stallion Enterprises proposed rejuvenation plans when he suddenly lost his train of thought. Thoughts of Marah swept through his head, a cold chill flushing his body. The sensation was so unnerving that he had to excuse himself from the room, making a beeline straight to his office. As he moved down the length of hallway to his office, he pulled his cell phone from the breast pocket of his suit jacket and dialed Marah's number. Three rings and he was switched into her voice mail to leave a message. Depressing the Off button he immediately dialed her office, hoping to reach her there. No one answered.

Juanita was suddenly on his heels, concern washing over her face. "What's wrong, John?"

"I don't know. Something's not right though. I can feel it."

"Feel what, John?"

"It's like—" the man paused, distress suddenly painting his expression "—I suddenly felt like I did when my parents had their accident. I knew something was wrong then, I just didn't know what. Call it intuition."

Juanita nodded slowly. "I'm sure everything is fine. Your brothers are all…"

John shook his head vehemently. "It's not them. It's Marah. Something's wrong with Marah."

Juanita moved ahead of him into the office. Reaching for the telephone she dialed the ranch. Marla answered the phone, her voice edged in tension.

"Marla, honey, it's Juanita. Is everything okay?"

Juanita could hear the young woman's voice swell with tears. "No," Marla answered. "Something's happened to Marah," she said, filling the woman in on the few details she was aware of. "They're out search-ing for her now."

Juanita nodded, casting a look toward John. "Okay. Tell your father John and I are on the way. If you hear anything before we get there call me on my cell phone. Do you have the number?"

Marla nodded into the receiver. "I will, Juanita," she said before she disconnected the line.

Before John could ask her what was wrong, Juanita depressed the intercom and called for the driver to bring the company car around. As she pulled her purse from her desk drawer, Matthew, Mark and Luke came barreling into the room.

"What's going on?" Mark asked, looking from John to Juanita and back.

"Did you forget we're in an important meeting?" Matthew interjected.

John shook his head, dismissing them both with a wave of his hand. Juanita pushed him toward the door.

"There's an emergency," she said, gesturing for the three men to follow her. "Something's happened to Marah."

The three brothers looked at each other. Luke pulled a phone into his hand as he followed behind the others. "I'll get one of the secretaries to make our apologies. We'll reschedule later," he said as they all headed for the door and the ranch, neither giving any thought to anyone staying behind.

Minutes later they were pulling in front of the Briscoe home. John jumped from the vehicle before the driver could come to a full stop. Marla and Eden met them on the front porch, the twin sister cradling baby Michael tightly in her arms. Her face was streaked with tears, she and Eden both pacing anxiously as they waited for information.

"Anything yet?" John asked, his gaze racing from one sister to the other.

Marla shook her head no.

Eden pressed a shaky hand against his arm. "Everyone's out looking. I'm sure we'll hear something very soon."

John nodded, then turned, taking the steps two at a time.

"Where are you going?" Matthew asked, racing to catch up with him, Mark and Luke close behind.

"To look for Marah."

The brothers cut an eye at each other. Luke nodded. "Well, I guess we're all riding then."

John turned to look at his younger sibling. "You can't ride."

Luke chuckled. "Who can't ride? I took lessons for years."

"You did?"

Matthew patted his brother on the back. "We all did. Horseback riding, dance, piano. You name it, we took it."

"While you were out building your empire," Mark said. "Aunt Juanita made us."

John smiled, a mild bend of his lips. "Goes to show you what I know," he said as they made their way into the stables.

Edward and two of the ranch hands were inside, co-ordinating horses and riders and relaying transmissions from one search party to the other. A tall, wispy man with long black hair that hung in a ponytail down his back immediately moved to find them all a change of clothing as Edward and John hugged, Edward patting the man anxiously against his back.

"We haven't covered a quarter of the ranch yet," Edward said, swiping at his eyes with the back of his hand. "And it's going to be dark soon. I appreciate you boys coming to help."

"We wouldn't be anywhere else," Matthew said as he stepped out of his suit and into a pair of oversized jeans and a plaid shirt.

Minutes later they were combing the western end of the large homestead, calling out Marah's name as they prayed steadily for some response. John couldn't believe this was happening and he was imagining the worst. Marah was a true horsewoman. She knew how to handle the animals she loved so dearly. She was a master at her art, always prepared, and for something like this to have happened, she would have to have been taken totally by surprise. Business had taught John that it was those surprises thrown at you when you least expected them that could make or break a body.

His brother Matthew seemed to be reading his mind as the man sidled up to his side, more at ease atop the horse than John would have imagined. The two smiled weakly at each other.

"She's going to be fine," Matthew said. "We're going to find her."

John could feel hot tears burning against the back of his eyelids, fighting to rain down over his cheeks. "I can't lose her, Matthew. I can't."

"You're not going to lose her, big brother. I'm telling you. We will find her," the man said firmly.

John nodded his head, not totally convinced. "I remember when the police came to the door to tell us about Mom and Dad's accident. I knew they were gone before the officer could get the words out. I could feel it, Matt. I could feel it and this afternoon, during that meeting, I suddenly thought about Marah and I felt the same way as I did back then. My whole body went cold and I felt like I couldn't breathe."

Matthew said nothing, not sure there was anything for him to say. They had always trusted John's intuition, his keen sense of things going right or wrong. He wanted to believe that John might be wrong about this, but he wasn't sure and he didn't want his brother to know that.

He nodded his head slowly. "Do yourself a favor and take a deep breath," Matthew said, bringing his horse to a halt. "You need to try and relax. You can't be any good to Marah if you're not calm."

Pausing with him, John took a deep inhale of oxygen, allowing it to fill his lungs to capacity before blowing it slowly past his full lips. He took a second and then a third, feeling his whole body begin to ease just a hint of tension away. He was worried sick about Marah but deep down he was trusting that they would find her safe and sound. He was holding on to hope that the sick feeling in the pit of his stomach had nothing to do with any predictions of dread and doom, but was just his nerves working on him.

Ahead of them, Luke and Mark had continued on, their gazes sweeping over the landscape as they periodically called for Marah's attention. Both John and Matthew saw them come to a full pause, a cell phone pulled to Mark's ear. Mark's head was waving up and down as he listened to what was being said on the other end then both men turned and galloped back in their brothers' direction.

"That was Eden. They found her," Mark said, as he

came to John's side. "She's been injured but no one knows how bad yet. Paramedics are on their way."

Without another word, John and the stallion he was riding spun back in the direction they'd come from, his brothers following closely behind.

Chapter 20

An air ambulance had been called in to transport Marah from Briscoe Ranch to Doctors Hospital of Dallas. No one was allowed to make the short flight with her so everyone climbed into the Stallion limousine to make the ride to the hospital. As the car maneuvered its way through downtown Dallas, John called in every favor owed him, requesting the services of the most prestigious medical personnel he was acquainted with.

Dr. Marcus Shepard, one of Dallas's premier surgeons and John's fraternity brother, met them all at the entrance to the emergency room. The man's demeanor was stoic, his expression a mask as he extended his hand in John's direction, shaking it firmly.

"How's Marah?" John and Edward both asked simultaneously.

"She's still being examined. She hasn't regained consciousness yet. She's badly bruised from the fall. There are some broken bones and evidence of a severe head injury. Until all the doctors are finished there's not much else I can tell you. I've arranged for the family to wait in a private room outside of the ICU area. Ms. Briscoe will be moved there as soon as they've run some additional tests on her. As soon as I have some news I'll be up to talk with you."

The doctor gestured for one of the nurses. "Lynda will show you where you can wait. I'll be up as soon as I can." As soon as he finished, he spun around and marched back down.

Edward reached to wrap his arms around Eden and Marla. "She's going to be fine. She's going to be just fine," he said, conviction flooding his tone.

Eden nodded. "We know, Daddy."

Marla nodded her head, tears welling in her eyes. "I swear if she doesn't wake up soon I'm going to kill her!" she exclaimed, her body shaking.

Michael drew a palm down his wife's back, pulling her close as he kissed her forehead.

Juanita took control. "Let's get comfortable. We might be here awhile," she said, the first to follow behind the nurse named Lynda. "As soon as I find out where we are, Luke and I will go get us all some coffee."

An hour later John was pacing the floor outside of the waiting room. Dr. Shepard had come back once to tell them Marah was being transferred to surgery to stop some internal bleeding. A CAT scan of her head, chest and extremities had unmasked a pelvic fracture, a broken leg and collarbone, and a significant increase in her intracranial pressure.

"What does that mean?" Marla had asked.

"It may be an indication that there is some swelling of her brain matter," the doctor answered matter-of-factly. "She may be hemorrhaging. We're concerned that there may be further damage to her central nervous system since the swelling can cause compression of important brain structures."

"What's her prognosis?" Edward had asked, looking from one daughter to the other as he did.

Dr. Shepard's gaze locked with John's before he answered. Then, looking Edward directly in the eye he said, "Mr. Briscoe, your daughter's condition is critical. Right now it doesn't look good. But until we go in and see what's going on internally, I can't answer your question with any certainty. What I can tell you, though, is that clearly she's a fighter. She's strong and she's in excellent health and both are in her favor. As soon as I know more you'll be the first to know."

Eden drew a palm to her chest as she drew in air swiftly. Marla dropped down into the seat beside her husband, turning to sob against the man's chest. Edward closed his eyes, fighting not to break out into tears himself; Juanita moved to wrap her arms around him, hugging him tightly.

Marcus had tapped his friend against the back as he'd moved past him, his eyes sharing more than he'd voiced. As John watched Dr. Shepard exit the room, a look of complete despair washed over his face. He'd been pacing the floor ever since, waiting, hoping, praying that somehow this would all be over and he and

Marah would be back home, snuggled close together in the comfort of their bed.

He prayed daily and he'd been praying steadily since they'd been out looking for her. For him, all that mattered was that he loved her more than his next breath. He didn't even want to begin to imagine his life without her. The thought of losing Marah had his pulse racing out of control as he walked back and forth, panic washing over him.

John had nothing to say when his brothers joined him in the hallway, commanding him to follow where they were leading. For once in his life he had no desire to be in charge, unable to demand anything if he couldn't demand Marah well. Mark led the way as they sought out the hospital chapel. Once inside, Matthew and Luke guided him to one of the front pews and the four men sat down side by side. Growing up they'd attended church religiously, joining their parents every Sunday at Greater Bethlehem Baptist Church. John had insisted they continue doing such while each of them had still been in school, but over the past few years all four of them had slacked off badly, other things always maneuvering in the way. There was a quiet serenity that dropped down over them as each man found himself in the company of his brothers in a house of God.

John closed his eyes, allowing the fullness of the moment to wash over him, its warmth filling him with comfort. One brother's arm rested against the back of his shoulders. Another's hand patted him lightly against his leg. The four sat in quiet reflection for some time, praying silently for Marah and each other. Mark eventually broke the silence.

"You and Marah will get through this, big brother," he said softly. "Together."

Luke echoed his sibling's sentiments. "This thing won't beat what you two share, John."

John nodded, still not speaking, wanting to believe them both. He dropped his chin down against his chest, heaving a deep sigh. Only once before had he felt so lost. Back then he'd thrown himself and his heartache into finishing school and keeping what remained of his family intact and functional. This time he couldn't think of anything he could throw himself into.

Time ticked by slowly as they waited. Periodically one or the other would step out of the room to go check on Marah's progress, the surgery taking hours longer than had been anticipated. When Edward, Eden and Marla joined them the two families prayed side by side, holding each other up in support.

Late afternoon had turned into evening and the evening into a dark night when Juanita poked her head in, gesturing for them to all come. The doctor was finally delivering some news. Marcus Shepard was sitting in the center of the large couch, his body slumped over from exhaustion when they all returned to the waiting room. His surgical cap was in his hands, the man twisting it round and round between his fingers. He smiled slightly, nodding his head in greeting as the family surrounded him, anxious to hear what needed to be said.

"Marah's in the recovery room. The surgery went well. There was more internal damage than we'd anticipated and she's lost a good deal of blood. Right now she's in a drug-induced coma. We want her body to get as much rest as it can before we allow her to regain consciousness. If we can get her through the next twenty-four to forty-eight hours then I think the worst of it will be over," the man said softly.

"What then, doctor? Can we expect a full recovery?" Edward asked, his tone hopeful.

The man nodded. "She'll definitely have a long recovery ahead of her, but it's doable. I imagine we'll have her up and walking out of here before you know it.

"Can we see her?" John asked.

The man shook his head, waving it from side to side. "Not tonight. In the morning and definitely not all of you."

Edward nodded with him. "I just need to make sure my baby girl is okay. And I know John here does as well. I don't think the rest of my family will mind waiting."

Eden and Marla hugged each other tightly, tears of joy streaming down both their faces. Edward punched a fist into the air, a silent prayer of thanks floating skyward. Juanita moved in to hug him close.

"Like I said," the doctor reiterated, moving onto his feet. "We're not over the hump yet. The next forty-eight hours are going to be crucial," he said as he shook a round of hands and made his way out of the room.

Pushing his hands deep into the pockets of his slacks, John leaned his head back against his neck, staring up at the ceiling. Forty-eight hours. Marah could survive forty-eight hours. And he would be right there to see that she did.

The family held a bedside vigil for two weeks straight. The doctors had no answer for why Marah hadn't yet regained consciousness, but her condition had been upgraded from critical to serious as she'd been moved from ICU into a private room. The Stallion men had returned to their daily business, each of them stopping in periodically to check in on her. John hadn't left her side, insisting that when she opened her eyes for the first time that he would be right there for her to see. Wanting Marah to know that nothing, business or otherwise, had kept him from her.

Marah's eyes fluttered open and then closed and open again as she slowly took in her surroundings. The nurse looking down on her waved an index finger at her, cautioning her not to say anything.

"Welcome back, sleepyhead," the woman said, smiling. "You have a tube down your throat so you can't speak just yet. As soon as I get the doctor we'll see if we can't get that thing out."

Marah's eyes skated left and then right, her body feeling unusually heavy and out of sorts. Turning her head slightly she saw him sitting to her left, his arms crossed over his chest, his eyes closed as he snored lightly. John was sound asleep. Marah managed to point a finger in the man's direction. The nurse nodded her head, a wide grin filling her face.

"Mr. Stallion hasn't left your side. He's been here night and day," she said, moving to his side. She tapped his arm gently, mindful not to startle him from his moment of repose. "Mr. Stallion?" she called softly.

John jumped, the touch against his arm sending a jolt of electricity through him. "What's wrong?"

The nurse pressed a calming hand against his forearm. "Everything is just fine, sir. Ms. Briscoe is awake. The doctor will be in shortly to check her and remove the incubation tube."

John jumped to his feet, almost tripping to the bedside to see for himself that Marah was finally back.

Her eyes widened as he knelt down against the floor by her bed, wrapping one arm above her head and the other across her torso. His kissed her cheek, allowing his lips to linger there, a tear rolling out of the corner of his eyes.

"Hey, you," he whispered into her ear. "It's about time. I was starting to wonder how long you planned to keep me waiting."

Marah met his gaze with one of her own. She had a million questions to ask him, having no coherent memory of why she was lying there in a hospital bed. An hour later the doctor had checked all her vital signs, pleased that she was responding as well as she was.

"Okay, Marah," Dr. Shepard said, gently easing the medical tape from around the mask that covered her mouth and nose. "When I say three you're going to blow out hard, like you're trying to blow air into a balloon. I don't want you to try talking right off. Just take your time. Your throat will probably be sore for a day or two, but that's normal. Are you ready?"

Marah nodded her head. John held tightly onto her hand.

"One. Two. Three."

Marah blew, feeling the long tube being pulled quickly from her throat. Her first inhale of oxygen burned slightly, causing her to cough from the disruption. She looked up to see John smiling down at her. Her father and sisters were smiling excitedly from the foot of the bed. Marah swallowed, saliva moistening her dry mouth and lips.

"You had us worried, Marah," Edward said, his hand tapping against her foot.

Marah smiled, her mouth opening and closing as she struggled to speak. "Sorry," she finally whispered, her scratchy voice sounding odd to her ears. "What happened?" she asked, looking from one face to the other.

Eden smiled back. "You had an accident when you went riding with Brutus. You were thrown off and hit your head."

Marah suddenly had a vague recollection of the moment. "A snake," she whispered, her eyes racing from side to side. "Brutus?"

Edward nodded. "Brutus is fine. Missing you is all. He didn't get a scratch on him."

Marah smiled, closing her eyes for a brief moment. When she opened them again she looked up at John who was still holding on tightly to her fingers. The man beamed down at her.

"I love you," Marah whispered, her gaze caressing his face.

John leaned down to kiss her forehead. "I love you, too."

Marah peered out from under her bedcovers, the bright morning sun pouring into the room through the opened window blinds, due to one of the hospital's many nurses, no doubt. Wishing herself back to sleep, she shook her head, annoyed by the intrusion. The intentions were good but Marah wasn't in the mood to be light and cheery, her spirit inviting her to her own personal pity party. Heaving a deep sigh she rolled onto her back, stretching her body against the mattress. She hurt, her body still wounded with pain from her accident. Every morning started with more hurt than Marah cared to claim, the wealth of it increasing as the day wore on. Sleep was the only thing that seemed to bring her any comfort. She sighed again.

Her lips and face felt dry, her skin pulling taut and uncomfortable. Running her tongue across the bottom lip there was no moisture to be found; the skin was sore and cracked. *Okay, sit yourself up,* Marah thought, commanding herself to move. She slowly eased her legs off the side of the bed, willing her feet to touch the floor until she was sitting upright against the pillows, her legs dangling off the side. Reaching toward the nightstand, Marah poured water from a pitcher into a glass that sat in the center. Holding the glass to her lips she sipped it slowly, forcing the fluid down. She knew the risks of dehydration and she didn't relish the prospect of them keeping her confined in the hospital any longer than was absolutely necessary.

Getting started in the mornings always seemed to require more energy than she possessed. She desperately wanted to take a shower but the mere thought of making her way to the small bathroom and out of her clothes felt like more than she could handle. She knew someone would come to help if she called, but she was determined to not be any more of a burden than was absolutely necessary. Unfortunately, more was necessary than Marah cared to admit.

She struggled to move onto her feet, to lift her body from where she sat, but when it was just too much for her to maneuver, she lay back against the mattress, pulling the covers back up and over her head. Without warning, tears began to drip from her closed eyes.

There was a reason all of this was happening to her Marah thought, believing that the plans she'd had for herself had been usurped by a higher power. One day there was nothing she couldn't accomplish and in the fraction of a second she suddenly couldn't accomplish much of anything at all. Were she a pessimist, she'd believe it to be a cruel joke being played against her.

Curling herself into a fetal position, Marah's thoughts moved to John. Just days earlier she'd been thinking about breaking up with him. Although he'd been a rock, supporting every step of her recovery, she couldn't help but wonder if all of her issues might be too much to burden him with.

Her sisters had convinced her to not make any rash decisions and Marah trusted that for the moment they knew better than she did. And, truth be told, she didn't want to lose him, the thought sending her into a deep depression. Knowing he was willing and wanting to stand by her side gave Marah the courage to do what the doctors asked of her no matter how much hurt and pain she had to endure. John's support fueled Marah's drive and she didn't want to disappoint the man.

John's love was consuming. Marah would never have believed that love could be so encompassing, so energizing. Thinking of their future together made her smile at the possibilities. They shared the same dreams for each other and right now both were dreaming of the day when Marah would be well again and all of this bad business would be far behind them.

Chapter 21

A line of perspiration dotted Marah's face, moisture beading up over her brow and along the side of her nose as she struggled to get through the last repetitions of her therapy. The physical therapist counting out each push of the padded hand weight had just about gotten on Marah's last nerve but, before she could say so, John, standing in the doorway watching her, gave her kudos for a job well done.

"That's my girl! Good work, honey!"

Marah rolled her eyes skyward, frustration wrinkling her forehead. "I hate this," she said, letting go of the weights and reaching for her walker. "When is this all going to be over?"

John gestured for the physical therapist to give them a moment of privacy. He moved to Marah's side, wrapping his arms around her as he kissed her lips. She leaned into his chest, affording him a quick moment to bear the heaviness of her stress. Marah's recovery had been all-consuming. John had moved a team of nurses and medical personnel into her family's home to assist with her care. He had wanted Marah to move in with him where he could keep an eye on her 24/7 but Edward wouldn't hear of it.

"My baby girl is still a Briscoe," he'd said, his head shaking vehemently. "When she's wearing the Stallion name I can't say where she's going to stay. Until then though I have the final word for now."

"I'll marry her today, sir," John had answered, ready and willing to legitimize their relationship.

Marah had laughed, the two men she loved most in her life, acting as if she herself didn't have a say in what she wanted.

"I'm just *temporarily* incapacitated, you two," she'd quipped. "I'm not dead or deaf."

Knowing her father didn't appreciate her "shackin' up" with a man she wasn't married to, Marah respected the man's wishes. Not wanting to commit to John until she could walk on her own two feet down an aisle, Marah had negotiated a compromise, agreeing to stay at the ranch but allowing John to commandeer the medical team who would assist in her rehabilitation. Her father had balked at the offer, insisting that he could well afford to provide for his daughter's health care, but in the end, everyone had been appreciative of what each of them had all been able to do for her.

For almost four months she'd been diligently working to relearn simple motor skills; her walking, standing, feeding herself, even talking, had been impeded by the severity of her injuries. But the doctors were bowled over by her progress, Marah having come farther in the short span of time than any of them could have imagined.

Despite her improvement, though, Marah still wished she were farther along, able to do what she had before the accident had happened. John also knew that what she wanted more than anything else was to be able to get back onto a horse and ride. He sighed and kissed her again.

"Patience is not one of your virtues," he said with a soft chuckle.

Marah shook her head. "No, it isn't. And I'm tired of trying to be patient. I want my body to be better *now*."

"It'll happen soon enough," John said, guiding her to a seat.

Marah shook her head vehemently, tears welling in her eyes. "I hate this so much," she said, her voice dropping low. "I hate everything about this."

John said nothing, understanding seeming to flow between them. He listened as Marah wept quietly, spilling out her fears and frustrations against his broad shoulder.

"I feel so selfish," Marah was saying, gripping his hand between the palms of hers. "Everyone has been so good to me, doing everything for me, but I would give anything to just make them all go away and leave me alone so I can do it for myself. What's wrong with me, John?"

"You're frustrated, honey. You and that independent streak of yours have never had to rely on anyone and you're not use to it. I can only imagine what that might feel like and I'm sure I wouldn't like it much either."

Marah nodded slowly as John continued to encourage her.

"It's only temporary, darling. You just have to keep telling yourself that. This will be over before you know it. Look how far you've come in the past few weeks alone! You're making strides that others will only be able to dream about. So, focus on what you've accomplished and not what you can't do yet. In time you'll be able to do it all."

Marah blew a gust of air out of her lungs, her gaze meeting his. The man smiled down at her, the sweetness of it melting into her heart. She suddenly paused, realizing the time of day. "What are you doing here?" Marah asked, her eyes moving to the large clock on the opposite wall as she changed the subject. "Don't you have a big meeting to be in, John Stallion? You can't miss any more work just trying to look after me."

"I'm not missing anything. I have an hour before I have to be anywhere and I wanted to spend that hour with my baby."

"Sure," Marah said eyeing him with some reservation. "If I find out from Juanita that you missed any time from work to be here with me I'm breaking up with you."

John laughed. "You can't break up with me."

"Why not?"

"Because I don't have any intentions of ever letting you go." He snuggled down in the seat beside her, drawing her into the warmth of his embrace. "You're stuck with me good, kiddo. Like it or not."

Marah smiled. "I do like it. I like it very much. But I hate you letting your business suffer on my account."

"Marah, nothing is suffering. When I can't do what needs to be done I have three very capable brothers who can step in. We're doing just fine so you stop worrying."

The woman heaved a deep sigh. "Are you coming back later?"

"Don't I always come back?"

"Maybe we can go out for a while," Marah said, her voice dropping low and husky. She brushed her fingers against his thigh, her hand quivering ever so slightly. Her fingertips lightly grazed his groin. "Maybe we can spend some quality time alone."

John's gaze swept to the door and back to Marah's face. He pulled her palm into his hand, pressing a moist kiss against her flesh. "You need to stop that. You're trying to start something, aren't you."

"Yes, I am. I miss you," she said, nuzzling her mouth into his neck. "Don't you miss me?"

John allowed himself to briefly savor the sensation of her tongue trailing against his neck before he answered. "You know I miss you. You also know that the doctor said you and I have to show some restraint for just a little longer."

"Marcus doesn't have a clue what he's talking about. I know that being with you is the best medicine I could probably get and I could really use some good medicine right about now," she said seductively, nibbling at his earlobe.

John tilted his head toward her mouth, her warm breath blowing heat straight through him. "You need to stop that," he said, his hands pressed against her shoulders as he eased himself away from her. "If you leave me all hot and bothered, I won't be any good this afternoon."

"See, it'll be good medicine for you, too."

John shook his head. "Marah Briscoe, you need to behave or I'm telling. Where's your father?" John said, laughing warmly.

Marah shook her head as John gave her a tight hug.

"I'm coming back early," John said lifting himself from the seat. "Finish your therapy and then get some rest. I have a surprise for you when I get back."

"What kind of surprise?" Marah asked excitedly.

John smiled. "I imagine it's one you'll like even better than teasing and tempting me."

Marah grinned. "I wouldn't be so sure of that if I were you. Tempting you is the highlight of my day."

Her sisters were all grin as they came to rouse her from her nap. The daily siesta she took was ordered by the doctor, a ritual that Marah could easily have done without. Inevitably though, every time Marah lay down, she would drift off thinking about John. Today had been no different and as Marla had shaken her gently from her slumber, thoughts of John were still tripping through her mind.

"What's going on?" Marah asked as she slowly opened her eyes, stretching her body against the padded mattress.

"We need you to go with us," Eden said softly, her wide smile filling her face.

Marah rubbed her eyes with the back of her hands. "Where are we going?"

"To meet your man," Marla said. "We've been instructed to have you down at the barn at five o'clock."

Marah grinned herself as she sat upright in the bed, easing her legs off the side and onto the floor. "He said he had a surprise for me. What is it?"

The two women laughed. "It wouldn't be a surprise if we told you," Eden said, helping her to her feet and into her shoes.

The duo stood in wait as she maneuvered herself and her walker into the adjoining bathroom to rinse her mouth and wash her face. Pulling the length of her curly locks into a ponytail, she secured it with an elastic band at the nape of her neck. A touch of lip gloss across her lips and Marah was ready to go.

Outside the family home a golf cart sat in wait, Edward sitting behind the driver's wheel. "Took you girls long enough. What were you all doing in there?"

"Marah had to get pretty for John, Daddy," Marla said with a giggle.

Eden nodded. "It takes Marah a long time to get pretty."

Marah rolled her eyes at her sisters as they helped her into the cart, leaving the walker at the edge of the porch steps. Just minutes later, the family pulled up to the barn. Marah's eyes were wide with anticipation as John stood in the entranceway, his own broad smile washing over them.

Marah felt herself hum with appreciation. Her man looked good and she was suddenly breathing heavy with wanting. Tight Levi's jeans fit the high shelf of his very round behind, the length of blue denim falling down over black cowboy boots. A bright white cotton shirt was buttoned midway up his broad chest, exposing just a hint of dark skin, and a classic black Stetson hat sat perched on top of his head. He was cowboy through and through as he offered Marah his arm and guided her into the paddock where Brutus waited in full saddle.

"What's going on?" Marah asked, curiosity getting the better of her. She brushed a flat palm against her horse's nose as he nuzzled her arm.

"We thought you deserved a treat," John said, guiding her to the side of the horse. "I talked to Marcus and it took some persuasion, but he gave his permission for you to take a ride."

Marah's eyes widened even more. "I can take the horse out?"

Edward chuckled behind them. "There's a catch, munchkin. You can't ride alone just yet. John here is going to ride behind you."

Marah reached up to wrap her arms around John's neck. She kissed his cheek, her lips gently brushing the side of his face as she lifted her gaze to stare into his eyes. Moisture puddled beneath her lids, joy shimmering in the look she gave him.

"Thank you," Marah whispered softly, her lips brushing against the line of his earlobe.

John nodded. "Let's do this, Ms. Briscoe," he said as he and her father maneuvered to get her into the saddle.

After Marah was settled atop the horse, Brutus braying his approval, John swung himself up and onto the back of the horse behind the saddle, the saddle blanket cushioning his seat. He reached his arms around Marah's waist as she took the reins and nudged her horse into a slow gait around the fenced field. At one point she swiped at the tears falling down her cheek with her fingers, tears blurring her vision ever so slightly.

When all were comfortable, John signaled for

Edward to open the gates and he and Marah rode toward the paths, Marah eager to reacquaint herself with the routine she loved so dearly.

Down by the large pond they came to a halt and John swung himself off of Brutus's back and then helped Marah down to the ground. Brutus moved to a patch of freshly bloomed grass and grazed comfortably as the couple took a seat against the ground. Marah settled herself down between John's legs as he wrapped himself around her, the woman leaning into his broad chest.

He hugged her tightly as Marah thanked him again for riding with her. "I didn't realize how much I missed this," she said as he leaned to kiss her forehead.

"I'm glad," John answered, his hands gently stroking the length of her arms. "I want you happy and I know how much riding your horse makes you happy."

Marah nodded. "I miss this, too," she said her voice dropping low.

"What's that?"

"Being alone with you. We haven't had a moment like this since my accident. I miss you holding me without folks poking their heads in to see if I'm okay."

John chuckled. "Everyone was worried about you. When you were in the hospital, Marah, we were scared to death. Me especially."

"Why?"

"Because I don't know what I would have done if I'd lost you. Don't you know how much I love you, woman?" He gave her a quick squeeze.

"Now you're stuck with me for a very long time."

"It won't be long enough."

"I know that's right," Marah said teasingly. "So, what kind of trouble do you think you and I can get into since we're all alone."

John laughed warmly. "No trouble at all. And we're not alone. There's a horse watching us."

"Brutus won't tell. Will you, boy," Marah said, her gaze shifting toward the horse then back out over the pond. "See? He won't say a word."

"And just what kind of trouble are you thinking about getting into, Ms. Briscoe?"

"The kind of trouble that has you and me making up for lost time. It's been a long time, John. I'm hungry for you."

John nodded as Marah grazed his taut thighs with her small palms. A quiver of energy pulsed through his groin. "Just how hungry are you?"

"I'm craving you, John Stallion. I'm craving you like I'm addicted and in need of a John Stallion fix. The way I feel you'd think I'd been starved all my life."

"That sounds serious," John said as he closed his eyes, enjoying the pressure of her hands against him.

"It's very serious. So serious that I might slip into another coma if you don't do something about it very soon."

"Well, we sure can't let that happen, can we," he said, easing his body to the side of hers. Holding her gently, John dropped his mouth against Marah's and kissed her, his own desire fervent against her lips. When he lifted his mouth from hers, Marah allowed the heat of the moment to flow from one end of her body to the other.

"Oh, yeah," she whispered huskily, the words falling

like saltwater taffy from her mouth. "Oh, sweet goodness, yeah."

John chuckled again as he suckled her bottom lip and then her top. His tongue darted back and forth across the line of her mouth and Marah felt herself growing anxious with wanting. When John pulled away, lifting his body from hers, it took everything she had not to strip out of her clothes and demand his attention.

"Why'd you stop?" she asked, her gaze meeting his.

"Because we are not doing this now. And definitely not here. The doctor didn't give us permission for that kind of extracurricular activity. So if I don't stop it now, we probably won't stop and then we'll both be in some deep mess. What if I hurt something?"

"But I feel fine."

"I'm not talking about your something. I'm talking about my something!"

Marah laughed as John gave her a teasing stare. "And what about my love Jones? You're actually going to leave me hanging like this?"

John nodded, moving to lift her from the ground onto her feet. "You and your Jones thing will be just fine. Trust me."

Marah pouted, moving back to Brutus as John helped her to get on top. "You owe me big time," she said, guiding the horse back in the direction they'd come from. "And I plan to collect very soon."

John squeezed his hands around her waist. "When you come to collect, I promise to pay you with interest and then some. Deal?"

Marah nodded, leaning comfortably back against him. "Deal."

* * *

Marah, meet me at the pond at 7:00 p.m. John

The note, scribbled on Stallion Enterprises letterhead, was resting on the glass tabletop in the family
kitchen when Marah made her way into the room for a
late breakfast. No one else was around, her father and
Marla having gone into downtown Dallas to run errands
and Eden was pulling double duty at the office to make
up for Marah's slack.

Marah read it curiously, wondering what John could
possibly have in mind to want her to meet him later on
that day. Their riding together had become a daily ritual,
John ending his business day at the ranch with Marah.
She was usually ready and waiting in the barn for him
when his car pulled into the drive, but clearly he had
something else on his mind for the evening. Marah
wondered at the possibility.

The doctors had finally given their approval for
Marah to ride alone and, despite the assurances that she
could, she'd not yet ventured the undertaking by her
lonesome. She'd grown comfortable with John's
presence. Him riding behind her, holding her tightly
around the waist, felt as natural to her as breathing. Her
rehabilitation was going nicely and Marah could almost
predict the time and date when she would be back to
her normal self. The walker had gone by the wayside
weeks earlier and even the carved wooden cane she'd
used for support rested in a corner no longer needed.

She had grown to like the routine they had with each
other and here John was wanting to shake things up by
doing something different. She took a glance down to

her watch, tossing back the last mouthful of orange juice that had been left for her. She had a midday appointment with the doctor before meeting her sisters and Juanita for lunch. Marah was anxious to have a conversation with the good doctor. Due to her pelvic injuries, the man had adamantly refused to let her resume certain activities that she'd been missing dearly and she was determined that today would be the day that he would give her and John the okay to rekindle their romantic flames. Marah had already decided as well that if the doctor told her no again she had no intention of listening to him. She missed being with John. She wanted to make love to him, to feel him connected to her. That part of their relationship had been better than good and Marah was intent on ensuring it stayed that way.

She could only imagine the conversation between John and Marcus during her last visit when she'd asked about sex, John cutting his eye at her as a wave of heat warmed his cheeks with embarrassment. Marcus had told her to be patient and John had been adamant about not going against the doctor's wishes. Every time she'd tried to get him into a compromising position the man had outmaneuvered her, slipping out of her clutches like a wet fish out of water. *Humph,* Marah grunted as she made her way out of the house and to her car. The doctor could say no all he wanted. She fully intended to pull a Stella and get her groove back on before the weekend ended.

Brutus was saddled and waiting for her when Marah made her way down to the barn. Papa Chico held the horse's reins, helping her to maneuver on top before sending her on her way. "Take it slow, Miss Marah," the man had exclaimed over and over again as she'd gotten comfortable with being alone on the massive animal again. As she and Brutus became adjusted one to the other, Marah took off across the fields, maneuvering the horse in a slow gallop.

With the wind blowing briskly, Marah felt her body finally relax, her and her horse doing what they did best together. She felt herself grinning, knowing that although she'd thoroughly enjoyed her rides with John, those rides didn't hold a candle to the experience of controlling the horse by her lonesome.

Brutus and Marah rode down to the southern pastures and across the back fields before shifting right toward the wooded acreage and the pond that had become her and John's private sanctuary. As she neared the water's edge, John was waiting for her, his hands pushed deep into the pockets of his denim jeans as he stood grinning in her direction.

Pulling the horse up to a halt, Marah allowed John to guide the animal to a tree, tethering him to a massive trunk as Marah eased herself down to the ground. When both were comfortable that Brutus was secure, Marah wrapped her thin arms around John's neck and pulled him to her. She hugged him tightly then pressed a damp kiss against his cheek.

"Hey you," she whispered huskily, her voice dropping low and seductive. "What are you up to?"

John nuzzled his face into her curls, allowing his hands to glide down the length of her back. "I made us a picnic," he said, gesturing to a red plaid blanket that covered the ground at the water's edge. A large picnic basket sat in the center, waiting for attention.

"Oooh!" Marah exclaimed. "What's the occasion?"

"Does there have to be an occasion? I just thought we'd do something special," John answered as he guided her to the blanket where they both took a seat.

Marah eased the lid of the basket up to peek inside. She smiled up at him as John took the top completely off and began to unpack its contents.

"We have garlic fried chicken, potato salad, fresh fruit and cheese, and strawberries for dessert."

Marah popped a green grape into her mouth, savoring the chill of it. "Mmm," she hummed, appreciation washing over her expression. "A girl could get used to this, Mr. Stallion."

"My girl should," John replied, leaning to give her a quick peck on her lips as they began to devour the food, chatting comfortably together.

Marah grinned. "So, how was your day."

"I had a good day. Closed a major deal and hammered out the negotiations for another. We're in a good place right now."

"I'm glad to hear it," she said softly. "I was worried with all the time you've missed these past few months."

The man shrugged. "You shouldn't worry. I have three capable partners who more than pull their weight. Mark and Matthew have done an excellent job and Luke is learning well from them both."

"Mark is leaving for his trip soon, isn't he?" Marah asked.

John nodded. "This weekend as a matter of fact. The

boy can't wait. He does this every year. Riding that bike across country is one of his biggest thrills."

"When you see him, tell him I said to have a good time and to stay safe."

"I will." John sighed as Marah fed him a strawberry, the sugar and sweet of it melting like butter against his tongue.

When the last piece of fruit had been consumed and everything was packed back into the wicker container, Marah leaned back against John's chest, his arms cradling her torso. She brushed both her palms against his thighs, the duo trading easy caresses between them.

"I saw Marcus today," Marah said, shifting slightly against him.

John nodded. "Is everything okay?"

"Better than okay. The good doctor gave me a clean bill of health."

"Did he now?"

"Yes, he did. But I still have one more thing that needs to be fixed and he gave me a prescription for it."

"And what's that?"

"He didn't tell you? I know you two are good friends. I would have thought he'd have called you."

John smiled, his mouth pulling up into a wide grin. "You know he's not allowed to discuss your case with me without your permission."

"I know…but under the circumstances…" Her voice trailed off teasingly.

John chuckled. "And what circumstances might those be?"

"You being my prescription and all."

"Me?"

"That's right. You're the cure for what's ailing me."

John laughed as Marah turned to straddle his legs, pressing her pelvis against his. "I should call Marcus and check on that myself. You might have misunderstood him."

"I didn't misunderstand a thing. I know the exact dose and how many times I'm supposed to take my medicine tonight."

"Just tonight?"

"No. I'm going to be on this prescription indefinitely."

The man waved his head up and down, savoring the sensation of Marah's hands gently caressing his broad chest. "I'm sure I can handle that."

Marah kissed his mouth, allowing her lips to glide easily across his.

"What time's your first dose?" John asked playfully, breaking the connection between them.

Marah checked a nonexistent watch. "Soon. I'm thinking we should probably go home to your house just in case I have a reaction to the medicine."

The two laughed warmly together before John responded. "Well, before we do that, there's another reason I wanted you to meet me here tonight."

Marah eyed him curiously.

John motioned for Marah to let him up. As she came to her feet, standing above him, he reached into the pocket of his pants and pulled out the black box that he'd been keeping since forever. Easing up onto one knee, he opened the top and pulled out the diamond engagement ring.

Marah's eyes widened with joy as she pulled a palm to her face, pressing her fingers against her lips. Tears misted her eyes.

"Don't get teary on me, Marah Jean Briscoe," John said, the warmth of his expression seeping straight through her. He pulled her left hand into his.

"I was thinking," John said as he eased the ring onto her ring finger. "I was thinking that you and I make quite a team. Don't you agree?"

Marah's head bobbed up and down slowly. "We do."

"And when two people make as magnificent a team as we do, then they should make their merger a permanent arrangement. What do you think?"

Marah shrugged. "That depends."

"On what?"

"Negotiations like this usually take some maneuvering, Mr. Stallion. You should know that."

"I do."

"The parties involved can't just jump into something without thinking it through first. Did you think this through?"

"I certainly did."

"And?"

"And I love you. You have my heart and my soul. I want to give you the world. If I can make every one of your dreams come true then I'll do it. You complete me. Without you I wouldn't be half the man that I am," John said, his expression serious.

Marah smiled down at him, pressing her palm to the side of his face. "I love you, too, John Stallion. Will you marry me?" she asked, kneeling down to the ground beside him.

John laughed. "I thought I was the one controlling this negotiation?"

Marah tossed him a coy wink. "John Stallion

Business 101. Always let the other guy think he's in control, but never let him get the upper hand. So what do you say?" Marah said, laughing with him. "Because I love you just as much. You're my rock, John. You're everything I could ever want and with you I am a better woman."

"Yes," John said, sliding the ring onto her hand. "Yes, I will," he repeated.

Marah looped her arms around his neck and kissed him deeply. "I really like how this merger is going to go," she said softly.

John nodded his agreement. "So do I. Now why don't we go see what we can do about getting you that medicine you needed."

The couple arrived at the door of John's home out of breath with anticipation. As John pushed the key into the lock, Marah hugged him around the waist, her touch sending shivers up and down his spine. Inside, both moved about as if they'd been living side by side forever, Marah as comfortable in the surroundings as John was having her there with him.

Expecting a chilly evening, John lit a fire in the main room where the rock chimney reached up toward the ceiling. Although it wasn't quite dark out, the first flickers of light from the embers seemed to fill the space with a warm glow. Marah curled up on the chenille love seat, pulling her legs up beneath her body as John moved into the kitchen to retrieve a bottle of wine and two glasses. At one point, John paused, turning to stare in her direction, his gaze meeting hers, and Marah's heart skipped a beat.

Neither said anything, there being no need for words between them.

As John passed her a glass of chardonnay, his fingers brushing lightly against hers, Marah felt her body warm nicely, his heat mixing with her own. The man dropped down onto the seat beside her and as they sipped their nightcap, they chatted easily, the conversation revolving around their wedding wishes. Time passed easily, evening slipping quietly into night as they laughed and joked together. Marah eased her body against his, dropping her head to rest against John's shoulder. Side by side they enjoyed each other's company, the moment feeling right and good between them.

As John stroked the length of her arm, heat burning in his fingertips, Marah could feel herself getting aroused. Looking up at John she smiled and the man responded with a warm and knowing smile of his own. Marah turned her body against the sofa, dropping her head into John's lap as he stroked her hair and shoulders. Her breathing suddenly became static as she remembered the last time the two of them had been alone there together, savoring time with each other. She turned her face up to his and as if she'd asked, John leaned down to press his lips against hers.

His mouth was full and soft and when the tip of his tongue slipped between her lips, Marah opened her mouth to let him in. She suckled him slowly, teasing his tongue with her own as he teased back. Marah was lost in the moment when she felt his lips leave hers and his kisses trail gently across her cheek and down her neck. John stopped to linger at the lobe of her ear, his mouth brushing against the line of it. When he slid his tongue into her ear, Marah felt as if a jolt of electricity had shot straight through her.

John took Marah's face into his hands and kissed her deeply. Marah couldn't remember when she'd ever been kissed so completely, the man's mouth dancing like silk atop hers. She was completely lost in the beauty of his touch when John slid his hands around to cup her breasts, caressing them gently as they pressed against her cotton blouse. Marah could feel her nipples harden beneath his touch, each one swelling full and firm. Marah was breathing heavily with excitement.

Without warning, John suddenly swept Marah up into his arms, lying her against the carpeted floor in front of the fireplace. The flames were raging now in vibrant shades of red and orange. John moved down to her feet, pulling her shoes off as he gently massaged one foot and then the other. His fingers tickled the bottoms of her perfectly manicured toes and Marah giggled. When the man began to kiss and lick her foot, Marah was overcome by the adoration. He sucked each toe into his mouth, one by one and she shuddered from the pleasure. His kisses slowly moved up the length of her bare legs and beneath the linen skirt that fell against her knees.

Marah leaned up on her elbows as John moved above her, rising to his feet. He slowly stripped his clothes off, stepping out of his jeans and trunks and pulling his T-shirt up and over his head. Marah grinned. "I really want my medicine now," she breathed heavily, her voice a deep whisper.

John laughed as he dropped back to the floor beside her, pulling at her clothes until she was lying naked, her skirt and blouse tossed into a corner of the room. John laid himself over her, covering her body with his own. He caressed her, his hands reacquainting themselves with every curve and crevice. The two breathed in sync and every so often a groan or a whimper would escape from one of them. He leaned and kissed her neck, whispering into her ear. "You are so beautiful," he said, moving his mouth back to her mouth as he kissed her hungrily.

A firm hand ventured into Marah's nether regions, slick moisture dampening his fingers. He continued to kiss her, his hands teasing and taunting her femininity with exact precision. An orgasm suddenly shook Marah to her core, the sensation jolting her out of her erotic reverie. Before she realized it John had sheathed himself with a condom and had eased his body into hers. His strokes were slow and controlled, gaining in momentum as Marah moaned and whined with each thrust. John found himself lost in her, completely abandoned in everything he loved about Marah.

She pushed against him, meeting him stroke for stroke, harder and harder. Marah had missed his touch and he hers and they loved each other as if they might not ever be able to love each other again. John savored the sensation of hot, wet velvet wrapped tightly around him and when his orgasm erupted it was powerful and loud as he screamed with pleasure, Marah unrelenting in her ministrations. As his body erupted in pleasure Marah shrieked his name over and over, her nails digging into the flesh along his back. Between them the air was thick and heavy and both felt as though they might never catch their breath.

Marah gasped as she pressed herself beneath him, holding on tightly. She nuzzled her face into his neck, lightly lapping at the salty perspiration that moistened his flesh.

"Are you okay?" John asked, hugging her tightly.

Marah nodded her face against his chest. "Better than okay," she answered. "I think I just got the best medicine a girl could ever get."

Chapter 22

The two brothers stood side by side. John ran his hand across the handlebars of Mark's Gold Wing, the touring motorcycle a combination of power, luxury and extreme sporting capability. John had to admit that the dark blue metallic vehicle with its gleaming chrome accessories was truly a specimen of perfection if you liked that sort of thing. Mark called it his private jet on two wheels, one of the many expensive big-boy toys he'd acquired over the past few years.

John admired his brother's fortitude and free spirit, Mark rarely succumbing to tradition or directives. Of his siblings, Mark was the brother with a penchant for fast cars and even faster women, rarely slowing down as if he were afraid he might miss something in his young life. With more than four million miles of paved road across the United States, Mark was intent on satisfying his wanderlust every which way he could and his annual jaunt to the South Carolina coast for the Black Bike week was only one of those ways.

"You're looking good, boy!" John exclaimed, admiring Mark's black leather jacket and pants.

The other man nodded, his head bobbing up and down against his thick neck. "You're not looking so bad yourself, big brother. Congratulations! I'm really happy for you," Mark said extending his hand to shake John's.

John grinned. "Thanks. Marah and I are really excited."

"Have you two set a date yet?"

"Not officially, but I'm thinking it would be a good idea to do it during the rodeo. I think a down-home Southern celebration would be just the place for me to let everyone know how much I love that woman."

Mark shook his head, a wide grin filling his face. "Look at you! You're gushing!" The man shuddered, pretending to shake his body vehemently. "There's something not right about that, John. Don't get too close to me with that mess. It might be catching."

"You could stand to catch some of this. This is good for the soul."

Mark rolled his eyes, swinging his leg over to straddle his bike. "I don't want any part of that mess. Too many beautiful women out here in need of attention. I've still got my work cut out for me."

John chuckled. "I'm sure some woman will slow you down soon enough, my friend. I use to say the same thing, remember? Then I met Marah. When that bug bites, it bites hard."

"Sounds like something I need to get an inoculation

for," Mark said, laughing. He checked his equipment one last time, then started the engine.

John took a step back out of his way. "Stay in touch. Let us know where we can find you," he said, brotherly concern wafting into his tone. "And keep yourself safe. I need me a best man when you get back."

"You've already got two of them," Mark said.

John smiled. "It wouldn't be the same without you. Don't you know three's a charm?"

Mark smiled back. "Always has been in my book, as well." He gave his brother a wink as he adjusted his helmet. "I love you, bro!"

"I love you, too. Have some fun!" John chimed.

As Mark gunned the bike's engine and headed out the driveway of the family estate, John waved his hand after him. He knew all would be well and Mark would soon be back home to help him celebrate his love for Marah. He was meeting her for dinner later and he put it in the back of his mind to ask her if she might have a friend or two that might be interested in his brothers. He just had to ask because what he was feeling was too good not to share it and pass it around.

Edward and his grandson sat together in front of the television set, a rerun of Sesame Street playing on the big screen. The baby's eyes were wide with enthusiasm, racing back and forth as he tried to take in the flash of color and noise. Every so often he would coo happily as he sucked on his toes, a small foot pulled cheek high. Edward marveled at the youthful flexibility.

Juanita stepped in beside them, reaching to wipe a

line of baby drool from the infant's face with a cotton bib. She paused, a palm resting on Edward's shoulder as she leaned to press a light kiss against the spreading bald spot on top of his head.

"What are you two scamps up to?" she asked cheerfully.

The man beamed as he passed the kiss down to the baby boy. "Little Mike and I were just plotting our day. He and Grandpa are hanging out all day together. Aren't we, big boy?" the man said as if the child might actually answer.

Little Mike gurgled contentedly.

"Well," Juanita said, dropping down to the seat beside the man, "Mark and Matthew would like to talk with you later today if you have some time. Something about the paperwork for the ranch."

Edward grinned. "I can't wait until we tell Marah and John. Do you think he suspects anything?"

The woman shook her head from side to side. "Not a thing. He stopped asking about the sale weeks ago. I think he thinks we all forgot about it."

Edward chuckled. "That boy's slipping. He's not been on top of his game."

"A good woman will do that to you. You should know," Juanita said teasingly.

He laughed, shifting the baby up and onto his shoulder. "That I should, Miss Juanita. That I should."

Juanita smiled. "Don't worry, though. Marah will get him back on track soon enough. That's what a good woman will do for you as well."

Edward moved to kiss her mouth, allowing his lips to linger in the beauty of the touch.

"I think we should have two weddings around here. What do you think?" he asked.

"I think you and I should just elope. We could sneak off to the justice of the peace and just do it. This is Marah's time. I want her to enjoy every moment of it."

"What about you? You deserve your time, too!"

Juanita's smile brightened. "I'll enjoy it every day for the rest of my life as long as I'm with you."

Edward grinned. "I'm not doing anything tomorrow morning. How about you?"

"Tomorrow morning sounds perfect," the woman answered, snuggling down against him, a palm stroking the baby's back as he drifted off to sleep. "Just perfect."

Eden and Marla were both humming the wedding march as they waited for Marah to come of the bridal shop's fitting room. They'd been trying on dresses for well over two hours and Marah still hadn't found one that moved her or them to a state of happiness.

"What's taking you so long?" Marla chimed, peeking behind the curtain where her twin sister stood.

Marah stood staring into a full-length mirror, an ivory sheath-style dress flattering her petite figure. She scowled, a deep frown pulling at her facial muscles.

"What's the matter with that one?" Marla asked, moving to stand behind her sister. "It's beautiful on you, Marah."

Marah heaved a deep sigh. "It just doesn't feel right. It's so…so…girlie!"

Eden chuckled from the entranceway. "Bridal gowns are supposed to be girlie, Marah. They're bridal gowns, for Pete's sake!"

"This isn't working for me. I don't know that I want a traditional gown. It's not like we're having so traditional a wedding ceremony."

"You got that right," Eden exclaimed, rolling her eyes. "I mean really, Marah. Did the invitations have to look like wanted posters?"

Marah grinned. "Nice touch, huh?"

Marla beamed back. "They really were cute," she said, quoting the text from the invites. "*Wanted. A posse alive and willing to witness the marryin' of John Stallion and Marah Briscoe!* Very creative, sister dear."

Marah chuckled. "Burning the edges of the paper gave it that final touch. They were very authentic. But this dress isn't. It's very pretty but it's not working for me at all."

Eden's head waved from side to side as Marah moved to step out of the dress she was trying on. She suddenly jumped with enthusiasm. "I know, I know!" she chimed excitedly. "I know exactly where to go for your dress. Put your clothes back on and hurry up."

Some thirty-odd minutes later the three women were laughing hysterically as they entered Miss Hazel's Tack and Supply Shop. Marah was shaking her head from side to side as Eden explained to the sales clerk what they hoped to find.

The young woman smiled, nodding confidently. "I actually think we can help you out," she said, her blond head bobbing against her thin neck. "We outfit bridal parties all the time," she finished as she guided them to the back of the overstocked store.

In a rear corner a line of dresses blanketed the wall. Leslie, the young woman who'd introduced herself as

Miss Hazel's granddaughter, appraised Marah's size then pulled three selections from the rack. Marah's eyes widened with excitement as she reached to take one from the woman.

"I have to try this one!" Marah exclaimed excitedly. Her sisters laughed, both knowing that Marah had finally found a dress that had her name written all over it.

In no time at all Marah stepped out of the dressing room, the lace and denim dress fitting her to a tee. The top was a boned, corset-style bodice that laced up the back. Constructed of re-embroidered lace it was generously embellished with sequins and host of pearl beading. The bottom skirt was stonewashed denim, the trumpet flare flattering Marah's petite frame. Leslie completed Marah's ensemble with a straw cowboy hat the color of buttermilk, a lace bow and veil cascading down the back and classic ivory sahara boots. Marah was grinning from ear to ear.

"You look beautiful," Marla gushed, clasping her hands together, tears misting her eyes. "Absolutely beautiful, Marah. It's perfect."

Eden nodded her agreement. "I think flared denim skirts and denim blouses with white cowboy boots would make great bridesmaid outfits. What do you think, Marla?" she asked.

Marla looked from one sister to the other. "I think Marah's going to have her dream wedding."

Marah reached out to hug both women. "I think so, too!"

Chapter 23

John held Marah's hand tightly as they made their way off the center stage positioned at the far end of the north field. The annual invitational rodeo had started off with a big bang and Edward welcomed a large crowd of western enthusiasts to the homestead. Marah's father had joked once again that putting together such an extravaganza had been much like bull riding. Everyone's insides had gotten tossed around and jostled but they were all still on top, enjoying every minute of a ride that had been more than worth it. His greeting had been followed by the announcement that Stallion Enterprises had assumed full corporate sponsorship of the event and included all of the Stallion brothers passing the Briscoe family an oversized cardboard check. Edward had ended by thanking the men and women who participated and all the fans who came year after year to see some of the greatest horsemanship in the world.

The welcome had been followed by a reading of black cowboy history, the performance acted out by one of the founding fathers of the Federation of Black Cowboys, an elderly gray-haired man who came every year without fail. John had wrapped his arms around Marah's torso, bearing her weight against his broad chest as they listened intently, the old storyteller regaling them with the legend of Bill Pickett, the black cowboy born in 1870 who invented the rodeo sport of bulldogging wrestling. The children in the audience were enthralled by the tales being told, their excitement shimmering in their eyes as they heard the true sagas of America's black cowboys. The stories that segregation and discrimination had wiped from the history books.

The official rodeo events would follow, everyone entertained by an impressive cast of top-notch cowboys, some wearing trademark angora chaps and tall Stetsons, followed by a tried and true Wild West show. It was tradition at its finest with some three hundred plus cowboys and cowgirls having come to compete.

"I can't believe this is your first time at one of these," Marah said as she and John made their way back to the main house.

"It is," John responded, squeezing her fingers lightly. "Mark and Matthew have come a few years in a row, apparently. Luke, too. It seems like I was always working or away on business."

Marah shook her head. "Well, the first time is always the best." She pointed to group of little boys who stood peering through the fence at a gathering of older riders prepping their horses for one of the events. "I never get tired of seeing smiles like that," she said, a big grin filling her face.

John nodded. "It's definitely a sight to behold," he responded, moving to wrap his arm around her shoulder. "So, what's on your agenda today?" he asked playfully.

Marah pretended to be in deep thought as she gave his questions some consideration. "I have a very busy schedule," she finally answered. "I'm competing in two events, judging the little Miss Briscoe Ranch competition and then there's something else I'm doing…" Marah said with a long pause. "Oh, that's right. I'm getting married to that Stallion guy today."

John chuckled. "Thanks! I'm glad you remembered."

The two giggled together, moving up the expanse of stairwell to the front porch and into the home. Everyone else was gathered in the family room waiting for them.

"Took you two long enough," Edward muttered, glancing quickly to his watch. "Don't you know we have an event to run?"

"It was her fault! It was his fault!" both chimed simultaneously, Marah pointing to John and he to her.

The family laughed with them as they broke out into guffaws. Edward only shook his head, rolling his eyes skyward.

"Marah Jean, you play too much and John, son, I expected so much more from you."

John stifled a laugh. "Sorry about that, sir."

Edward grinned. "Well, let's make this brief. First,

Juanita and I have a quick announcement to make. Now I know this may come as a shock to you, but…"

Marah and her sisters all cut an eye toward each other, the trio breaking out into laughter for the umpteenth time.

"What's so funny?" Edward asked, his gaze sweeping from one to the other.

Marah waved her head from side to side. "You are. We all know you two got married."

"We do, Daddy," Eden and Marla echoed.

"And we're very happy for you both," John and his brothers chimed in as they all reached out to give the older couple warm hugs.

"Well, how in the world…" Juanita started.

John smiled. "Judge Barrows. You really shouldn't call my friend to marry you if you don't want me to find out about it."

"And he just had to tell me because I would have killed him if he didn't," Marah added.

"And Marah couldn't keep it a secret from me or Eden," Marla said.

The duo both nodded. "Well, thank you all," Juanita said, looping her arm through Edward's. "I so happy that you all are accepting of me and Edward being together."

Marah moved to the woman's side, wrapping her arms around Juanita's shoulders. "Welcome to the family, Juanita. I know you'll continue to make our father a very happy man."

"I will," Juanita answered, hugging Marah back. "I promise.

Marah wiped a tear from her eye as she moved back to John, who hugged her again tightly.

Edward looked from one face to the other and beamed at how nicely his family had grown. He moved to the countertop, lifting a large manila envelope off the granite counter. Mark and Matthew moved to stand at the patriarch's side.

"Marah, John," Edward started clearing his voice before continuing. "We all wanted you two to have the best possible beginning for your marriage that we could imagine and so your brothers and I got together and did some serious negotiating to figure out what we could do for you two."

Edward passed John the envelope and paused as the man opened it. Marah peeked excitedly over his shoulder. Both came to a complete halt, mouths falling wide open as they studied the document that had been hidden inside.

The deed to Briscoe Ranch, signed and sealed, stared up from John's hand, the envelope falling to the floor below. John and Marah both were listed as the property owners.

"We decided that the best merger between our two organizations started with you two," Mark said softly. "We knew that when this day came and Marah officially became a Stallion that our two families could come to a mutually beneficial agreement about the ranch."

"And so we decided that you two would have joint ownership of the ranch. The property will fall under Stallion Enterprises legal umbrella, but the Briscoe sisters would still retain the right to vote on any decisions we make regarding its operation."

Luke nodded. "Our executive board now has three new members and once you officially say 'I do,' you two got one heck of a wedding gift."

"And, ultimately, whatever happens, this ranch stays in the family for you and Marah to pass down to your own children some day," Edward concluded.

Marah didn't think she would ever stop crying, the tears streaming down her cheeks as she wrapped her arms around her father's neck and hugged him tightly. When she finally let go, his red plaid shirt damp from her tears, everyone in the room was misty with emotion. Spinning around, Marah moved back into John's arms to be held, waves of emotion washing over them both.

"Thank you," John said, Marah pressed against him. "This means the world to Marah and to me. We love you all so much," he finished, his own tears pressing hot against the back of his eyelids.

Edward waved a dismissive hand toward both of them. "Y'all leave that blubbering for the wedding. We're having a rodeo and I need to get back to our guests. Marah, don't you and your sisters have a competition to judge?"

Marah nodded, swiping at her eyes with the back of her hand. "Yes, sir."

"Then get to it."

"John, you and the boys follow me. Let me go show you what real rodeo riding is all about."

John smiled. "We're right behind you, sir." He tossed a wink to his brothers as they all moved to follow the man.

As her old family and her new family all made their way out in different directions, Juanita moved to the door, stopping on the front porch to stare after them. The sun was beaming overhead, warmth radiating energy in every direction. Noise and laughter rang from every conceivable direction, hoops and hollers denoting the good time being had by all. Juanita reveled in the sheer beauty of the moment, her own laugher shaking her body with glee.

Marah was preparing for her turn in the ladies barrel racing competition, an event she'd won some three times in the past five years. John sat waiting for her to go, mulling over everything she'd explained to him about the ride. The importance of the rider and the horse working together as a team was never more evident than when she and Brutus had first started practicing weeks ago, Marah putting the horse through his paces to get them both ready. The two had moved as one and John was never more confident that Marah was truly back on point than he was that first time he'd come to watch. Marah had almost fallen off the horse but recovered like it was something she did every day of her life.

The moment had scared the life out of him as he'd fathomed Marah ever being hurt again. And when he'd caught his breath and his heartbeat had dropped back to normal, it had taken everything in him not to smother her with overprotective concern. Recalling the moment sent a wave of anxiety through him and John shook the emotion away as quickly as it had risen. The thought of how close he had almost come to losing Marah was never far from John's mind and so he was diligent to ensure that whatever time they shared was quality time, Marah never having to doubt his love.

At the sound of the horn, John sat on the edge of his seat watching as Marah and Brutus raced around three barrels set up in a cloverleaf pattern. Brutus moved easily, seeming to possess the spirit and speed of a

quarter horse and the agility of a polo pony. The rider
and horse required excellent coordination to turn tightly
around the barrels and sprint back home, and when all
was said and done, with no penalties against them, the
family was certain Marah had run an impressive time.
Minutes later, they celebrated her first-place victory
and John clapped loudly as the crowd cheered their
approval.

Marah's face beamed with joy as he made his way
to her side, sweeping her up into his arms.

"That's my girl!" he exclaimed excitedly, his enthusiasm as intense as hers.

"That felt so good," Marah said, laughing and talking
at the same time. "I can't believe how good that felt."

"You did your thing, honey. I'm so proud of you."

Marah hugged his neck and kissed his cheek. "I need
to go get ready. I'm getting married in two hours."

John grinned. "You're sure about this now?"

Marah's wide smile greeted his. "I've never been so
sure about anything in my entire life as I am about
marrying you, John Stallion."

Leaning up to kiss his mouth, Marah allowed her
lips to lightly caress his before she pulled away,
waving goodbye as she moved away from him. "See
you at the altar!"

"I'll be waiting," John answered, his eyes wide with
anticipation. "Nothing could keep me from you."

A tent had been erected on the grounds of the homestead. Yards of sheer fabric cascaded from the arched top,
transforming the interior space into something out of
wonderland. Ceremony seating occupied one end with

a makeshift altar at the front. The room was filled to capacity, friends and family anxious to be a part of the joyous occasion. The back wall was open to the exterior and outside. Twelve black stallions were tied to a center post, six horses flanking Brutus on the left and six on the right. Four horsemen stood at attention, their hands clasped behind their backs. The other end of the large space was adorned for the reception that would immediately follow the ceremony, an arched partition dividing the two areas one from the other. Marah and John had arranged that when the ceremony was over and everyone was seated for dinner, the seating would be arranged to accommodate the dance floor beneath their feet.

The family's pastor stood in wait as John and his brothers made their way into the space, John twisting his hands nervously in front of him. They greeted the man warmly, the elderly minister offering him a few welcome words of advice. Taking their positions, John grinned widely, his brothers grinning back.

Mark was the first to chuckle, his laughter drawing the same from Matthew and Luke. "Look at you," the man exclaimed, shaking his head in John's direction. "You look like you're scared to death," he said, his voice dropping low so as not to be heard.

John laughed with them. "Is it that obvious?"

The three other men nodded.

"You can always change your mind," Luke said jokingly. "We'll sneak you out if you want."

Matthew fanned a hand in the younger sibling's direction. "Oh, no we won't. Big brother is getting this over with. We won't be able to live with him if he doesn't marry that woman today."

John shook his head at the three. "You all need to stop. I'm doing this. I have no intentions of letting Marah get away from me."

John took a quick glance down to his watch when Juanita came into the room, making her way to her seat in the front row after whispering to them that Marah would only be a few minutes more then they could begin. She reached up to kiss his cheek, pressing her warm palm to his face as she told him how much she loved him. The man took an inhale of air, holding it deep in his lungs before blowing it slowly past his full lips. Time seemed to be ticking by too slowly and he wished for the moment when Marah would officially be his wife.

Mark patted him on the shoulder, hoping to alleviate just a touch of his anxiety. "I can't wait to tell you about my trip," he said, trying to divert his brother's attention for a moment.

"So you had a good time?" John asked.

Mark grinned. "It was better than good. In fact, I think I'm going to take some time off after you and Marah get back from your honeymoon to head back in that direction for a few days."

John eyed the man curiously as Matthew leaned in toward them. "You know there has to be a woman involved," Matthew said teasingly.

Mark's wide smiled filled his dark face. "You don't know what you're talking about."

John and Luke chuckled. "It's a woman," they both chimed in unison.

Mark shook his head. "I think we're ready to start," he said, grateful to change the subject as he gestured to the other end where Eden and Marla had appeared in the entranceway.

John glanced up excitedly, everything suddenly moving in slow motion. A trio of electric guitars began to play as the two women slowly made their way down the aisle. As both stepped into place, the musicians transitioned to the wedding march and Marah stepped into sight, clasping her father's arms as Edward guided her in John's direction. Tears swelled, dripping from the corners of John's eyes as his gaze met hers. Marah was a beautiful bride.

Chapter 24

The reception had gone on well past midnight, guests shimmying and shaking across the dance floor. With every passing hour, Marah and John felt reenergized, both enjoying every new minute as husband and wife. The clock struck one in the morning when both finally decided to retire for the night, the party still going on strong around them.

Summoning the driver, the couple settled down in the back of the limousine, delighted to finally be alone and headed back to their home. As the car pulled off, leaving them at the front door, Marah could only imagine what surprises her sister had in store for them, memories of their brief capture etched deeply in their minds.

Just as she expected, candles burned softly from one

end of the house to the other. John nodded his head, taking in the brilliance of the view. "It's a wonder they didn't burn my house down!" he exclaimed.

Marah laughed. "These have just been lit. Someone knew we were coming. I don't doubt they were pulling out as we pulled in." She moved slowly through the living room toward the bedroom. White pillars burned softly, the room glowing from the illumination. "It's absolutely stunning, though," she said, her eyes sweeping from one end of the space to the other.

The man sighed. "Not nearly as stunning as you are," he said, his gaze locked on her as he moved into the room on her heels.

Marah smiled, turning back to face him. All of her attention was on his eyes, his stare drawing her in like a cobra entranced by the melody of the flute. John was playing a seductive song with his dark gaze and Marah could feel herself falling headfirst into a trance.

When he leaned to kiss her lips, his hands resting against her upper arms, she closed her eyes, tilting her head back to savor the moment, a flood of heat washing over her body. She suddenly felt empty when he broke the connection.

"Don't stop, Mr. Stallion," Marah whispered. "I love it when you kiss me like that."

John smiled. "I love kissing you, Mrs. Stallion. And I don't ever plan to stop," he said as he drew her closer until their lips met for the second time.

Passion took over as her mouth opened, their tongues mingling and dancing an erotic dance of ecstasy. Marah loved being that close to him, feeling as if she were being transported to some heavenly space where only the two of them existed. It was a glorious feeling like nothing she'd ever experienced before. They stood there motionless for a minute or two, his mouth dancing a slow drag across her lips. When he released her, both were breathing heavily with wanting.

"Why don't we get a warm bath together," John suggested, moving in the direction of the bathroom.

Marah nodded her head, following behind him. She watched as he reached for the bottle of ocean-scented body and bath oil that she favored from Carol's Daughters beauty line.

John turned on the hot water pipe, pausing as a stream of lukewarm water became hot before he opened the bottle and allowed the bath oil to drizzle into the warming stream. As the water and oil mixed, then formed light bubbles. Marah took a deep inhale, the bathroom filling with the scent of wildflowers and fruit. Shutting off the hot water, John added just a hint of cold to balance out the warmth and when he was satisfied with the temperature he turned his attention back to Marah.

Marah reached to unbutton her dress and John stalled her efforts, his hands grasping hers and drawing them back down to her sides. "Let me undress you," he said, his gaze compelling her to comply. She watched as he slowly unbuttoned her dress, easing the straps off one shoulder and then the other before allowing it to slide to the floor at her feet. Underneath she wore white lace, the bra and G-string causing him to harden with desire at the sight. Marah was beautiful, her caramel complexion complementing the garment nicely. He stopped to admire her, his fingers slowly brushing a heated path along her torso. Marah thought her knees might buckle from the attention, his touch inciting heat through every blood vessel in her body. When she was naked, John having slid her undergarments slowly away, Marah climbed into the tub, the lower half of her body disappearing in the cloud of scented bubbles. She settled down comfortably and watched as John began to undress himself.

Teasing her, he removed his clothes slowly, his white dress shirt first, each button taking longer than necessary to undo, then his denim jeans and his briefs. Marah could feel herself salivating, every inch of his Olympian physique stunning. He was glorious from the top of his head down to his pectorals, his bulging biceps, his chiseled abdomen, taut calves and the impressive display of maleness that swayed between his parted, tree-trunk thighs. Marah imagined that every square inch of him was beckoning for her attention.

Stepping into the large tub with her, John eased his body behind hers, Marah settling between his legs, her back pressed against his chest. He took a sponge from the side of the tub and began to run it over her body, gently stroking Marah's tight flesh. He dipped it into the warm water, soaking it, then brought it back out and resumed his ministrations, gently rubbing every inch of her body.

He glided the sponge over her breasts, leaving a trail of wetness that faded into drips that ran down her midriff and back into the water. He brushed along her neckline, over her collarbone, down across her back and shoulders. Marah allowed her eyes to close, enjoying the sensation.

John bathed her slowly, gently massaging away

every ounce of tension for the better part of an hour before allowing Marah to reciprocate. As the water grew cold, John stood, pulling Marah up with him as he turned on the shower, allowing a spray of hot water to warm them.

Stepping out of the tub Marah drew a plush towel over his body, his muscles sparkling from the water. As he flexed, the wet and smooth feel of his tight muscles flooded Marah with erotic fantasies that shimmered a current of electricity over her nerves. John's eyes closed in anticipation as Marah glided her body against his, bare skin embracing bare skin.

As he held her, Marah felt as if their love was an eternal, ethereal thing, a blessing so magnanimous that there were no words that could do it justice. As if reading her mind, the man lifted her chin into the palm of his hand, tilting her gaze up to meet his. He stared into her eyes, joy shimmering in the dark orbs, then he kissed her, sweetly molding his mouth to hers. As Marah fell into the beauty of it, her senses magnified by every touch and caress, she felt her body quiver with excitement.

John suddenly swept Marah up into his arms and carried her into the bedroom, laying her across the bed. He continued to tease her with his kisses, taunting her with his touch until he made her moan loudly. Caressing her from head to toe, he finally eased his body against her, his fingers pulling through her hair gently as he twisted the curls down about her shoulders.

Marah allowed herself to savor the sensations, enjoying the attention John was giving her. She pressed her hands to his chest, her palms sliding across the taut muscle as she leaned to nibble on his neck until he was humming her name as if he were in prayer.

"Thank you," Marah whispered, her mouth pressed against his cheek. "Thank you very much."

John stared down at her, confused. "What did I do?"

"You've given me a bright future," Marah whispered, snuggling close against him. "I have so much to look forward to, I don't know where to even start."

John smiled broadly, wrapping her in a tight embrace. "I'm the one who should be thanking you," he responded as he hugged her tightly.

Marah smiled. "I love you, John. I love you very much."

John acknowledged the sentiment with a kiss as he pressed his mouth to hers. "I love you, too," he finally answered, pulling away. "More than you can even begin to imagine."

Nodding her head, Marah suddenly pushed against him, rolling him onto his back against the mattress as she lifted her body up and over his.

"Whoa!" John hummed, chuckling deeply as Marah dropped her body against his, drawing him deep into her secret chamber. "Easy on my stallion, girl!"

"Whoa, nothing," Marah answered, her own giggles rippling through them as she pulled and pressed her body against his. "This stallion is all mine."

Marah didn't think they'd gotten any rest at all when John roused her from her sleep, his lips dancing against the side of her face. "What's wrong?" she asked, rubbing at the sleep that held her eyes closed. "Has something happened?"

"Nothing's wrong," he answered, pulling her to her feet. "I have something I want to show you," he said, handing her a pair of sweat pants.

Marah shook her head, curiosity pulling at her attention. She reached for the T-shirt that John handed to her and then slipped her feet into a pair of well-worn sneakers. "This better be good, John Stallion," she said, following behind him. "You've kept me up all night making love to me and now you've got me up and it's not even light out yet."

"Stop whining," John said as he maneuvered them out the house and into his car and started the engine. "You're going to love this."

Marah only shook her head as she settled into the passenger seat, her arms crossed over her chest. Minutes later they pulled into the family's ranch, John guiding the car straight to the barn. Marah eyed him with some reservation as he gestured for her to get out and follow him.

"What are we doing here?" Marah asked, her voice a hushed whisper as if she were afraid someone might hear them.

John only laughed as he pulled the barn door open and stepped inside. On the other side of the door, Papa Chico stood prepping John's new horse for the ride. Marah looked from one to the other, a wide grin filling her face.

"What are you up to?" she asked again.

The two men exchanged a look, both breaking out into laughter though neither answered her.

John extended his hand to the elderly man. "Thank you, sir," he said as Papa Chico nodded his own gray head.

"You two be careful," Papa Chico said, moving out of the way as John mounted the horse and gestured for Marah to take the seat in front of him.

Once she was seated atop the animal, John's arms wrapped around her waist, Papa Chico opened the barn door, leading the horse outside. When they were clear, John tapped the horse with the heel of his boot and the animal set off on an easy gait across the expanse of open fields.

Marah took a deep breath, filling her lungs with fresh air as she took in the view around them. The tent now stood empty, only memories left of the wedding that had happened just hours earlier. Above them, the dark sky was beginning to turn, the first hint of a rising sun beginning to lift itself up. John pulled the horse up to a halt in the center of the north field, the location giving them full view of the homestead and the surrounding land. Marah leaned back against him, dropping into the warmth of his embrace as his arms held her steady. Together they sat in silence, watching as the beginnings of a new day began to take shape before them.

The sky was glowing a deep shade of orange with sweeping striations of yellows and reds cascading across the clear landscape. A hint of pale blue was peeking from beneath the bright coloration, the first promise of a clear morning sky. John could feel the smile that filled Marah's face, the beauty of it as magnanimous as the morning sunrise. He pressed a light kiss to the back of her neck, his lips lingering for just a brief moment.

Marah nodded slowly, her gaze sweeping across the

To Love a Stallion

expanse of landscape. "One day this will all belong to our children, John Stallion."

He nodded his agreement. "Yes, it will. And God willing, we'll be here to share it with them for a very long time."

Marah twisted her body just enough to press her lips against his. "Promise me we'll do this often. I'd forgotten just how beautiful the sunrise could be out here."

John smiled. "I promise."

"I do love me a Stallion," she said, her gaze meeting his.

John chuckled softly. "It just so happens, Mrs. Stallion, that I love me one as well."

ESSENCE **Bestselling Author**

DONNA HILL

SEX AND LIES

Book 1 of the new T.L.C. miniseries

Their job hawking body products for Tender Loving Care
is a cover for their true identities as undercover operatives for
a covert organization. And when Savannah Fields investigates
a case of corporate espionage, the trail of corruption leads
right back to her husband!

Coming the first week of February wherever books are sold.

KIMANI™
ROMANCE

www.kimanipress.com

KPDH0520208

Mixing business with pleasure...

Acclaimed author

ANGIE DANIELS

the
PLAYBOY'S
PROPOSITION

Sheyna and her sexy boss, Jace, have a long history
of competition. Despite their mutual attraction, Sheyna
refuses to fall for the playboy. But when Jace wins a trip
with Sheyna at a bachelorette auction, the competition's
not over...until he loses his heart.

"Each new [Angie] Daniels romance is a true joy."
—*Romantic Times BOOKreviews*

Coming the first week of February wherever books are sold.

KIMANI™
ROMANCE

www.kimanipress.com   KPAD0530208

The game of love...

PLAYING *for* KEEPS

Favorite author

YAHRAH ST. JOHN

Ambitious Avery knows laid-back Quentin isn't her type—until a crisis drives her into his arms for comfort, and fierce attraction takes over. Quentin's life leaves no room for relationships...until he realizes he can't picture the future without Avery.

Coming the first week of February wherever books are sold.

KIMANI™
ROMANCE

A compelling short story collection...

New York Times Bestselling Author

CONNIE BRISCOE

&

ESSENCE Bestselling Authors

LOLITA FILES
ANITA BUNKLEY

YOU ONLY GET *Better*

Three successful women find themselves on
the road to redemption and self-discovery as
they realize that happiness comes from within...
and that life doesn't end at forty.

"This wonderful anthology presents very human
characters, sometimes flawed but always
heartwarmingly developed and sympathetic.
Each heroine makes changes for the better that
demonstrate the power of love. Don't miss this book."
—*Romantic Times BOOKreviews* Top Pick on
You Only Get Better

**Coming the first week of February
wherever books are sold.**

KIMANI PRESS™

www.kimanipress.com   KPYOGBI540208

A Man Who Has Everything Needs...

More Than a Woman

National Bestselling Author

MARCIA KING-GAMBLE

Anais Cooper put her savvy and savings into creating a
charming day spa. The only problem is...her neighbor.
Former baseball star turned celebrity real estate mogul
Palmer Freeman has declared unofficial war on
her business venture. So she decides it's time to
add a little sugar to the mix!

*Coming the first week of February
wherever books are sold.*

ARABESQUE®

www.kimanipress.com

KPMKG0830208

"*Eternally Yours*...A truly touching and heartfelt story that
is guaranteed to melt the hardest of hearts."
—*Rendezvous*

USA TODAY Bestselling Author

BRENDA
JACKSON

ETERNALLY YOURS

A Madaris Family Novel

Attorney Syneda Walter and fellow attorney
Clayton Madaris are friends—and the last two people
likely to end up as lovers. But things start to heat up
during a Florida getaway and Clayton realizes Syneda
is the woman for him. Can he help her heal old wounds
and convince her that she will always be eternally his?

"Ms. Jackson has done it again!...another Madaris brother
sweeps us off to fantasyland..."
—*Romantic Times BOOKreviews*

**Coming the first week of February
wherever books are sold.**

ARABESQUE®